Prince of The City

City

by
Jason Poole

Copyright © 2013 by Jason Poole

Editor: Linda Wilson
Book Interior Layout: Nuance Art,LLC Book
Cover Design: Glenn Modlin - asantegln@aol.com
ISBN#: 13-digit: 978-0-9913294-0-3
ISBN#: 10-digit: 0-9913294-0-6

Published by:
Gangster Chronicles Books
PO Box 31086
Washington, DC 20030

Other Best-Selling Classics

by Jason Poole

Larceny

Convict's Candy

Victoria's Secret

-Dedication-

To the next Prince of Chocolate City seeking his place upon a Throne. This one's for you!

Pay attention and peep game 'cause you're definitely gonna need it.

Acknowledgments

I'd first like to thank my creator. I thank him for my loved ones and for all those who remained loyal during my struggles. Wahida Clark, for remaining true to a bond we have created almost a decade ago, and for conducting business how it's supposed to be done. Thank you for helping me make this project a success. I am deeply grateful and loyally indebted to you.

T. Styles and Charisse Washington (Cartel Publications), thanks for encouraging me to take the necessary steps to become my own boss, and recognizing a Boss when you see one. I am now proud to say that I am President and CEO of Gangster Chronicles Books, and that I did all of this from a prison cell. Thank you for everything.

To my brothers, my best friends, and my comrades for life, James "Fry" Fowler, Short Dogg, Draco, and Ishmael Ford-Bey, CEO of Gangster Chronicles Music. Thanks for letting my company become a subsidiary of your music label and providing me with the soundtrack for my movies and books. You are what every person wants, a loyal, true friend and a comrade with honor.

My business partner and co-executive producer of our reality show. "Pierre 'BET' Antonio", continue to negotiate our project, and tell them people out in Hollywood that the next time I come out there to have those contracts ready. Get the deal done. We can party some other time.

For all the homies locked behind bars, continue to stick together and represent our city to the fullest, and get into that Law Library and give that time back. It's too much talent being wasted in prison . . .

To all the entertainers and authors from D.C. that continue to represent, Wale, Taraji P. Henson, Raheem Devahn, Lola Luv AKA Lola Monroe, Villian Style, 30/30, Fat Trell, Boobie, Eyone Williams, Anthony Fields, Nathan Welch, Antonio "Yo" Jones, and many, many more. Continue to do your thang in that industry and don't hesitate to extend your hand to one another, (Keep it D.C.). To Toney Lewis Jr. for being that positive force for our city. You really need to run for mayor, homie. This city loves you and needs you (D.C. or nothing).

And last but most importantly, to my fans and my city Washington D.C. and the entire DMV (D.C., Maryland, and Virginia). Thank you for supporting me from day one with my first project (Larceny) and for giving me the strength to never give up. This is our most prized project. This is the project that's gonna break barriers and get us into that music and major motion picture industry and create opportunities for the raw and hidden talent that D.C. has to offer. So continue to support and help break barriers. Like I said, I did my job. It's in your hands now.

For all those who wish to view videos and hear music for the sound track to this project, please visit www.gangsterchroniclesmusic.com. I guarantee you won't be disappointed.

Big shout out to my PR rep, Ms. Shante Brisco of Prep Media Group. Contact info: preready1@gmail.com

Peace!
Jason Poole
President & CEO
Gangster Chronicles Books

"Even if I knew it would cost me life in The Pen, I would have put at least seven shells in the head of a snake that deserved it . . ."

-The Notorious Wayne Perry
A True D.C. Legend
Feds magazine interview

Introduction

Damn! One slip up and that's my life. The thought stampeded through his mind like a herd of wild buffalo. Standing upright on the balcony of his tenth floor apartment at the Wingate Condominiums, Malik Jabril Perry took a deep breath, inhaling the various pollutants that Washington, D.C. had to offer. For some odd reason, the foul smell of bus exhaust always reminded him that only a select few had ever been placed in his position. Malik held a glass of Remy Martin XO, his signature drink—the same drink preferred by his father, who was also his mentor. As he raised his glass to take a sip, a rainbow reflected off the diamond bezel of his watch. Anxiously, he awaited the proper time to make his move. Oblivious to the winter's blistering chill, Malik's fur coat flapped open like a sail in the breeze, exposing his beltline where his .45 automatic handgun rested.

"Fuck!" he said quietly, disappointed with his careless actions. He'd got caught slipping, but truth be told he knew it was coming. There's only one way I can get out of this situation, he thought. Taking another deep breath, Malik sighed and continued to look over the entire Southeast side of D.C., which was considered the most crime-ridden section of the city, infamously known as the Concrete Jungle. Southeast was a place where only the strong survived, and Malik had always considered himself a warrior of great strength.

Although rapid gunfire rang out in the distance, sirens whistled in the night, and homeless dogs howled like wolves during a full moon. On this balcony, Malik found solace, peace, and tranquility. His mind began to race back to his childhood, and he remembered that here is where he learned morals and principles. Here, priceless jewels of knowledge were dropped and strategies were planned and executed. Every lesson for a prince was taught on that balcony, and Malik was that prince.

"I knew you'd come," Malik said to the person who crept up behind him with a gun pointed at his head. The cold steel pressed hard into the crease of his neck, sending chills down his spine. He knew the person behind the trigger was someone who would kill on instinct, and had every intention of doing so. "Before you pull that trigger, I think there's something you need to know," he said calmly. Without giving his attacker enough time to respond, Malik began to recite his life story. He told his attacker everything he was, is, and ever would be, and thankfully the killer chose to listen.

Chapter 1

-ROYAL LOVE-

The King stood outside the cool confines of his balcony on a warm summer day with his Remy Martin glass half-full and his .38 snubnose revolver neatly tucked. Along side him stood a little boy, no older than ten years old. Together they looked out into the sky and noticed how the sun dominated it. A moment later, a soft rumble took over, turning the sky into a purple hue. Just as he figured, a storm was definitely approaching. But as fate would have it, the storm that nature was bringing couldn't compare to the storm that this ten-year-old boy was soon to endure.

"Son, if you lie down with snakes, they gonna bite you. No matter how long they take; you better believe that before you get up they gonna bite. You understand me, son?"

Malik would just look up at his father in admiration and smile warmly. He knew the man who towered over him with a sincere and stern face was of some importance. He just didn't know how much, or better yet, why? None of these things meant anything to him as an innocent child, but later in life they would mean more to him than any gift a father can give. Malik was the son of Michael Perry, a major hustler and well-

1

respected gangster who received profits from a majority of every drug strip in Southeast D.C. A man of great wisdom, with the ability and power to rule. A boss, who controlled and employed those whom everyone thought were big boys, shot callers, and heavyhitters. They all answered to him and his most trusted comrade and childhood friend, Black Sam.

Michael stood about six feet tall, medium complexion, with dark wavy hair and a long scar racing down the right side of his cheek. A symbol that served as a sign of victory in war, and a constant reminder of things he endured while climbing the ladder of success. A diamond flooded band adorned his wedding finger, another symbol that served as a constant reminder that he wouldn't be alone. It assured him that there was someone he loved who would remain loyal and faithfully by his side. Connie was Michael's wife and the mother of his child, a son who came bursting into this cold, corrupted world without any defect. Mental or physical.

Malik's parents met at a high school homecoming dance during the late 70s Go-Go scene, a time when almost every speaker in the ghettos of D.C. blasted the new wave baseline music with an uptempo beat played by live bands.

One evening after coming home from the nearby carryout with their favorite grape soda and French fries, both Connie and Linda sat in Connie's bedroom getting prepared to watch their favorite show, Goodtimes. As Connie reached for the remote, Linda got up, stood in front of the television, and blocked her view.

"Girl, move your crazy ass out the way. My show 'bout to come on—ooh it's gonna be good too. I think this the one when Penny gets burned by her momma," Connie said with excitement. Linda still didn't move, instead she just stood there looking at her friend with a spoiled girlish pout. "What?"

Connie asked, looking annoyed, knowing her friend had something sneaky up her sleeve."

"Dag, you acting like you gonna die if you don't see this show," Linda retorted and then folded her arms.

"No, it's just that I know that sneaky ass look all too well." Connie always could tell when Linda wanted something. She'd often put on some type of spoiled girl pity party seeking her friend's sympathy.

"Connie, I need you this time. I really need you," she pleaded, putting both hands together as if saying a prayer.

"Need me for what?" Connie asked, almost irritated. By now her show had started, and her French fries were getting cold. But that still didn't stop her from dumping almost half the bottle of ketchup on her food.

While Connie prepared her food, Linda was plotting, determined to convince her friend to attend the upcoming dance. Linda always felt that she would get more attention from the type of guys she liked, but only if she'd brought Connie with her. To Linda, Connie was more like the bait while she would be the catch. At sixteen years old, Connie was already developed like an exotic dancer, with flawless milk chocolate skin and long, shiny hair. She was considered very pretty, with the likes of a centerfold model. Linda, on the other hand, wasn't as pretty, but her caramel complexion was unblemished and beautiful. Although her stature was tall, her tomboyish build left her without curves. But what Linda lacked in sex appeal, she more than made up for by her eagerness to live life in the fast lane. So whenever an event would come up, Linda would do any and everything to persuade her friend to join her.

"I need you to go to Ballou's homecoming with me tomorrow," Linda said in her little girl tone. Before Connie could open her mouth to say no, Linda got on the floor and began to beg as if it was a dire need. "Please–please–please! I'm begging you, Connie. I need you this time. Please!" Linda held her hands together as if praying to God.

"I don't know, Linda," Connie replied, hunching her shoulders. "I mean, Ballou High is kinda rough. Them niggas gonna be out there fighting and what not. And besides, I ain't got nothing to wear."

Seeing that her friend didn't say no, Linda jumped up quickly. "Good, I knew your scary ass was gonna say that. That's why I came prepared." She then reached in her bookbag and pulled out a set of clothes. "Here, take this," Linda said, throwing the clothes on her friend's bed. "And fuck them punk ass niggas. We coming to have fun," she proudly announced while resting her hands on both hips.

"Hmph! You all Miss Sassy now. Just a minute ago you was a cry baby," Connie teased. "And what's this anyway?" she asked, fumbling through the clothes and checking for labels.

"It's your new outfit, bitch. Try it on."

Connie examined the new outfit with suspicion and wondered how her friend was able to purchase such expensive clothes. "Ooh Linda! This is Calvin Klein. How did you get this?"

"I stole it from Iverson Mall today. Look, I got one too," she replied proudly, showing off the stolen goods. "So are you going or what?"

Connie tried on her new outfit, pleased as she turned in front of the mirror, admiring how the new jeans perfectly fit her round ass. "Shit, from the way I look in this outfit . . . hell yeah, I'm going." She grinned. "Thanks Linda. Well, the best I can do for you to return the favor is to fix your hair," she offered.

"Good, bitch. Let's hurry up 'cause we got a dance to attend tomorrow, and we gonna be the baddest bitches up in that joint," Linda said with confidence. She then sat between Connie's legs and freed her hair from the scrunchie. "Make me look like Pam Grier," she demanded playfully.

"Damn, you coulda at least let me eat my food first."

"Connie, them French fries is cold as ice by now. Tell you what. When you finish my hair, I will personally walk down to the carryout and get you some more. Deal?"

"Shut up!" Connie replied, pushing her friend's head to the side. With comb in hand, Connie tried to figure out where to start. Linda sat back, closed her eyes, and smiled. The only thing she had on her mind was the upcoming event for tomorrow. Mission complete, she proudly thought.

The next Saturday night was the homecoming dance, and all eyes were on Linda and Connie as they danced to Chuck Brown's song "Bustin' Loose." Guys moved in closer in an effort to dance with the two girls. While Linda enjoyed the attention, Connie didn't. She immediately stopped dancing and stood with her back against the wall, watching her friend get freaked on the dance floor by two guys.

From across the room, Connie felt someone watching her. She glanced in all directions, but never made eye contact with anyone. However, she still felt creepy and desperately wanted to shake off her uneasiness.

"Hey Linda. Hey Linda!" Connie said, walking over and interrupting her friend's fun by tapping her shoulder.

"What, girl? Can't you see I'm getting my freak on?" Linda stated in an irritated tone.

"Yeah, bitch, it's obvious. I'm just letting you know I'm going to the bathroom."

"Okay. But if you ain't back in ten minutes, I'm coming wit' my knife out, stabbin' first and asking questions later."

"Shut up, girl. Your ass know you crazy. I'll be right back." Connie left the gym and went to the restroom.

After freshening up, Connie pushed the bathroom door open and made her exit. She stopped dead in her tracks, seeing a handsome, familiar face. Although she didn't know him personally, she knew exactly who he was, as his reputation in school was well known.

"How you doing, Connie?" the guy asked coolly.

"Excuse me? Do I know you?" Connie squinted, checking him out as if she didn't know him.

"No, not exactly, but we do go to the same school. My name is Michael, and I was wondering if I could have a minute of your time?"

Connie took a second to re-examine the handsome teenager, who was quickly blossoming into manhood. She was pleased with his handsome looks, yet wasn't too sure of his thuggish swag. Connie was a square, oftentimes being called naive. Intrigued by his interest in her, she decided to take a chance since there was nothing else better to do. After all, she wasn't worried about going on the dance floor anytime soon.

"Well, I guess I could give you a minute. How do you know my name anyway?" she asked.

"We had history class together, but I guess you didn't notice me. I always sat in the back. Anyway, I've always admired you and wanted to say something, but figured you wouldn't give me the time of day."

At that statement, Connie blushed, but before she could reply, Linda came bursting out of the gymnasium door.

"Okay, didn't I say ten minutes? And who the hell is this? Is he bothering you?" Linda asked Connie as she pointed her finger at Michael.

"No. This is—"

Before Connie could finish her sentence, Michael butted in. "How you doing? I'm Michael. I was just talking to your friend, tryna get to know her better. I can see you're very overprotective. I respect that," he said, nodding his head.

Linda folded her arms and looked him up and down. Although she could sense Connie's interest in Michael, Linda wasn't going for his charm. It was obvious from the burgundy Pierre Cardin sweatsuit, and the latest shell toe Adidas on his feet, along with two gold chains around his neck, that he was a thug. His outfit alone complemented a hustler's lifestyle, and Linda wasn't about to let Connie get caught up in his web.

"Okay, uhhhh Michael. I'm really sorry, but we gotta go home now. It's getting late," Linda said, grabbing Connie's arm and pulling her away.

At the same time, Michael looked Connie deep in her eyes and shouted out his phone number.

"I'll call you first chance I get," Connie shouted back while memorizing his number.

"I'll be waiting," he yelled, hoping she wouldn't play him like a sucker by not calling at all.

Chapter 2

-A LION'S PREY-

One year later . . .

The night of Connie and Michael's high school graduation was a memorable time. Over the past year, Michael started doing well for himself. A life of crime had earned him more money than he had ever seen. He purchased an all-white Cadillac Eldorado, and couldn't wait to pick up the love of his life. He was going to take her to one of the finest restaurants in Georgetown, and then to the waterfront pier in Southwest. But Connie had different plans.

Michael pulled up in front of theBarry Farms projects and took a deep breath. Then he hopped out of his Caddy and walked up to the door.

Knock, knock, knock!

"Who is it?" Connie asked, acting as if she hadn't watched him pull into her driveway from her bedroom window.

"It's Mike! You ready to go?"

"Uhhhh, come in for a minute," Connie yelled down from the window.

"Okay, baby, but we should be going. It's getting kinda late," he said, glancing at his watch.

"Just come in the house for a minute."

Once Michael went inside, Connie came downstairs and took his hand.

"Baby, what you doing?" he asked as she led him up to her room. Not another word was spoken. Only the smooth voice of Marvin Gaye's hit "Let's Get It On" played from the radio. They finally reached her room, and Connie took charge, kissing him passionately and holding him tight. As she began to remove his clothes, he stopped her.

"Baby, are you sure about this?" Michael asked. "Do you know what you're doing?"

"No. No. I really don't know what I'm doing, but I know in my heart I love you. Michael, I'm ready . . ."

Connie slipped off her clothes, revealing her nakedness to a man for the very first time. After some thorough kissing and foreplay, he laid her soft, perfect frame down on the bed and began to insert his manhood inside her. At first she winced and then whispered, "Sssssss . . . ouch!" The more Michael eased inside of her she grimaced in pain. Gently, he rocked his body against hers as she cried out. Soon, the loud screams that escaped her mouth scared him. But no matter how painful it felt, Connie still searched for pleasure.

"I love you, Michael . . . Please, Michael. It hurts sooo bad. Ooooh, Mike, stop!" she begged. His narrowed brows showed his confusion as he tried to get up, but she dug her nails deep into his back and pulled him closer. This was his first time ever being with a virgin, but also his first time being in love.

After a long session of lovemaking, Connie experienced an orgasm for the first time. Then she lay in Michael's arms and they cuddled, talking of their future. Connie believed that no one could ever love her like Michael. He too believed the same about her.

With something special on his mind, Michael got up and started to dress.

"Where are you going?" she asked.

"I left something in the car. I'll be right back," he responded as he slipped his shoes on.

"Okay, but hurry up, 'cause I want to do it again." She grinned.

"From the way your ass was screaming, I'm not sure if you're ready for another round yet," he teased.

Connie blushed. "Don't tease me, Michael," she replied in a whiny voice.

He smiled and kissed her forehead. "I'm sorry, baby. You know I love you," he said, and then dashed outside to his Cadillac to retrieve the fourteen-karat gold ring he had purchased earlier.

Michael planned to propose to her while they were walking on the waterfront, but since there had been a change of plans, he felt now was an even better time to pop the question.

Inside the car, he took one last look at the ring, certain this was indeed the woman he wanted to marry. Although nervous about the outcome, he knew in his heart that he was ready to build a life with Connie. He took a deep breath and exited the car.

Two unfamiliar faces approaching startled Michael. One dude looked like an old junkie while the other was younger and much bigger. Both were armed with knives.

"Look here, nigga. We don't know you, so what the fuck you doin' 'round here?" the junkie asked, closing in on him. His partner joined him, cutting Michael off from walking away.

PRINCE OF THE CITY

"I'm visiting my girl. What business is it of yours?" Michael asked.

"Hold up, nigga. I know the fuck you ain't gettin' slick outta the mouth, and on top of that, your pretty ass down here fuckin' one of our bitches. Matter fact, empty your pockets, nigga," the younger guy said, holding his knife in a striking position.

"And don't try nuttin' stupid," the junkie said. "I'll drive this joint in your ass so deep, you'll be dead before you realize you've been hit. Now do what the fuck he said. Hurry up and empty those pockets, nigga."

At that very moment, Michael touched the pocket where he had placed the ring and then began to size up the situation. Naw, this shit can't happen like this, he thought. This ring belongs to my future wife. I just can't give it up like that.

Before he could think of a way to get out of the mess, he felt the knife slash his face. It didn't hurt much, but the wound felt warm. As the junkie took another swing, Michael ducked and delivered a vicious blow to his nut sack.

"AHHHH, FUCK!" the junkie yelled, dropping to his knees.

The other guy attacked Michael from behind and stabbed him in the rib cage. This weakened Michael, but still, he fought back with vengeance. His adrenaline pumped vigorously, allowing him to brawl like a lion in the heat of an attack by hyenas—never backing down and fighting until the bloody end. He turned toward his attacker and delivered a crushing left hook to his chin, followed by a hard right to the jawbone. Having dazed the attacker, Michael grabbed his attacker's wrist, twisted it, and turned it upward. Instantly, he heard a crack.

11

JASON POOLE

"AHHHH!" the younger guy screamed in pain.

Michael knew he had broken his attacker's wrist. When the knife fell to the ground, Michael retrieved it and held up the weapon in anger, now becoming the aggressor. Nothing could hold him back as he plunged the knife deep into the younger guy's lung, causing him to collapse. He stabbed him at least five more times before turning his attention back to the junkie, who quickly fled the scene.

Michael looked at the man that he had just killed. He didn't feel sorry for him, since this man had attacked him first, but Michael did start to feel lightheaded and dizzy. He reached at his side and felt a thick wetness surrounding his wound. Realizing he had lost a lot of blood, Michael quickly fell unconscious.

By the time Michael woke up from his two-week coma, a bandage covered his face with nineteen butterfly stitches underneath. Also, his right lung had been punctured badly, which required him to undergo a blood transfusion.

As soon as he regained consciousness, police detectives charged him with second-degree murder. Although Michael was only seventeen, he was still charged as an adult because of the nature of the crime. He wanted to go to trial and argue self-defense, but the prosecutor had an eyewitness who said he only saw Michael stabbing the guy. There was no way he could win. During this same time, he also found out that Connie was pregnant. If he had gone to trial and lost, he would have definitely gotten twenty years to life. So instead, he took his lawyer's advice and copped seven to twenty-one years.

While Michael was serving time in Lorton Prison, one of the deadliest prisons in the nation, Connie visited him every visiting day, all the way up until her ninth month.

On the fourth day of July in 1979, Connie went into labor at D.C. General Hospital, where she endured nine painful hours of labor and produced a little boy into this world. The baby boy's dark caramel complexion was a mixture of both his mother and father's skin tones, but he inheriteda head full of dark, curly hair solely from his father. The baby's features already looked as if they were chiseled from a sculpture.

"Damn, Connie, this boy is too handsome," Linda said, taking him out of his bassinet.

"Let me see my baby," Connie whined, eager to give him his first feeding.

Linda took the small child over to his mother.

"Oh my God. He is adorable," Connie said, staring at him with amazement.

"I know . . . Now what's his name?" Linda asked, irritated that Connie hadn't yet decided on a name before giving birth.

Connie laughed. "I don't know."

"Well, did Michael suggest anything?"

"No. He said that whatever name I chose would be the name that fits him."

"Well, he is an angel."

"Okay then. Since you say he's an angel, I'm a name him after an angel."

"Whoa!" Linda exclaimed. "'Cause the only angel I've ever heard of was the one in the Bible that turned out to be the devil."

"Linda, your ass is crazy." Connie chuckled. "I guess we can name him after one of the angels in the Holy Quran." As they continued to talk, Linda's pager went off several times and Connie took notice.

"Let me find out Mike went to jail and turned Muslim, and now you're supposed to be one too."

"Shut up, stupid!" Connie smirked. "And no, I'm not one. But I do read the Quran."

"Then, which angel we gonna name him after?"

"We can name him Malik. That's the angel that guards your soul from evil."

"Malik sounds good. Okay, now what's his middle name?" Linda asked while checking her pager again.

"Jabril. He's the angel that told Mary that she was gonna have Jesus. Also, he was the angel that revealed the Quran to Prophet Muhammad."

"Connie, are you sure you ain't no Muslim?"

"No, silly. Are you sure you ain't on call? 'Cause it seems like somebody is really tryna reach your ass."

"Well, girl. Look, I gotta be going. In case you forgot, it's the Fourth of July. I gotta go party and celebrate my new nephew being born," Linda said, ignoring her friend's concern.

"Okay," Connie replied with uneasiness. She knew Linda was headed down to the track to turn tricks for Butter, who had been paging her all day long. Although Connie hated Butter, she was glad he never laid a hand on Linda. She knew she didn't need to worry though, because Linda knew how to take care of herself.

Chapter 3

-THE LION'S DEN-

Perry! Perry!" the corrections officer called out onto the basketball court. Michael was in the middle of an intense basketball game. Right after he made the last three-point jump shot to end the game, he turned to the CO.

"Yeah. Carter, what's up?" Michael asked.

"You got a visit," the small, chubby, old head replied. Carter had been working at Lorton for almost twenty years. He knew how to deal with convicts the way they wanted to be treated. He also made money on the side smuggling drugs in for certain inmates who paid him well and Michael was one of those inmates.

"Okay, thanks," Michael responded. He walked off the court without an explanation.

"Hey, Mike! Where you goin'? We got one more game," one of his fellow inmates asked.

"I got a visit, Slim," he answered without breaking his stride.

Slim James was Michael's prison partner and cellmate. The two men became partners when Michael first arrived at Lorton. Although Slim was older and had been in the streets a

15

lot longer than Michael had, he still looked up to the younger man. Michael Perry had leadership qualities, and Slim James respected that. They established an unbreakable bond after one particular incident that happened in prison.

Michael had just finished his visit with Connie and returned to his dorm to find all of his things had been stolen. He never expressed any anger, but just walked away calmly to another dorm. There, Michael called out for Jason, Connie's older brother, who was also serving a lengthy sentence for murder.

"Hey Jason! I need to holla at you for a sec."

"Yeah. What's up, Mike? You a'ight?" he asked, sensing something was wrong.

"Nah, slim. I need a knife," Michael replied, looking around to make sure no one peeped his move.

"Whazzup? You got some beef with them suckers in your dorm?"

"Ain't nuttin' I can't handle myself."

"Okay. Give me a minute."

Within seconds, Jason returned with the biggest knife Michael had ever seen. "Here you go," he said, passing him the blade.

"Damn, Jay. What the fuck is this? A sword?"

"Nah, young nigga, that's a lawnmower blade. I call her Betsy. Now look, whatever you do make sure you get away with it. 'Cause once you hit a nigga with that, ain't no coming back. He's through," Jason instructed.

"A'ight. Thanks," Michael said, tucking the knife away.

"Anytime. Now how's my nephew?"

"I just got back from a visit with them. He's chillin', looking good and healthy."

"And my sister?"

"She's fine, as always."

"Take care of my lil sis, a'ight?"

16

PRINCE OF THE CITY

"Man, Jay, you ain't never gotta worry 'bout that. I love my wife and son."

"Then think about what you're getting ready to do," Jason replied.

"I already did. But you know how it is. You can't violate a man, no matter what condition you in. For my respect, I'd go to hell and fight the devil himself."

Jason looked at the young but wise man. "I fully understand. Just be careful," he advised.

"A'ight" Michael said, and then walked over to the other dorm where an associate by the name of Donnie G stayed.

"Hey, Donnie G!" he called out at the front entrance.

Donnie came to the door with two other convicts. He held something that appeared to be a knife covered up with a towel.

Michael and Donnie G had known each other from the streets. They once robbed a bank together somewhere in a suburb of Virginia and had what one would call a "men of understanding" relationship. Donnie G was known as the kingpin of Lorton. He was responsible for majority of the heroin being smuggled inside the prison. Whatever a prisoner wanted, Donnie G had it. Fiends would come to him with everything just to get high—shoes, sweat suits, snacks, cigarettes, money, etc. Anything dope fiends could get their hands on, they brought to Donnie G.

"What's up? How can I help you?" Donnie G asked Michael.

"Ay look, Donnie. I'm coming to you as a man and I respect you as a man."

"That's vice versa. So what's up?"

"I need to ask you a serious question, and I ask that it be kept between us."

17

JASON POOLE

"Okay. What's your question?"

"Did the nigga Brutus come and get some blow from you today?"

"Yeah, he came 'bout a half hour ago. Had some cigarettes and some brand-new Nikes. Don't tell me that was your shit, Mike. If it was, I can get it back for you. That nigga Brutus must don't know who he's dealing wit'."

"Yeah, I know. Look, I'll be back to get my shit later, but like I said, keep this between us. A'ight?"

"Understood. Go 'head and handle your business," Donnie G said.

* * * * * * *

Brutus was Lorton's worst nightmare and the king of advantage-takers. If another inmate had something he wanted, he was going to take it. No matter the consequences, it was going to be his. Everyone in the prison was petrified of Brutus's big, ugly ass. He'd been down for about fifteen years, and everyone had heard the stories of how he raped and robbed people. He ran the compound as if it were his kingdom, and whenever some good heroin hit the compound, all inmates had better watch their belongings, because either he was pulling a knife to take it, or he was breaking into someone's locker. Brutus was considered without a doubt or contradiction, a real gorilla within a jungle of men.

* * * * * * *

As Michael reached the dorm, his mind raced back and forth from his child to his wife. He knew he was going up against death itself. If he came bullshitting with this gorilla, most likely he would be killed. On the other hand, if he killed this gorilla and got caught, he could get life and remain in prison until his death. Either way, Michael knew he was faced with death, but something inside him wouldn't let it go. He had to claim his mark, state his position, and become the ruler of his surroundings.

Michael went into the dorm, wet a towel with water, rolled it up, and neatly placed it around his neck to protect his jugular vein, and then tucked the tails inside his sweatshirt. He then taped a thick stack of National Geographic magazines to his chest and sides. Since Brutus had just gotten his dope a half hour ago, he would still be high, so this was the proper time for Michael to make his move.

Before going into the back of the dorm where Brutus normally got high, Michael looked around for any signs of the CO or known snitches. Seeing that his way was perfectly clear, he headed toward the back, not knowing what his fate would be, but having no fear. When he walked into the bathroom and closed the door, he saw Brutus sitting on the sink nodding from his last blast. As Brutus looked up at Michael, a sneaky grin appeared on his face.

"Yeah, nigga, I took your shit. And from now on, whenever you go to the canteen, you make sure you come and get my list first," Brutus said. "Now get your bitch ass outta here before I take your manhood and stick my dick in your ass."

Brutus was enormously big and known to have a one-punch knockout. On top of that, he stayed strapped. Michael knew he couldn't turn back. Brutus had crossed the line of no return. Although it was over some petty-ass tennis shoes and cigarettes, the value of the items weren't the point. It was about principle and respect, and whenever a man's principle and respect were violated, justice must then take its course. On top of that, if Michael were to let it slide, every gorilla on the compound would be taking shots at him, assuming he was weak.

19

When Brutus got down off the sink, he gave Michael the coldest stare, and his eyes reflected death. "Nigga, didn't I tell your bitch ass to get the fuck outta here? What's wrong? Is you deaf? Did I stutta, muthafucka?"

As Brutus reached into his waist for his knife, Michael slid the long blade from under the sleeve of his sweatshirt while looking Brutus directly in the eyes. Just as Brutus pulled his knife from the front of his waistband, Michael plunged the lawnmower blade straight through the middle of his torso. The blade was so sharp that when he pushed inward, it went through Brutus's body as if he were cutting butter.

Before Michael could remove the knife from Brutus's stomach, Brutus grabbed Michael's sweatshirt and stabbed Michael on the right side of his body near his lungs. Although Michael was strapped with magazines, Brutus exerted so much force that his knife went straight through the magazines and poked Michael's flesh, luckily never breaking the skin. Brutus held Michael so close that he didn't have enough room to pull his blade from Brutus's stomach. So instead of taking it out, Michael grabbed hold of the lawnmower blade with both hands and jerked it upward, tearing the insides of Brutus's guts. The harder he jerked, the lighter Brutus's hold became until finally he let go.

When Michael noticed Brutus weakening, he pulled the long blade out, held it up like a sword, and chopped the right side of Brutus' neck, cutting deep into his jugular vein. Blood gushed out of his neck like a waterfall, while at the same time his intestines fell out of his stomach. Brutus fell to the floor, dying instantly.

Michael stood over Brutus's body much like a lion after killing its prey. Although his victim was dead, Michael wanted to send a message to the rest of the convicts at Lorton. He wanted to make it fully known that he, Michael Antonio Perry, was not to be fucked with, and whoever violated him in any way would be treated the same. So he reached down, grabbed Brutus by the head, and began chopping at his neck. As he looked down at the body lying in a pool of blood, and now disconnected from the head, Michael mumbled, "Nigga, the only manhood you took today was your very own." Then he spat on Brutus.

At that very moment, Slim James burst into the bathroom. Instantly, Michael became alarmed. Still clutching his blade, he turned to look Slim in the eyes and noticed Slim wasn't strapped. Instead, he held a fresh prison uniform in his hand.

"Look, nigga, I ain't come in here to do you any harm. I came to save your life," Slim said, standing face-to-face with the young but fearless warrior. "Now wipe that blade with this towel and put on these clothes. Leave the blade and throw the clothes in the toilet," Slim James instructed. "Hurry up before the CO comes to make his rounds."

As Slim looked over at Brutus and noticed his headless body, he said, "You know you sending a vicious message, right?"

Michael never answered.

In the following weeks, Slim James and Michael became close friends. They ate, worked out, and played ball together. They walked the yard while learning more about each other. Michael thanked Slim for saving his life. Right after the incident, the CO came around to make his rounds and found Brutus decapitated. If Slim had never walked in, Michael would be doing a life sentence behind the walls of Lorton. Michael would never forget what Slim James did, and for that, Slim James had his respect.

Michael and Slim became cellmates for the remainder of Michael's sentence. They shared their dreams of becoming young millionaires. Also, they had talks of getting out of the game and going legit. They talked about women, but most of all, they talked about a plan to get on top and remain on top. None of these plans would ever work for Slim though. They were more of a fantasy for him since he was serving thirty-five years to life for two murders. As for Michael, it was just a matter of time. So instead, Slim's plan was to stay close to Michael until his release, and then take over the throne and run the prison compound.

After Brutus's murder, Michael became the most talked about convict in the compound. Niggas respected and feared Michael. He held his position with style. During the last two years of his sentence, he put together a most vicious team that would rule Lorton Prison until the walls fell down. His right-hand man was Slim James, and his advisor was his brother-in-law, Jason. Also, he had two vicious youngins around, Gerald and Carlos, both hailing from a crime-ridden neighborhood in Southeast that obviously lived up to its name. They began moving all the drugs once he took over Donnie G's business. Michael always knew Donnie G was a cruddy nigga. Donnie had known that the items Brutus gave him belonged to Michael. He was the only person in the jail with those Nikes, and weeks before the incident, Donnie had asked Michael about the sneaks. It was Donnie who'd sent Brutus on that mission. Donnie tried to kill two birds with one stone—get the shoes and give up Brutus. That way, he didn't have to worry about Brutus extorting him anymore.

Once Michael got his crew together and his connections with Slim James's older brother on the outside, he put his move down on Donnie G. Donnie had raw dope coming in by the ounces. In Lorton, you could make some real money, but you had to have your operation tight. And Donnie G's operation was skintight. He had a lil crew from Northeast that held him down, but there was no other team as vicious as Michael's. Michael realized he needed to have some start-up money when he got out, and the only way to get it was hustling while he was still locked up. After all, his best friend Black Sam wasn't doing too well on the outside, and surely, he didn't want to come home and have to rob a bank after doing seven years.

One morning, Michael and his crew got up and strapped themselves with knives at breakfast time. They went into Donnie G's dorm while he was still at breakfast. The two youngins from Simple City, Gerald and Carlos, stood outside the dormitory as lookouts while Slim James and Jason waited in the back for the signal. Michael broke into Donnie's cell and hid under the bed. When Donnie came back, the youngins gave the signal. Slim James and Jason let him through, but cut off any familiar faces in Donnie's crew. Donnie didn't even realize what was going on. He thought they were there to bring someone else a move, not knowing he was the victim all along.

As Donnie walked into his room, Jason and Slim James stood in front of the cell blocking the door.

"Hey!" Donnie said after looking back. "What the fuck y'all doing?"

At that moment, Michael rolled out from under the bed with two knives taped to his hands. "Surprise, Donnie! I came for what's rightfully mine."

"Heeeeeeeey, Mike . . . if you're talkin' 'bout that thing with Brutus, you ain't gotta go like this."

"Don't tell me what I don't gotta do. I'm the one in charge. I'm the aggressor in this situation, and I make the calls. Now sit your ass on that toilet and listen carefully," Michael said. Donnie did as he was told. "Now look, Donnie. I want everything."

"Everything? What you mean you want everything?"

"If I have to repeat myself, you'll be the next nigga they'll be sending home in a box. Now, like I said—everything. Put it in the pillowcase." When Donnie went to reach behind the toilet, Michael said, "Don't even think about making a move. You're outnumbered. I got two niggas out front holding off your crew and two niggas holding this cell, and I alone have two knives on you. That's five against one. Either way, you come out dead."

"I ain't that stupid, Mike. I'm just getting out the dope. Here, that's one ounce of raw dope." Donnie reached into a hollow brick in the wall. "And that's one ounce of weed and a half ounce of coke."

"Okay, now where's the money?" Michael asked.

Donnie went into his locker and pulled out about fifteen cartons of cigarettes. "There's fifty dollars in each pack. That's all I got, slim. I swear. You can turn this muthafuckin' cell upside down."

"Okay, but before I leave, I'm gonna let you know something. I always knew you were a cruddy nigga. I knew you set up the move for Brutus, but I also knew when we robbed that bank with them uptown niggas, you stashed some money in your nuts."

"Mike, man, that was years ago."

"Yeah, but I'm letting you know that you ain't get nothing past me, nigga. I'm like God. I see everything. Now move your bitch ass the fuck outta my way."

PRINCE OF THE CITY

Relieved that his life had been spared, Donnie quickly moved out of the way to let Michael pass.

With his back facing Donnie, Michael said, "I want to thank you for something."

"What's that, Mike?"

When Michael turned, he looked Donnie straight in the eyes and replied, "For giving me the opportunity to send your bitch ass to hell." He then stabbed Donnie a total of twenty-two times in the stomach, neck, and head.

In the following months, Michael made more money in prison than he did on the streets. After selling all the dope he had gotten from Donnie G, he sent half the money home to Connie and copped with the other half.

Connie was still in his corner, and although it was hard raising a child while his father was living in a prison environment, they managed to make the best of it. Malik respected and loved his father, something his mother had instilled in him. Connie was the perfect wife. No other woman could ever fill her place. She was his queen. From prison, Michael paid the rent for their two-bedroom condo at Wingate Condominiums in Southwest D.C., and he also paid for Connie to attend nursing school. In addition, he had Connie trade in the Cadillac for a reliable car that would make it down to Lorton in any weather.

Michael was making at least five thousand dollars every three weeks selling dope. He'd often get three ounces of raw from Slim James's brother, Sonny. He'd get Sonny to give it to Connie, and she would give it to CO Carter to bring in. Slim James and Jason would cut the dope and bag it up, while Gerald and Carlos flat-footed the compound. Michael just sat back, collected, and smiled. He didn't have to put in any work

25

to keep the compound level. All he had to do was keep his crew in check and let them run the joint while he sat on the throne.

In 1985, Michael's parole hearing came up. This was the most critical stage of his bid. This was the time when he needed God the most. Michael had everything he needed to get paroled, a clear conduct sheet and a degree in marketing from attending the University of D.C. prison college program. Also, he had earned all kinds of certificates in anger management, A.A., N.A., parenting, etc.

One day at mail call, Michael received a letter. He thought it was from the parole commission giving him an answer, but instead it was postmarked from New York with no return address. He eagerly wanted to know who was writing him from New York. As he opened the letter, he was aroused by the smell of a perfume that wasn't Connie's. Michael sat down on his bed and began reading.

Dear Michael,

How are you? I pray that when you receive this letter, you read it carefully and know that I love you. You were my first love and always will be. Before you got locked up, there was something I wanted to tell you. Even though you left me for Connie, I still tried to tell you, but was too scared to get my feelings hurt once again. I'm sorry it's taken me so long to tell you, but I have moved on with my life now and just thought you needed to know. When you got locked up, I was two months pregnant. Don't worry, I didn't have it, and yes, you were my only boyfriend at the time. It was your child, Michael, and now he's gone and I hate you for that. You left me for that bitch Connie. You made me have an abortion and move to New York just so I couldn't see your face. You humiliated me, nigga. I was pregnant with your child.

I HATE YOU, MICHAEL! I HOPE YOU DIE!
C.J.

Unfazed by the hatred of this woman from his past, but more concerned with his parole hearing, Michael quickly tore up the letter and envelope and threw them in the trash.

"Stupid bitch," he said while shaking his head.

Chapter 4

- (1985) A LION'S ROAR -

In the spring of '85, Michael Antonio Perry was paroled. When he left Lorton, he had accumulated one hundred thousand dollars, which was stashed in his and Connie's condo. He'd left Slim James and Jason with all the dope. While he was on the street, he was going to be their connect. Their plan was to keep the money flowing.

Connie sat in her brand-new Maxima in the prison parking lot, dressed in her best and awaiting the arrival of her king.

Michael left the prison in style. He wore his new Fila sweat suit and matching tennis shoes that Connie sent. His crew walked him down the corridor to the central office where he'd be officially released. Michael turned, and with a deep breath, he took one last look at Lorton's Youth Center. Then he embraced each of his comrades and told them he would never forget them and he would always be there for them no matter what.

As the gates opened, Connie ran up to him, embracing and kissing her husband so intensely that he could feel the missing years of their life apart.

"Connie, I'll never leave you again."

"You never left in the first place, Michael." She held his hand to her heart. "You were always right here, always."

PRINCE OF THE CITY

"I love you, Connie."

"I love you too, baby."

On the drive back to their new home, Connie told him everything he had missed. She talked about Malik and how smart he was. She also mentioned Linda and Butter breaking up. The words that put a smile on his face was hearing Connie say that while he was paying the rent from prison, she saved and deposited all of her checks into Malik's savings account. Also, she told him about her job and how much she loved it.

As the car stopped at a red light, Connie looked over at Michael, whose eyes watered.

"What's wrong, Michael?" Connie asked.

He looked into her eyes and said, "Connie, you are truly a queen, and I will always treat you royally. I missed you so much."

"I missed you too, baby."

"Now, why isn't my son with you?" Michael asked.

"Well, since me and you have a little making up to do, I had Linda babysit for a while."

With that, he smiled. Connie and Michael were married three years ago in prison, and although they had sex at the prison a few times, they had only made love once, and that was their first time together seven years ago. He knew he had to make passionate love to her, and she knew she had to give herself totally to him.

Once inside his home, Michael loved his surroundings. The condo was neatly furnished with thick black carpet and cream leather furniture. They had a forty-two-inch color TV, and Connie had even purchased Michael his own lounge chair, which she called the king's chair. He looked around at all the

JASON POOLE

pictures of him, Connie, and Malik that she had blown up and framed.

"You want a drink, Michael?"

"Yeah, baby."

While Connie fixed his drink, he walked out on the balcony to look at the scenery, which was breathtaking. From the tenth floor, he could see the whole Southeast side of D.C. For the first time in his life, Michael had reached the top of his throne.

Connie came out on the balcony and handed her man his drink.

"Come here." He pulled her close and planted a kiss on her soft lips.

"Do you like it, baby?"

"I love it."

"The view is nice too. Isn't it?"

He held her hand and looked out into the world. "Connie, this is ours."

"What do you mean?"

He extended his hand out over the balcony and looked at her. "This. This is ours, baby. The entire southside of D.C. and everything in it."

Connie smiled and grabbed her husband by the hand. "Come here. Let me show you something." She led him into their bedroom, which looked like a master suite. Michael loved it. Their bed was enormous. Yet, it was being occupied by a pile of shoeboxes.

"Connie, why you got shoe boxes on the bed?"

"'Cause, baby, I wanted to show you something."

"Show me what?" he asked.

"This." Connie opened all the boxes. "These are all the letters you sent me. I kept every last one of them. They're in order by date. I read them from time to time just to get through the days. There are 956 letters here." Connie then dumped all

30

the letters on the bed. "Michael, make love to me on top of these letters." She unsnapped her sundress, revealing her full nakedness. He kissed his wife passionately, removed his clothes, and made love to her for the second time in their lives.

They made love all day and night. In between taking a drink and smoking a joint out on the balcony, they would talk a little and then go back to making love. They fucked in the living room, kitchen, shower, balcony—everywhere. They felt the apartment needed to be broken in, and they did just that.

Some months later, once Michael was out and settled, he got with Sonny James, Slim's brother. Sonny was from Seventh and T Streets, NW. He was a mid-level hustler, moving ounces of heroin for Big Luke. Michael first approached Sonny after getting back with his best friend Black Sam, who had a strip on Sixth Street, SE that was moving approximately two thousand dollars worth of blow a day. To Michael, the strip had potential, but not a good quality of dope. The product that Black Sam was getting was only strong enough to take three times the amount of cut, and he'd be putting three and a half of cut on it. So actually, he was selling garbage. This was the reason Black Sam only had about thirty-five thousand dollars to his name when Michael came home.

"Damn, Sam. You mean to tell me in seven years, you only got thirty-five thou'?"

"Nah, Mike. You know I've been taking falls. Plus, the blow I be getting don't be nothing. I can't find a connect for shit. Them niggas uptown got all the plugs and ain't trying to share 'em."

"Shit, Sam. I don't blame 'em. If you had the connect would you share 'im with a bunch of ruthless, disloyal niggas?" Michael asked. "The reason why they don't fuck

31

with Southeast niggas like that is 'cause we always tryna take something from a nigga."

"Yeah, out here it's like the fuckin' jungle. Ain't no order out here in these streets. Every man for himself and only the strong survive."

"You got that right," Michael agreed. "Look, Sam, I got a plan that's gonna get us rich. All you gotta do is follow my lead. It takes money to make money. Now, you got a few loyal customers over on Sixth Street. Where else do you be moving your shit?"

"Sometimes I go around the Lane or over to Fifteenth Place, and you know my cousin is over in Potomac Gardens," Sam replied.

"There's four strips in Southeast that we gonna take over first."

"What the fuck are you getting at, Mike?"

"Nigga, we 'bout to take over the whole Southside! After all, like you said, this is the jungle, right? And if we want to survive, we gotta think and act just like the lions do."

As Michael and Sam rode down Alabama Avenue in Sam's 190E Mercedes Benz, they began to talk more about their future.

"Now, what's this you're talking about taking over the whole southeast? You know niggas ain't gonna just let you come here and take their spots like that," Sam told Mike.

"Yeah, I know. But like I said—I got a plan. It's all about finesse. We gotta finesse our way in, just like a pussy, and once we get in, we gotta fuck the hell outta it and then pull out. You see, that's where other niggas go wrong. They don't know when to pull out."

"So, you're telling me that we 'bout to make enough money to quit this shit for good?" Sam asked.

"Yeah, that's what I'm saying, Sammy."

"I don't know 'bout that, Mike. I ain't ever heard of a nigga getting what he wants and getting out that easy. The only thing I know, which is reality so far, is that a nigga gets so big that he ends up in jail forever or six feet under."

"Well, that's the difference. We ain't them other niggas. So the first thing we gonna do is take over Sixth Street since that's one of your major spots."

"Yeah, but how we gonna do that? You know the nigga Kojack is the one who really got it locked down."

"So we take it from him," Michael said.

"Like I said, Mike. How?"

"You ever see the movie The Godfather?"

"Yeah."

"Do you remember this part: 'We'll make him an offer he can't refuse'?"

"I hear you, Mike, and you know I'm down till the end," Sam told him.

"Good . . . Hey, Sam?" Michael asked, turning in his direction to face him.

"Yeah."

"Question. Why you ain't ever come see me?"

Sam looked Michael in his eyes and answered, "For what? To see you get hauled off like an animal in a cage?"

"So you saying I'm an animal now? What? I ain't human no more?"

"Shit, Mike. Hell yeah! From the stories I heard about you cutting niggas heads off and rolling it down the tier like a bowling ball, only an animal could do some shit like that."

Sam and Michael laughed.

"I guess you're right then. But anyway, I do want to thank you for helping my family out when I called on you."

JASON POOLE

"That's nothing. I'm supposed to do that. We've been friends since elementary school." Silence filled the air.

Michael didn't respond, instead he looked out the passenger window and studied the Southeast jungle while also admiring his friend's loyalty.

"So where you wanna go now?" Sam asked, breaking his silence.

"Let's go to the Pancake House, get a bite to eat, and finish discussing how we gonna take over this muthafucka," Mike answered.

"Cool," Sam replied and then mashed the gas. Sam was eager to talk about taking over much more than Mike would realize.

Chapter 5

-THE TAKE OVER-

Within three months, Michael had taken over two strips—Sixth Street and Talbert Street Southeast. He and Sam were going hand-to-hand with some of the best heroin in Southeast. Sixth Street wasn't that hard to take over. Kojack had heard about Michael at Lorton. So before Michael could make him an offer he couldn't refuse, Kojack surrendered on his own. Now he was buying from Michael, and he was the best customer Michael had.

After Sixth Street got moving, it was pulling in an easy twenty thousand dollars per day. The more the strip pumped, the less Sam and Michael had to be on the streets. Eventually, they hired Kojack as a lieutenant. They would drop off the dope early in the morning and collect money at nine o'clock at night.

Money was coming in from Talbert Street and Sixth Street so fast that Michael had to find another supplier, because Sonny James couldn't handle the rush. Whenever Sonny would get down, Michael was the first to buy all of it and then ask if there was more. Since Michael needed more than Sonny could supply, Sonny turned him on to Big Luke, who was D.C.'s first real millionaire in the drug game. Big Luke sold kilos of dope to all the major hustlers in the city. Luke began selling Michael kilos at a wholesale price, so Michael would buy one kilo and then get the other fronted. In the process of moving the product, Mike and Sam took shifts. Michael would buy it, and Sam would package it and dish it out to customers and lieutenants.

The next year was booming. Michael bought a brand-new, pearl white, convertible Jaguar and Sam purchased an all-black 300E Mercedes Benz. After laying the hit on the Wilson brothers who ran Fifteenth Place, Sam suggested they take out Skinny Pimp, who ran Wahler Place, the deadliest and most profitable strip in Southeast.

"Look, Mike, the nigga Skinny Pimp runs this shit. If we kill this nigga, we can get the spot. And from what I hear, this muthafucka is moving anywhere from fifty to seventy-five thousand a day."

"Yeah, that shit sounds good, but like I said before, I ain't tryna deal with them niggas around there. They're snakes. Better yet, they're wolves. They run in packs. They kill each other. They ain't tryna get no money. They just got a pumpin' ass strip."

"I'm telling you, Mike. We can get this joint."

"A'ight. If you think so, we'll try it. But if anything goes wrong, I'm holding you responsible."

"Good. We can meet up first thing tomorrow morning and take care of everything."

The next morning, Sam and Michael dressed up as dope fiends. They drove Connie's Maxima and parked it around the corner on Ninth Street. While walking through the alley, they came across some other fiends.

PRINCE OF THE CITY

"Hey, where that good shit at? Who got that bomb? We sick as hell," Michael said. One fiend looked at them. Sensing something was up.

"Hey, where you from? We ain't never seen you coppin' 'round here."

"We usually cop from Kojack on Sixth Street, but he got locked up last night," Michael answered.

Then Sam interrupted. "Man, fuck where we from. We just tryna get our mix, man. We ill. Now is you gonna tell us where to get it?"

"Yeah. Go through the alley and look to your left. You'll see a line, but I don't think Skinny Pimp gonna serve no new faces. Y'all probably gotta pull up your sleeves and show 'im your tracks first."

"Shit, ain't nothing wrong with that. We got enough tracks to make 'im give us some dope," Michael said.

They walked through the alley and saw the longest dope line they had ever seen.

"See, Mike. Look. I told you this spot was pumpin'."

As they approached the long line, scratching their arms like true dope fiends, Michael scoped out the scene. Skinny Pimp had two other dudes with him. One was short, and anyone could tell by the way he walked that he was strapped. The other looked like a fiend. He was serving the blow while Skinny Pimp collected the money. As the line got shorter, their plan started to unfold.

Michael whispered in Sam's ear, "Make sure you hit him right between the eyes."

"I got you, Mike. Just watch my back."

As Sam approached Skinny Pimp, Michael was in line right behind him. Skinny Pimp looked at Sam and said, "Who the

37

fuck are you? You ain't never copped nothing around here before."

"I'm Jimmy, man, and I'm ill. I need a fix bad." He started scratching his arm. "Look, man, I know you don't know me, but I usually cop my shit from Black Sam and Mike Perry up on Fifteenth Place. Them niggas done got too big to come out and serve us early in the morning when we really need it."

"Oh yeah? You cop your shit from them bitch-ass niggas, huh? You know what? I'm glad you came over here, 'cause them punks just lost a customer. Now what you want?" Skinny Pimp asked.

Sam looked Skinny Pimp deep in his eyes and gave him an answer he didn't want to know. Sam pulled out his .38 Special and placed it between Skinny Pimp's eyes.

"Nigga, I'm Black Sam, and I don't want no blow. I want your life." With that, he pulled the trigger. *Boom!*

When the shorter guy started to reach for his gun, Michael eased up right beside him, put a .38 to his temple, and pulled the trigger. The fiend who was serving the blow dropped the package and ran back through the alley while all the other fiends stood and watched Skinny Pimp's brain ooze from his head.

Michael picked up the package of blow, held it up in the air, and said, "This strip is now under new management. Free blow for everybody courtesy of the old manager, Skinny Pimp." With that, he threw the package into the crowd of dope fiends and left.

After killing Skinny Pimp, Michael and Sam opened Wahler Place back up with raw dope. Fiends from all over were dying to get some of the brand named heroin they called Pink Panther. They were pulling in fifty thousand dollars a day from Wahler Place alone. It got to the point where they had to take all of their best lieutenants off the old strips and move them over to Wahler Place. Clientele was tremendous, and Michael Perry's name was the talk of Southeast.

Although Mike and Sam were equal partners, the streets respected Michael more. Sam treated dope fiends like trash, but Michael treated them with respect. If a fiend didn't have any money to cop when he was really ill, Michael would tell one of his workers to give him a blow, and sometimes Michael would even give the fiend a few dollars. While Sam was hard on the workers and lieutenants, Michael would sometimes work with them if they came up short. Sam looked down on those who didn't have anything, but Michael would buy kids in the neighborhood tennis shoes.

Although Michael was a gentleman, he knew how to turn into the devil when needed. He had charisma. The younger guys emulated him, the older guys respected and feared him, and the women adored him.

Unfortunately, while Michael was building an empire, Sam was tearing it down with a vicious gambling habit. Sometimes he'd win, but when he lost, he'd lose big. Michael and Sam were close to reaching the goal they had set to leave the game behind, which was two million dollars, but Sam's gambling was slowing down progress.

Inside Michael's condo, he and Sam rolled perfect joints while they gathered all the money they collected from that day's shift. Michael picked up thirty thousand from Sixth Street and twenty thousand from Fifteenth Place. He collected another thirty thousand from Talbert Street and twenty-eight thousand from Melon Street. These strips were Michael's responsibility. He was also in charge of the neighborhood he grew up in, Langston Lane.

The Lane wasn't a dope strip. The main drug of choice in that area was weed. Michael usually picked up about twenty thousand a week from Langston Lane.

"Hey, Sam, did you bring the money machine?" Michael asked.

"Yeah, I got it."

"How much you pick up from Wahler Place?"

"I got like thirty-five," he replied lowly.

"Thirty-five?" Michael said, shocked by the number.

"Yeah, Mike."

"Damn! What the fuck is going on over there? When we first got that joint it was moving no less than fifty." He looked at Sam with disappointment.

"Yeah, I know, but shit is moving slow now. For real, I think Kojack's been holdin' out lately."

"Well, that's your spot. When we first got it, it was understood that you'd be in charge. I think you need to change lieutenants if Kojack is stealing."

"I ain't saying the nigga's stealing, Mike," Sam said. "He just ain't paying like he usually does."

"If that ain't stealing, I don't know what is."

"Forget it, Mike. I'll talk to him."

"Okay, but remember, it's your responsibility to hold down that spot. That's our most valuable strip."

"Don't worry. I got it."

And Sam did have it. Once again Sam was blaming Kojack for his gambling habit. Sam had been uptown on Seventh and T Streets all day gambling with Butter, who had won thirty thousand from Black Sam, money that Kojack had earned on Wahler and given to Sam.

After counting the day's profit, they combined it with the rest of the money.

"Ay, Mike, this is 1.3 million. We only got seven hundred thousand to go. We should have it within the next six months if everything goes right."

"Yeah, let's just make sure everything goes right, 'cause I'm ready to pack up, relocate, and live a comfortable life. Fuck this game, Sammy. There are only two things that can happen if we continue—jail or death. And I don't want either one of 'em."

"I hear you, Mike. These cracker-ass Feds ain't gonna let a nigga get but so much before they arrest you and take it all."

"That's my worst nightmare, Sam."

"Mine too."

Connie walked into the living room to see if Mike and Sam were finished handling business. "Hey, honey," she said.

"Hey, baby, come here. I missed you." Mike kissed his wife passionately while Sam looked on with a smile.

"I guess I should be leaving," Sam said.

"Oh no. I'm sorry, Sam," Connie said. "I didn't mean to come in here and bother y'all."

"It's okay, Connie. We're finished anyway." Sam embraced his best friend and called for Malik before he left. "Ay Malik, come out here and give your Uncle Sam some dap."

Malik came running and gave Sam a smooth but firm handshake like his father had taught him.

"Hey, wazzup, lil soldier? You been doing good in school?"

"Yeah, I'm doing good, but my math needs a little work."

"Ah, man. You know you gotta get that math down pat. How else you gonna count all that money when you get rich, huh?"

Malik smiled. "I dunno."

Sam rubbed him on the head. "Look, I gotta go, but remember, get that math down."

"Okay, okay, Uncle Sam. I got you."

"Okay, lil man. See you later, Connie."

"Bye Sam."

"Tomorrow, Mike."

"Yeah Sam. Ay, don't forget what I said about Kojack."

"I got you."

After Sam left, Connie snuggled up with her man.

"Hey baby. Go 'head and get yourself together while I go out on the balcony and talk to my son."

"Okay, baby." Connie kissed him and started to walk off. However, before leaving the room, she stopped. "Oh yeah, Mike?"

"Wazzup, baby?"

"Talk to Malik about acting up in school. His teacher called me at work today and said he was fighting."

"Okay, baby. Now go ahead and freshen up, 'cause I'm a punish that pussy tonight."

"Oohhh, I love it when you talk like that." Connie went into the back room while Michael poured himself a glass of Remy Martin.

"Hey Malik! Come out here with me on the balcony."

At night, Southeast sounded even more gruesome than during the day. Gunshots rang out from way across the other side of Valley Green. Sirens went off and screams and laughter echoed throughout the streets. While Michael and his son looked out into the jungle of Southeast, a jewel was being dropped on an innocent child.

"Malik, look out there and tell me what you see."

"I see a jungle, Dad."

"That's right, son. And what kind of animal rules the jungle?"

"The lion does, Dad."

"Why is that, son?"

"Because he's brave and wise."

"That's right. But most of all, he is what?"

"A thinker, Dad. He studies his enemy before he attacks. That is why he remains on top and keeps order."

"Okay, Malik." Michael then pointed out to certain areas. "What am I pointing at?"

"That's Valley Green, Dad."

"And what did I say about the Valley?"

"That's where the wolves dwell. They run in packs. Always feed 'em and never let 'em go hungry, because when they're hungry, they'll turn on you. But as long as you feed 'em, they're cool. And whenever you stop feeding them, have a plan to get rid of 'em."

"Okay. Now what's that?" Michael pointed in a different direction.

"Barry Farms."

"And what did I tell you about the Farms?"

"They're like the gorillas. They take. Never be careless with your valuables when you go through there."

"And what's that?" Mike asked, pointing again.

"Oh, that's Third, Fourth, and Sixth Streets."

"And what do you know about that?"

"That's where the snakes lie. Never turn your head, 'cause once you do, they bite. Never trust 'em, no matter how pretty they seem to be. They are masters of trickery."

"Okay. Now what's that?"

"That's Alabama Avenue. Everything on that side is under the lion's rule. They comply with everything the lion says with no problem."

"Now, name all the spots on that side under the lion's rule."

"Well, Dad, we got Fifteenth Place, Robinson Place, Stanton Road, Savannah Terrace, Twenty-second Street, Shipley Terrace, Congress Park, Wellington Park, Ambassador Square, Langston Lane, and Butler Gardens. Oh, hold on, Dad. I forgot Sixteenth Street and W Street."

"That's right, son. Now tell me who the lion is?"

"He's the king of the jungle. He sits high on a throne watching over his subjects."

"And who is the king?"

Malik smiled and looked up at his father. "You Dad. You're the king."

"That's right, son. Now, if I'm the king, then what does that make you?"

"The prince."

At that moment Connie walked out onto the balcony. "Now, I'm the queen, and I run this part of the castle. And the queen says it's past your bedtime, Mr. Prince."

"Awww, Ma. Can I stay out here and talk to Daddy?"

"No sir. Not tonight. You've been out here long enough. Now give your daddy a kiss goodnight. He'll see you tomorrow."

Malik looked up to his father for some help.

"Sorry, son. She's the queen. I can't help you out on this one."

"Man, okay." Malik kissed his father and told him he loved him. "Oh. Dad, don't forget you said you were taking me to the carnival down RFK Stadium tomorrow."

"I haven't forgotten, son. I love you."

"I love you too, Dad."

PRINCE OF THE CITY

"Goodnight, son."

After Malik left, Michael took another sip of his drink and continued to stare out into the Jungle contemplating his next move. He knew that whatever he had to do, it had to be done fast and with caution.

Chapter 6

-1987 (THE CROWN)-

In the animal kingdom, the lion hunts with great skill so that their offspring or pride will have enough to eat. And in the spring of 1987, that's just what Michael set out to do, and there wasn't a better place to start than in Las Vegas at the Sugar Ray Leonard versus Tommy Hearns fight.

Michael had to get his things together before the fight. This was not just a vacation for him. It was the biggest break in his hustling career. Big Luke had set up a meeting for Michael with his connect. Luke was planning to disappear for about a year because he felt the Feds sniffing around. So before he let them get close enough to get a whiff, he was going to get ghost.

Michael and Sam were the only two hustlers in the city whom Luke respected enough to reveal his source. He liked Michael's style, and he understood Michael's plan to get rich and not go to jail. Although he never really knew how much they were collecting, he always thought they ran a smooth operation. Therefore, to keep the city moving, Luke stepped aside and gave up his position to a dynamic, aspiring, young hustler.

Within the first minute of the fourth round, Black Sam got up from his front row seat, fixed his clothes, and excused himself from the meeting.

"Does he always make that a habit?" the connect asked, nodding in Black Sam's direction.

"What are you talking 'bout?" Mike asked.

"The gambling, Michael. I bet you nine out of ten he's going down to the casinos."

"Nah, he just dibs and dabs a little."

Big Luke's connect was a smooth hustler out of Harlem, New York, and one of the richest black hustlers in his time. Frank Wallace Mathews had Harlem in an uproar with the purest dope coming in from China.

"Now Frank, are we going to sit here and talk about what my partner does in his spare time, or are we gonna talk business?"

"I like that in you, Michael. Your willingness to take advantage of an opportunity."

"Yeah, it's money out there to be made and I want it."

"Michael, the one reason I continue to make money in this game and stay alive and outta jail is because I don't go back on my word. My word is my bond, and whatever standards I set I keep to 'em, understand?"

"Yeah, Frank. Totally."

"Good then. Well, first of all, I can see you are more of the businessman between the two of you. So from now on, I deal strictly with you and no one else, understand?"

"Yeah, but before you go any further, I'd like to let you know that Sam is not only my partner, he's my best friend."

"Michael, in this game there are no friends. Money is truly the root of all evil, and when you get enough of it, you'll see for yourself. Just remember I told you that."

"I'll remember."

"Now, I know that Big Luke was giving it to you for a good number, but I want to see you move up a little faster. So what I'm a do is give it to you for ninety thousand a key, and after the first six months, I'll drop it to eighty. Also, I know Big Luke wasn't giving his to you in its purest form either. The shit I'm a give you can stand a fifteen. Can you deal with that?"

Michael knew the answer he was about to give would be the start of a new future. Also, he knew he was going to have to move fast before Big Luke came back home. He planned to be retired by the time Luke hit the streets.Micheal then placed his hand on Frank's shoulder and flashed a smile.

"Yeah, Frank. And furthermore, I'd like to thank you for giving me the opportunity to make money."

"Well, you know Luke highly recommended that I deal with you in his absence."

"Yeah, me and Luke's relationship is solid."

"Good then. That should seal the business side of the meeting. Now let's get some drinks."

While Mike and Frank sat at the bar talking about the finer things in life, a strikingly beautiful woman whispered something in Michael's ear.

"Hello, Mike. Your scar makes you look even sexier than I remember."

Michael quickly turned to see who was talking in his ear. He figured it had to be someone he knew as a teenager, because he'd had the scar ever since he was seventeen. Michael looked the woman in the eyes with shock. Of course he knew her. In fact, he knew her very well.

"Hello, Chevece. How are you? The last time I heard from you—"

She quickly cut him off. "Yeah, I know. A not too pleasant letter postmarked from New York."

Chevece and Michael were sweethearts before Connie entered the picture. Chevece always blamed Connie for taking Michael away from her, but never told Connie about her and Mike's relationship. She'd left that part up to Connie's friend, nosey-ass Linda.

"Well, Chevece, you still look fine. So tell me, what brings you to Vegas?" he asked while his eyes continued to survey her beautiful looks.

"You wanna know the truth?" Chevece smirked.

"Go ahead."

"Well, for your information, I'm married to the owner of this hotel." She held her diamond clad hand up as a gesture to show ownership.

"Oh yeah?"

"Yes. And yes, he's white and treats me well."

"That's nice to hear. I'm happy for you." Michael nodded his approval.

"Yeah, right. So how's your wife?" she asked, turning her smirk into a hard frown.

"How did you know I was married?"

"Come on, Mike. I may have left D.C., but I still got family."

"Well, Connie is doing good. She's happy."

"I bet she is. You have a son, don't you?" she asked with a devilish smile.

"Yes, I do. His name is Malik, and he's eight years old now."

"Same age, huh?" She folded her arms

"Same age as what?" Michael asked, quickly putting his drink down. He was curious about Chevece's antics, yet he was also ready to put a stop to it.

"Never mind, Mike," she said, putting up her hand as a gesture to stop. "Anyway, it was nice seeing you. Hope you enjoy your stay. Have fun," Chevece said, walking away from the bar

"I will," he responded, shaking his head.

"Damn, Mike, who was that fine-ass broad?" Frank asked, looking back at her as she walked toward an exit.

"Oh, she was a girl I used to mess with back in junior high."

"You mean to tell me you stopped messing with her?"

"I left her for my wife."

"Your wife must be a goddess, 'cause that broad is straight-up bad!"

"Yeah, she might be bad, but that bitch is crazy."

* * * * * * *

On the flight back home, Sam and Michael discussed their future. "Look, Mike, it's gonna take us only about three months to get to our two-million mark."

"What are you saying, Sam?"

"All I'm saying is that since Big Luke stepped off and now our prices are extremely low, we can do this for one more year and come out with four million."

"We agreed on two million."

"Yeah, I know. But I'm telling you, two million more won't hurt us, and you know if we move it with no problems, it'll come overnight."

Michael thought about Sam's proposal. Big Luke was gone and they had all the pumping strips in Southeast, plus a few of Big Luke's customers in Northeast and uptown. An extra two million would be cool. He and Connie could relocate and buy into a few businesses, get their dream house, and raise Malik in a better environment. Michael did want enough money so that his family could be secure.

"Okay, you got me, but on one condition."

"What's that?"

"We quit after six months. That's my word, and I'm not going back on my word for you anymore. I did it this one time because you my nigga and we came up together."

"Good then."

Black Sam and Mike shook on their decision.

"Ay, Sam?" Michael reached over and tapped his friend to make sure he had his full attention.

"Yeah, Mike?"

"There's something I've wanted to ask you since we got the time, and I want you to be straight up with me."

"What's up?"

"Man, have you developed a habit for gambling?"

"Fuck no! I just do it every now and then when I got some play money."

"Do you be winning?"

"Sometimes I do. Sometimes I don't."

"Well, tell me this. What's the most you won?"

"About seventy-five thousand uptown at the pool hall. I be bustin' they ass."

"You gotta watch those uptown niggas. They real smooth with that gambling shit. They'll let you win just so you'll come back and get your head cracked for triple of what you won."

"Nah, I'm too sharp for that. I know when to stop."

"I hope you do." Michael paused briefly. "So tell me this."

"What?" Sam asked, hoping his friend wouldn't ask another question that would make him lie.

"What's the most they ever got you for?" He then looked at him sternly, studying his face for the truth.

"Not as much as I won. Believe me. I'm a dice shootin' mothafucka." An arrogant smile beamed across his face.

"You probably are. I just hope you ain't taking no money out the kitty for that shit."

"Nah, slim. I only do it when I got play money. My stash is my last." Sam once again lied to his best friend, but he knew that Michael was no dummy. Sooner or later his wrongdoings would come to light.

As soon as they got home, Frank sent down ten kilos of pure heroin, which he called China White. Sam and Michael sold a few kilos straight up to some of Big Luke's old customers, and they stepped on the remaining bricks and put it on the market. For the next six months, Michael and Sam were getting so much money that they exceeded their four-million-dollar mark. They'd begun to move up in the game, and the more money they made, the more Michael's plans became crystal clear.

Chapter 7

-LION'S SHARE-

Six months later . . .

One day as Michael pulled his pearl white Jaguar into the car wash on Martin Luther King Jr. Avenue, a silver 735 BMW pulled up. Butter was behind the wheel and Linda sat in the passenger seat. They all exchanged greetings.

"What's up, Butter?" Mike had just asked the question that gave him the perfect opening for his proposition.

"Ain't nothing," Butter replied. "Just picked up Linda from your house."

"Yeah, I was getting tired of your lil bad-ass son, so I took him home to his mommy," Linda added, still seated in the passenger seat.

"What he do?" Michael asked with a curious expression.

"Oh, nothing." Linda waved her hand. "Malik's my angel. I just had to do something."

"Thanks anyway for keeping him."

"Anytime. You know I love my nephew."

"Mike, can I talk to you in private?" Butter asked, stepping out of his car.

"Yeah, what's up?" Michael leaned against his car and folded his arms. He knew that talking with Butter would be a potential meeting about making money.

"Linda, go get the car washed while I talk to Mike," Butter instructed and then walked over to Mike's car.

"Okay, daddy." Linda hopped over in the driver's seat and pulled into the car wash. After formerly greeting Mike with a handshake, Butter got right down to business.

"I know we ain't ever dealt with each other before. Although me and your partner Black Sam is cool, I thought it would be better if I hollered directly at you."

"Talk then." Mike shrugged.

"Look, I'm tryna open up Fourteenth and Clifton with some of that China White you got, but I need you to sell it to me raw. How much can I get it for?"

"I can give it to you for a hundred fifty a key."

"Got damn!" Butter yelled out in complaint.

"Shit, nigga. The blow can take a fifteen. I should be giving it to you for a hundred seventy-five, but on the strength of Linda, I cut you twenty-five thousand."

"A'ight then, I understand. Right now I only got a hundred thousand. Can I owe you the rest?"

"I don't know about that. I gotta call my partner first to see if we got enough left to do that."

"Oh shit! That'll be a blessing to call Sam, 'cause he owes me fifty thousand anyway."

"Oh yeah? What he doing owing you?" Mike tilted his head in curiosity.

"I busted his ass shooting craps last night, and he turned around and borrowed it back, just so he could lose it to another nigga."

"Damn. Well look, here's my pager number. Call me later, and I'll set it up for you." He then quickly paid for his car wash and walk toward his Jaguar. Before leaving, he turned to shake Butter's hand, not out of friendship but for the information he indirectly gave him.

"Thanks Mike," Butter yelled as he walked away.

"Anytime. See you later, Linda," he called out as she got out of the driver's seat.

"Bye. And don't forget to tell Connie to call me," Linda yelled out before getting back in the passenger seat.

Michael jumped into his freshly cleaned Jaguar and drove up to Wahler Place to pick up Gerald, a youngin' from Simple City who was in Mike's crew down Lorton. He had just come home, so Michael made Gerald his top lieutenant. Gerald was loyal and dependable. He handled everything from packages to murder.

As Mike pulled up, everybody stopped to speak to him.

"My muthafuckin' man, smooth-ass Mike P."

"What's up, Fats?"

"Ain't shit. Out here tryna make that money," he said while making a transaction.

Michael looked up and down the street, making sure Fats was safe while doing business. "Is everything cool?" he asked.

"Yeah, except the fact y'all pushed up the prices on a nigga," he said with his hands in the air.

"What are you talking 'bout?" Mike asked. For all he knew, their prices never changed.

"Man, Sam came through here earlier talking 'bout I owe him a thousand dollars 'cause the prices went up. Shit, man, it ain't even a drought."

Mike paused. "I know, Fats. Don't worry about it. You can keep paying your regular price. I'll talk to Sam."

"Thanks, Mike. You a good nigga. I wanna be just like you when I grow up."

"You're older than me, remember?" He chuckled and shook his head in amusement.

"Oh, that's right. Never mind me. You know I be trippin' sometimes."

Michael smiled, and then continued to walk down the alley where Gerald set up shop.

Gerald emerged from the alley with gun in hand and shouted, "So what? Nigga, you getting bored with sitting on top collecting all that money? You wanna come back on the strip to see if you still can slang?" He was happy and honored that the man he looked up to as a father figure would come all the way down to the strip just to check on him.

"Nah, I came to pick you up. I wanna talk to you for a minute."

"It ain't about my car. Is it, Mike?" Gerald was afraid that his mentor wouldn't approve of him buying a lavish gift.

"What car?"

"My new car. Sam ain't tell you?"

"Nah, I haven't seen Sam in two days," Mike replied, looking confused.

"Oh well, I couldn't wait. The joint was so pretty that I had to get it."

"Well, where's it at? Can I see it?"

"Come around back."

For the first time, Michael was happy to see that Gerald had gotten something he liked. He purchased a candy apple red, turbo Nissan 300ZX.

"This joint is fast. Get in and see," Gerald said.

"How much did you pay for this?" Mike asked as they took a drive up to the Starr carryout on Wheeler Road.

"Thirty thou'."

56

"That's cool. I thought these joints were more than that. Man, I hope you still got something nice put up. I hate to see niggas buy cars then end up broke 'cause they spent their last."

"I still got a hundred forty thousand in the stash. I got a good deal at a dealer auction."

"That's good. I'm glad you're taking my advice about hustling."

"You know we go a long way back, and whatever advice you give a nigga it's always in his best interest." Gerald dipped in and out of traffic as they continued to talk.

"Hey Gerald, tell me something. What do you want out this game?" Michael asked. He had bigger plans for Gerald and wanted to make sure he was able to handle the new responsibility.

"For real, I'm cool with five hundred thousand. I can do a lot with that. Remember, we're from Southeast, and we're used to having nothing. So when we finally get it, we live how we want."

"Yeah, I hear you, but I got an even better proposal."

"Yeah? What's that?" Gerald asked, almost spinning in his direction, but still keeping his eyes on the road.

"Slow down, nigga. What you tryna do? Kill me?" he asked playfully.

"Oh, my fault." He slowed down the sports car.

"Yeah, it's cool." Mike glanced at Gerald briefly. "I'm gonna fire you as lieutenant and hire you as a partner. How 'bout that?"

"Partner? What! Partner? Did you talk to Sam about this?" Gerald cocked his head, instantly becoming curious.

"No, not yet. But regardless, I'm still pulling you in. We only got a couple more months left before we quit, and I want you to at least have a million before we stop."

"A mill'? Damn, Mike!" he said, excited almost to the point of unbelief.

"What?"

"I mean, this shit is too damn good to be true."

"Yeah, but you know I have a special interest in you. We go way back, and I could never forget your loyalty to me while in Lorton."

"For real, Mike. I'll never forget that you saved my life. If it wasn't for you seeing my potential and pulling me up, I'd probably be on death-row or dead."

"The main reason why I pulled you up was because I saw a lot of myself in you."

"And the reason I'm accepting the position is because I want to be rich like you." They both smiled.

"Take me back to my car," Michael ordered. "I'll set up a meeting with the three of us later to discuss the rest of my plan."

Chapter 8

-THE MEETING-

As Michael, Sam, and their soon-to-be new partner, Gerald, sat in the living room of Michael's apartment discussing the next few months, Black Sam felt it was his time to speak up.

"Hey. No offense to you, Gerald, but we don't need a new partner, especially since we ain't got but a few months left anyway." Sam's eyes shifted from both Gerald to Mike as he spoke. He was looking for an agreement of some kind, but neither man answered. For a brief moment, silence filled the room. Mike stood up and went to fix a drink.

"Well, Sam, I see it like this. There's enough money for everyone here. I have a lot of respect for young Gerald. My mission is to see that everyone comes outta this comfortable."

"I'm sure Gerald is man enough to make it on his own."

"I have no doubt in that, but if we leave him in the same spot, then he'll never get out the game."

"Mike, explain what you're trying to say." Sam demanded while looking back at both he and Gerald.

"What I'm saying is that Gerald doesn't have a connect, and once we stop hustling it'll be like handing him out there to the wolves. Now, I fucks with this young nigga here, and I'm not about to just sell him out like that. I'd rather pull him in and let him get enough money so that when we pull out, he'll be able to step off also."

"What if he doesn't want to step off? What if he wants to continue hustling?" Sam asked.

"Then that's on him. But we already talked about that, and his decision is to get a meal ticket and step."

"So you're telling me that you and Gerald already had this meeting without me, huh? You done made your decision, huh? So you're saying fuck what I think. I ain't got any say-so, huh? The last time I checked we were equal partners, right?" Sam pounded his chest with his fist while giving Mike a hard stare.

Michael stood in the middle of the living room, and with fire in his eyes he pointed his finger in Black Sam's face.

"Nigga, what the fuck you mean equal partners? If it wasn't for me coming home and puttin' this shit together, your black ass would still be riding around in that raggedy-ass 190E Benz, making a punk-ass two thousand a week. Nigga, I had the money, the plan, the connect, the moves, the respect, and most of all, I got my loyalty. Where yours at? How come I gotta find out from other niggas uptown that you losing a hundred to two hundred thousand shootin' craps, huh? Nigga, the last two months you lost over five hundred thousand of our money! You think I ain't know? But Sam, I see everything. So nigga, don't ever try to talk to me about equal partnership. I'm the CEO of this organization. I built this shit from prison, had a vision, took it to the streets, and made it reality." While the two friends argued, Gerald sat back and watched in amazement. Things started to get so heated that he began to question if Michael's idea was a good one.

"I understand that. All I'm saying is that you made the decision without me. Personally, I like young Gerald. I have

60

no problem with him, but when you make a decision like that, it should be conducted properly," Sam advised through clenched teeth.

"That's the reason why we're sitting in my living room now, Sam. Making a decision. All we got is a couple months left. So what we do from here on out is make as much money as possible. No spending and no lavish gambling. Agreed?"

"What about Gerald? What position is he playing?" Sam asked, pointing at Gerald.

"Gerald is gonna handle the collection from every lieutenant and turn it in at the end of the day."

"Damn Mike. Not only did you make him a partner, but you gave him my job," Sam replied with confusion and disappointment. Instantly, he felt betrayed.

"I did that for a reason, Sam. I want us to spend more time together. I gotta keep you focused before you go off the limb with this gambling shit."

Wrinkles formed in the center of Sam's forehead. "I'm a grown-ass man. I don't need you babysitting me!" he snapped.

"Sam, sometimes grown-ass men make mistakes. Now I want you to take Gerald around and introduce him to all the lieutenants on every strip," Michael said, turning his attention to the new addition to their family.

"Gerald, after 9 pm, your job is to collect whatever money has been made for that day, then find out how much blow didn't sell. Whatever is left over; give it to the lieutenant for half the price. That way he can pay his workers. Can you handle that?"

"Yeah Mike," Gerald responded.

"Now, at nine o'clock, I don't care where you at or what you doing, make sure your ass is at them strips picking up that money. I don't care if you have to get out of some pussy to do it, but bring the money straight over here and take the remaining packages out for the morning. At five thirty in the morning, you're gonna pass off the packages to the lieutenants. The only lieutenant that has the right to request more blow is Kojack. Whatever he wants, give it to him. He moves the shit."

"I don't know about that, Mike, 'cause Fats been moving a lot of shit too," Sam said.

"Yeah, but did you know Fats had a warrant out for violation of his parole? Ain't no sense giving him a lot of shit and then finding out he got locked up. That's like giving it away."

"Yeah, I see what you mean," Sam agreed. "Ay, Gerald, you think you can handle that?"

"Yeah, I got it like clockwork."

"Good then. Mike, let me talk to you out here on the balcony in private," Sam said.

"Okay. You want a drink?" Michael asked Sam.

"Nah, I wanna be levelheaded when we talk."

They went out on the balcony and sat in silence for a moment while overlooking the Jungle of Southeast D.C.

Michael finally broke the silence. "What is it you want to talk about, Sam?"

"You're my best friend and I love you, but what you said to me in there was disrespectful. I'm not talkin' 'bout your statement about being CEO of this organization and how you built it. I understand all that, 'cause it's true. But when you questioned my loyalty, I felt disrespected."

"Well, look at it from where we stand. How would you feel if you had to find out from another nigga that I was doing something that could tear down this plan we got going?"

"To tell you the truth, Mike. I don't give a fuck what another nigga says," he fearlessly announced while staring him directly in his eyes.

Michael sighed before speaking. "Now you're putting your feelings in it, Sam. Look at what you're doing. Five hundred thousand, Sam? A half a mil' that could be sitting in them briefcases is uptown in somebody else's hands. That ain't no play money. Any nigga that got half a mil' to play with is a rich muthafucka. The last time I checked we ain't rich. We're just living comfortable."

"Yeah, that's the other reason I called you out here."

"What are you getting at? Spit it out."

"Well, I was thinking, man. All I got is myself. I ain't got no wife and kids and all that responsibility shit. I ain't got no degree in marketing. All I know is these streets, and this is where I wanna be, out here in the jungle with my kind. For real, Mike, I ain't tryna quit. I wanna be a multi-millionaire. Fuck two or three million. I want two hundred million. I wanna be that rich muthafucka you talkin' 'bout that can afford to gamble half a mil' whenever he wants. I don't want nobody holding my stash. I wanna hold my own stash."

Michael nodded. "I ain't got no problem with that. We only got a couple months left to do this shit, though. Right now, we working with 3.6 mil' plus the hundred forty Gerald got."

"You mean to tell me that he only got a hundred forty thousand and you still making him a partner? Then in a couple of months he walks away with an easy meal ticket?" The very idea made Sam's insides burn with jealous anger.

"When we first started, you only had thirty-five thousand to my hundred thousand. And did I piss a bitch 'bout that?" Michael cocked his head and narrowed his brows.

63

"Nah, but I've known you all my life. We've been best friends since elementary school. You've only known this nigga for seven years in the joint."

"Ten years, Sam. Get it right. We still kept in touch when I got out, and on top of that, he was a part of this when I first put it together in the joint. Technically, he was a partner long before you. Shit, he helped me build this shit. At least I owe him that much." Michael didn't understand why bringing Gerald in as a partner bothered Sam so much.

Sam just looked out into the jungle. "Well, I'm not quitting. You and that nigga can do whatcha want. But me, I'm hustling for life. This is all I know, and all I need you to do for me is call Frank and tell him that after you quit, I'm a still be copping from him. Can you do that? At least you owe me that much respect."

"I've always respected you, and I do respect your decision, although I think it's a bad move for you. Plus, Big Luke is 'bout to come back on the scene anyway."

"Man, fuck Big Luke! Luke got enough money to last a lifetime. Me, on the other hand, in all reality I'm broke compared to him."

"Yeah, but a nigga can be comfortable with what you got."

"Maybe. But for some reason, I don't feel comfortable."

"All right then. I'll call Frank later on today and talk to him for you."

"Good then."

"For right now, everything is still on schedule. But after these couple months pass, we can split. Then you can do your own thing. Agreed?"

"Agreed," Sam responded.

They shook hands and embraced. Afterward, Sam looked into the jungle and took a deep breath before the two returned to the living room.

"Well Gerald, welcome to the organization. You 'bout to witness more money than you ever seen in your life," Sam told him.

"Yeah, I know," Gerald replied, "and believe me, I appreciate it." He extended his hand for a shake. Sam left him hanging.

"I know your ass does. Now, you ready to roll? 'Cause as of right now, your ass is on the clock."

They laughed.

"Yeah, let's go."

Ten minutes later, as Gerald and Sam rode up Martin Luther King Jr. Avenue in Sam's Mercedes. Sam turned down the music on his radio.

"So, how do you feel about Mike?" he asked Gerald, taking a quick side-glance at him.

"I got a lot of respect and love for Mike. For real, Sam, Mike doesn't know it, but I look up to him in a father-son type of way."

"Yeah, I can see that. So what you plan on doing with a funky-ass million dollars when you quit?" Sam asked.

"I plan to get a few soul food restaurants out here. Then chill and lay back."

"Oh, yeah? You got a girl? Any kids?"

"Nah. All I got is Mike and my man Carlos down Lorton."

"Damn, slim, and you mean to tell me you wanna quit and give up all this money you're gonna be making?"

"Shit, you know this don't last a lifetime."

"Yeah, I know, but don't you want more than one mil'?"

"Sam, I ain't ever had a mil'. To me, that's filthy rich," Gerald replied with a chuckle.

"Nah, young nigga, two hundred mil' is filthy rich."

"I agree with that. So what are you getting at?"

"Look, Mike is gonna quit. There's no doubt about that. But me, I'm still gonna be moving and making a lot of money. I'm a take over Southeast, and I need a good, young nigga like you in my corner."

"I dunno 'bout that—" Before Gerald could finish his sentence, Sam cut him off.

"Fuck what Mike says!" Sam shouted, instantly irritated. He slammed his foot down on the brake, almost stopping the car in mid traffic. "I'm talking about getting rich. Mike's talking 'bout living happily ever after with his wife and kid."

At that moment, Gerald knew he could no longer share his true thoughts with Sam. Gerald saw deception in Sam's eyes the same way he saw it in Donnie G's eyes down Lorton. He knew Sam wanted to take Michael's place, but he didn't know just how badly Sam wanted to be Mike, or the things he was willing to do to be placed in that position.

Chapter 9

-THE CONNECT-

At 5 pm, Connie called home. "Hey baby, what's up?" she asked Michael.

"Nothing. I'm just standing out here on the balcony," he replied.

"Damn, Mike, you stay out there. You ain't planning on jumping one day, are you?"

"Come on. You know I'll never leave the two of you. I don't care what I'm facing, and anyway, only suckers take their own lives."

"Baby, I'm just playin'."

"I know. So are you ready for tonight?"

"Yeah, I'm ready, baby. Did you get the tickets?"

"Yeah, I got two seats in the front row. A nigga had to pay extra for that."

"I bet you did pay extra. I better not see you lusting over Patti LaBelle either."

"Baby, the only woman I got eyes for is you."

"You better. Well, I'm 'bout to go pick up Malik from aftercare and take him over to Linda's."

"Is Linda gonna be home to watch him?"

"Yeah, baby. Why you say that?"

67

"Come on, Connie, we both know Linda's a top-flight whore."

"Michael, don't talk about Linda like that. That's my best friend and sister, and besides, she been quit doing that."

"So what's her profession now? Call girl?"

"Fuck you, Mike. I'm hanging up."

"Okay baby, I'm sorry. I was just playing. You know I love Linda. If I didn't I wouldn't let you take my son around her."

"Well, don't play like that. You know how I am about Linda. Plus, if I tell her what you said, she'd probably kick your ass."

"Yeah, right." Michael laughed. "Linda may have some heart, but she ain't stupid."

"Shut up! Ooooo, you make me sick."

"Then go to the hospital."

"I already did. I work at one, fool! Remember?"

They both laughed.

"I love you, baby," Michael said.

"I love you too, and when I get home I want you to love me some more."

"You got that, baby. You're the queen."

"See you later."

"Bye baby. And tell Malik to call me when he gets over Linda's."

"Okay, baby."

Michael hung up the phone and began pacing the living room while drinking his glass of Remy Martin. He was contemplating his call to Frank Mathews. In the beginning, Frank said he only wanted to deal with Michael. Michael was trying to figure out a way to make him understand that Sam wanted to continue with the connection. He knew he couldn't make up a lie. The best thing he could do was try to persuade Frank to deal with Sam. Even if he wouldn't work with Sam,

Big Luke was coming back soon, and Sam personally knew Big Luke, so he could cop from Luke directly. Although his prices would be more, Sam would still have a steady flow.

As Michael paced, he began to wonder if Sam was capable of becoming the next king of the jungle. He always knew he had the heart. Sam was a killer. Not only that, but he killed without reason. The thing that kept Michael in doubt was if Sam had enough brains and patience to deal with making future decisions. Was he capable of making his enemies bow down to his rule? All this had to be done with finesse, and Sam was lacking in that area.

If anything happened to Sam after he quit, Michael would feel responsible for letting him continue. But as Sam had put it, he was a 'grown-ass' man. So Michael decided to let Sam be his own man.

Michael placed his call to Frank.

"Hello?"

"Hey, Frank, it's Mike."

"Hold on a minute. Where you at?"

"I'm at home."

"Is your line clear?"

"Yeah, it's clear."

"Give me five minutes. I'll call you back."

Frank never talked business on his phone. He'd always go to a phone booth and place long distance calls on his bogus calling card.

"Hello?" Michael answered.

"It's Frank. What's the problem?"

"What makes you think there's a problem?" Michael asked.

"Well, first of all, you don't call me during this time of the day unless you're on your way up. Also, I know you can't be finished with everything that fast. And you never call me from your home phone."

"Yeah, you're right, but there ain't no problem. I just need to talk to you about a few things."

"If it's about Big Luke coming back and you wanting to continue on, I can't do that. I only deal with you in his absence."

"I understand that, but this ain't got nothing to do with Luke."

"Then talk, Mike. Time is money."

"Well, you know I'm quitting in a few months, and Luke won't be coming home for at least another six months, which leaves the city four months without some good shit."

"What are you getting at?"

"Well, my partner, Sam, ain't tryna quit. He wants you to continue moving—"

"Now hold on, Mike. Let me refresh your memory. When we first met, I told you that I only wanted to deal with you and only you."

"I know that, but this is my man, my partner. We're in this shit together."

"I know how you feel about your man and all, but I stick to my word. Do you remember when I told you the only reason why I stay in this game alive and outta jail?"

"Yeah, I remember."

"Do you really?"

"Yeah."

"What did I say then?"

"You said the only reason you stay alive and outta jail is because you don't go back on your word."

"Now I've been doing this shit for almost thirty years, and I've never broken my own rules."

70

PRINCE OF THE CITY

"I understand, and still I respect your decision. Although I'm a little fucked up about it."

"Don't be, Mike. Now if you want to cop for him, you can do that. But I ain't doing no business with him personally. And no offense, Mike, but your partner gives me the creeps."

"That's just the way he looks. If you took the time to really know him—"

"Sorry, I can't do it."

"I understand."

"Good then. I'll talk to you later."

"Okay, but if you change your—"

"Don't even try it. Nothing could ever change my mind."

Chapter 10

-KING OF THE JUNGLE-

At eight thirty that night, Black Sam and Gerald began to collect the profits for the day. Sam showed Gerald everything there was to know about the business while still trying to persuade Gerald to take him up on his offer. At the first three strips they collected over a hundred thousand dollars.

"See Gerald, look at this money. This money only comes from three strips, and we still got five more to go. You mean to tell me you wanna give this up?"

Gerald didn't answer because he knew his answer would be offensive. Instead, he stayed quiet. His plan was not to let Sam know how he felt until they got back to Mike's apartment. Then he would expose Sam's deep hatred to Mike.

"Nigga, are you deaf? You hear me talking to you?"

"Yeah, Sam, I hear you, but I'm in another world right now."

"Well, nigga, you need to jump your ass back into reality."

They picked up the rest of the money from the remaining strips and left Wahler Place for last. All together they collected two hundred sixty-five thousand dollars.

"Where is your car parked?" Sam asked Gerald.

PRINCE OF THE CITY

"Around back on Wahler Place."

"Good. After we collect from Kojack, you can take the money to Mike. I gotta go uptown for a minute, but I'll be back through."

"Okay."

Sam didn't pull up on Wahler Place. Instead, he drove around back and parked next to Gerald's car. The moment they parked, Gerald was happy. This was their last pick up and soon he would meet back up with Mike and expose Sam's greed. Gerald then got out, jumped in his car, and started the ignition. He felt uneasy and couldn't wait for their last pick up.

"Stay here with the money. I'll go up and collect from Kojack," Sam said. He left Gerald sitting in his car while he walked up to Kojack's stash house to collect. Once Kojack answered the door, Sam held his hand out and asked, "Ay, Kojack, you got that ready?"

"Yeah, but ain't Gerald supposed to pick it up?"

"Yeah, but he's running late. So give it to me, and when he comes past, tell 'im I said next time have his ass up here before nine o'clock."

"A'ight. Look, this is seventy thousand. I ain't finished the rest. I got like a hundred more bundles."

"Well, Kojack, this is your lucky day. You can keep the bundles."

"Get the fuck outta here, Sam! You mean to tell me you're giving something away?"

"Yeah nigga, and in the future, I got plans for you."

"Yeah well, I hope it ain't the same plans you had for Skinny Pimp," Kojack replied.

73

"Nah, it ain't that. If so, that would've happened a long time ago."

Sam went back to where Gerald was waiting and put the money in the gym bag along with the rest of the money. While Gerald sat in his brand-new 300ZX, Black Sam walked over to Gerald's car with the bag of money with his snub .44 caliber revolver behind his back.

"Ay Gerald?"

"What's up, Sam?"

"Look, slim, this the last time I'm a make my offer to you before you go over to Mike's. Now, you wanna get down with me or what?"

Gerald looked Sam directly in his eyes. "Nah, I'm a take Mike's advice and get an easy mil', then step off."

Sam eased his gun from around his back and placed it in the middle of Gerald's forehead. "Sorry Gerald, but that wasn't the answer I was looking for."

Boom!Boom!

Gerald's head jerked back and then bounced off the headrest of his car before falling forward onto the steering wheel.

Sam put the money in his car and drove off, leaving Gerald slumped with his head pressing against the horn of his car. The long drawn out sound echoed throughout the entire block. Beeeeeeeeeeeeeeeeeeep . . .

An hour later at 9:30 p.m., Black Sam rang the door buzzer. After looking through the peephole, Connie opened the door dressed in her new Gucci outfit that Michael had brought back from Las Vegas.

"Hi Sam."

"Hey Connie." Sam kissed her on the cheek. "You look nice. Going somewhere tonight?"

"Yeah, if your friend would hurry his butt up."

PRINCE OF THE CITY

Michael came from the back dressed in his Armani suit and draped in his most prized jewels.

"Damn, nigga. You killin' 'em. Where are y'all going tonight?"

"Down Constitution Hall to see Patti LaBelle and Frankie Beverly."

"Damn, ain't nobody tell me."

"Cut that shit out, Sam. Nigga, I asked your ass a long time ago was you tryna go."

"Oh yeah? Well, I still don't remember. And what's that you're wearing?"

"Giorgio Armani."

"Damn, you're wearing that muthafucka, too. Is that the bracelet that's supposed to have come from Italy?"

"Yeah, this is it."

"How much you pay for that?" Sam asked.

"About two hundred thou'," Michael replied.

"And you're pitching a bitch 'cause I gamble? But you're walking around with a nigga's house on your arm."

"Yeah, but if I want, I can always take this back and get my full value from it. Can you go uptown and ask one of them niggas for your money back?"

"Nah, I'm afraid you got me on that one," Sam replied. He clenched his teeth firmly to curtail his anger.

"Where's Gerald? Wasn't he supposed to be here dropping off?"

"This bitch kept paging him. He was with me for a while, so I told him I would make the drop for him."

"You shouldn't have made his first day that easy, Sam."

"Don't worry 'bout it. He knows how everything runs. Believe me."

75

"Hey baby!" Connie yelled for Michael. "It'll be time to go soon. Are you almost ready?"

"I'll be ready in a little while. Just give me a few minutes with Sam."

"Okay. Just let me know when you two are done." Connie hoped those few minutes didn't turn into sixty minutes. She didn't want to miss any of the concert. Connie grinned, happy that soon these business meetings would be a thing of the past.

* * * * * * *

Connie closed the bedroom door and dialed Linda's number.

"Hello? Linda speaking. May I help you?"

"Yeah, you can start by not answering your phone like a secretary."

"Shut up, Connie. What you want anyway?"

"I'm just checking up on my baby while my husband is finishing up with his business in the living room."

"Damn, Connie, he got you shacked up in that room while he's out there entertaining company?"

"Yeah, but it's cool, 'cause we getting our house next month and all this shit will be over."

"I'm so happy for you. You got a husband that got everything—money, respect, style, and enough sense to know when to quit."

"Yeah, thanks to you. If you wouldn't have made me go to that homecoming at Ballou High, I would have never met my baby."

"Yeah, I know. So when he gives you that first million-dollar shopping spree, your ass better not forget me."

"Hold on for a minute," Connie said, becoming silent for a few moments. "Okay, I'm back. I thought I heard them in there arguing."

"Who's in your house?"

"Black-ass Sam. Him and Mike go through the same routine every night, and tonight ain't the night, 'cause I'm ready to see Patti."

"I hear you, girl."

"Where's Malik?"

"He's playing cards with Butter," Linda replied.

"Tell Butter don't be teaching my son how to gamble."

"Shut up, Connie. Ain't nobody gonna turn your baby into a gangsta. Besides, that shit runs in his blood. His daddy is the biggest gangsta in Southeast."

"Yeah, but Malik doesn't know that."

"You think he doesn't?"

* * * * * * *

Mike and Sam got right down to business.

"Have a seat, Sam. You want a drink?"

"Nah, I'm cool. Let's just get all this out the way before we talk."

"How much did you pick up all together?"

"We got like three hundred ten thousand."

"Damn, shit must be lovely out there."

"It could be better. Now, how much you say was in them suitcases?"

"We got like 3.6 mil', plus the three hundred you got. We're only a hundred thousand from four million. Plus, we got two kilos left."

"Did you call Frank and talk to him 'bout our plans?"

"Yeah, I talked to him, but the man ain't tryna do it."

"What you mean he 'ain't tryna do it'?"

"Like I said, I called him earlier. I even tried to plead with the nigga, but he won't break. He says he only deals with me and that he doesn't want to deal with you."

"Why'd he say that? I ain't done anything for him to act like that. I only met the nigga once. He doesn't even know me." Sam looked confused and undecided, as if his friend wasn't telling him the truth.

"That's the problem, Sam. When we first met him, you showed no interest."

"How the fuck am I supposed to show 'im interest when you was the one doing all the talking?"

"Well, that's what the man said. I can't argue with you on that. I even asked the man to bend his own rules for you. He still said no. Now, if you want me to cop from him after these two kilos are gone, I'll do that for you. But after that, I'm through. And anyway, Luke will be back. You can hold fast and cop from him."

"Man, fuck Big Luke and fuck Frank Mathews's bitch ass!" Sam stood over Mike. "You know what I think? I think you don't wanna turn me on to that connect 'cause you afraid I'ma be way more successful at this shit than you are."

Mike laughed. "Come on, Sam. Be for real." He tried hard to ignore his friend's aggressive stance.

"Nigga, I am for real. You always kept me in the dark ever since we were little. That's how you dominated everybody. You did it with finesse. Nigga, all this time we been hustling together you're the one who holds the money, makes all the moves, meets all the connects, and tells everybody what to do, while I'm out there in the blistering cold hustling my ass off." Sam pointed his finger in Mike's face. "Nigga, you ain't shit. You don't wanna see me with nothing. You talk about me losing money gambling, but you got a fucking two-hundred-thousand-dollar bracelet. You sit up here looking over that

fucking balcony, thinking you're the fucking king for real."
Tears rolled down Sam's face while Michael looked at Sam
with love. Michael loved Sam, but Michael would still have to
deal with him. After gulping down his Remy, Michael sat
back, looked Sam deep in his eyes, and pointed his finger.

"Nigga, don't you ever in your fuckin' life raise your voice
in my house. Like I told your ass before. Nigga, I do run this
shit. Yeah nigga, I am the king. And if you ever in your life
stand over top of me like that again, nigga, I swear I'll cut
your dick and balls off and throw your ass over that balcony.
Now sit your muthafuckin' stupid ass down and take a chill,
nigga!"

Sam stood his ground as tears rolled down his face like a
water fountain. Michael looked at him with disgust. "Nigga,
didn't I tell you to sit your ass down?"

With that, Sam pulled out his Bulldog .44 revolver and
pointed it in Michael's face. Michael looked Sam in the eyes
and knew this man would kill. Sam also knew that if he let
Michael live, then he would be killed. They both understood
this reality, and Sam was the one with the upper hand. Michael
knew there was no way he could finesse his way out of this
one. Sam was a true killer. Michael knew it because he was
the one who made him like that.

"Now you know you're gonna have to use that," Michael
told Sam.

Tears rolled down both their faces.

"I was taught this by you: If you ever pull a gun on a man,
then you better use it. If you don't, then that same gun will be
the one that closes your own casket."

With that, Sam placed the gun to Mike's temple and pulled
the trigger.

Boom!

* * * * * * *

"Connie, what was that noise?"

"Hold up, Linda." Connie dropped the phone and ran out into the living room where Michael and Sam were conducting business.

Seeing her husband's brains splattered on the living room floor, she screamed as Sam pointed the .44 revolver at her chest.

"Oh my God! No, no Sam!" were the last words she uttered.

Boom!Boom!

Black Sam shot Connie twice in the chest. The impact sent her body flying across the room.

"Connie!" Linda yelled from the other end of the phone when she heard the gunshots. "Oh my God, Connie!"

* * * * * * *

Sam retrieved the suitcases of money and two kilos of heroin, while also relieving Connie of her diamond necklace that Michael had given her for their anniversary. He then wiped off the gun and placed it in Michael's hand, making it look like a murder-suicide. Since Connie was his wife, most likely the police would think he caught her having an affair, killed her, and then killed himself. Michael had previously done time for murder, so there wouldn't be much of an investigation.

While Sam was cleaning up and wiping off anything that could link him to the crime scene, he looked down at the person who was once his mentor and best friend. Sam loved Michael dearly, regardless of what he had just done. He bent over Michael's body and kissed his forehead.

PRINCE OF THE CITY

"You held it down strong while you had it, but you fell weak, Mike. Now it's my turn to wear the crown."

Chapter 11

-BURY ME A GANGSTER-

As Linda frantically kept calling Connie back, Malik could sense something was wrong. "Aunt Linda, what's wrong?"

"Nothing, Malik. Go back in the room and play cards with Butter." Linda grabbed her keys and headed for the door.

"Hey, where the fuck are you going?" Butter asked her.

"Something's wrong at Connie's. I gotta go over there." A few tears fell down Linda's worried face.

"What's wrong?" Butter asked her once he saw her crying.

"I don't know yet," Linda replied.

"Well, call me when you get there."

"Okay, I will. Keep Malik until I get back."

"Don't worry 'bout him. Just go ahead and do what you gotta do."

Linda drove Butter's BMW full speed while her mind replayed everything Connie had said on the phone.

"Oh no! Sam!" Tears rushed down Linda's face.

If anything had happened to Connie, Sam would be to blame and she would do whatever she had to do to get back at him. She knew the kind of man that Sam was.

PRINCE OF THE CITY

As she pulled up to the front of the Wingate Condominiums, paramedics brought out two bodies. Police were everywhere. The crowd was eerily still, some crying and others shaking their heads.

As Linda walked up, she could hear the conversation from people in the crowd. Although she knew they were talking about her best friend, she still had to see for herself.

Linda wanted to break down and cry, but she had to be strong, at least until she was able to find some place to go and let it out. There wasn't a doubt in Linda's mind that Black Sam had killed her friend. She was the only witness to this homicide. Although she'd never go to the police, she was still determined to get revenge.

Back in the car, Linda rode down Martin Luther King Jr. Avenue until she found a secluded spot. She pulled the BMW over, put it in park, got out, and screamed the loudest she could. "Oh my God, Connie! No, this can't be! No God, no!"

Linda felt her prayers wouldn't be answered, so she got up off her knees, wiped her tears, and made a vow to Connie and Michael. "I want you to know that Malik is now my son, and I will raise him like a warrior just like both of you. My love for you will last forever, and I promise you this. No matter how long it takes me, Black Sam will never get away with this. There are only two people alive that knows what he did, and before I leave this earth, I promise there will only be one. I love both of you, and I promise I'll protect Malik by any means necessary." She then looked up to the sky and blew a kiss.

"Love you two. You were my true family."

* * * * * *

Michael and Connie's funeral and wake were held at Mason's Funeral Home on Good Hope Road in Southeast. Major players from all over attended. The whole jungle came to pay their respects to the king and queen.

Lavish cars pulled up with people dressed in their best attire. Women who loved Michael cried their eyes out, and old ladies who loved his gentleness prayed over his body. Malik stood silently.

Linda broke it down to Malik hard. It was all she knew. She was raised hard, and she planned to raise Malik even harder. His understanding was beyond normal. Malik wasn't sad that his mother and father had been killed. Instead, he was angry their killer had gotten away. He was confused at how his father could fall victim to this. All he knew was that his father was king, and the king was invincible. Malik learned to accept that at some point in time, every animal in the jungle fell victim to prey.

This wasn't a funeral. It was a gangsta's goodbye party, a time when hustlers met connects and gangsters ordered hits. Pretty women attended just to meet these gangsters.

Right before the sermon, the funeral became silent, as if people had seen a ghost. Linda held Malik's hand tightly as Black Sam entered the funeral like a king. All he needed was a red carpet. He wore a black suit and the diamond in his ear was about five carats, setting off his shiny black head.

After Sam walked through, all the hustlers and gangsters started whispering to each other. Word on the street was that Gerald had robbed and killed Michael and Connie, and when Black Sam caught him getting in his 300ZX with the money, he put two bullets in his head and took over the operation.

Black Sam was now officially the new king, boss man, and CEO of Southeast. He came out looking like a hero, but deep down inside, he was too hurt to look at his friend lying in the casket. Linda peeped all the signs, and it was official that he was the killer.

When Sam came over to Malik, he jumped up to embrace him. "Uncle Sam!"

"Hey, lil man. Everything's gonna be all right."

As Linda stared Black Sam in the eyes, he looked away and held Malik even tighter. "Everything's gonna be all right, Malik. I promise."

Malik couldn't fight back the tears anymore. Sam was the closest thing he had to his father, and Linda was the closest thing he had to his mother.

Linda didn't talk, but her eyes pierced Sam's eyes. Nigga, your bitch ass killed them, and now you're gonna come in here and try to console their son? I swear on my life you will answer for this, she thought. With all her strength, Linda held her thoughts inside and grabbed Malik. "Come on, Malik. We gotta get going. Say goodbye to Sam."

"Bye, Uncle Sam."

"Bye, young soldier. Always remember everything your father taught you, okay?"

"I will, Uncle Sam. Are you gonna come pick me up from Linda's sometime?"

"Yeah, Malik. I'm a come and get you all the time. We gonna do everything together."

With that, Linda headed out the door while mumbling under her breath, "Bitch-ass nigga, lying to my nephew. He doesn't give a fuck about you, Malik. He killed your parents."

"What did you say, Aunt Linda?" Malik asked.

"Oh, nothing, baby."

Chapter 12

-GANGSTER ACADEMY-

1990 . . .

By the time Malik turned twelve, he was a full bred, seasoned youngster that was soon to come up in the ranks as a gangster. Linda lived uptown with Butter on Seventh Street Northwest, which was the busiest market for crime. It was considered a gangster's paradise. Everything moved on Seventh Street, from drugs to prostitution, gambling to murder, life to death. This was where Linda raised Malik.

Uptown was more like Las Vegas, where tricks were constantly being played. If someone wasn't sharp enough to recognize game, then he would fall victim to everyone's play.

Linda taught Malik everything she knew about surviving the streets. Although Linda knew Connie would never raise her child this way, she also knew that whenever Michael had a chance, he planted the seed of the streets in Malik. It was Linda's turn to make sure the seed blossomed into a full-fledged gangsta.

She brought Malik up hard. At ten, Malik's first lesson from Linda was to fight back, no matter what, and to come out the winner. Linda signed Malik up for boxing, and within the first six months, Malik caught on fast. He became skilled in throwing every blow with speed, power, and precision.

The coach took an extreme liking to Malik. He told Linda that Malik was a natural born champion. Malik had power in both hands, the heart of a lion, and the cleverness of a fox. He couldn't understand how a ten-year-old kid was able to fight and think at the same time. Although Linda knew how, she still kept it to herself. Malik had built-up anger, and whenever he put gloves on, it was his way to release it.

After learning he was well-trained in throwing hands, Linda took Malik out of boxing class and put him straight into the gangster's academy. She didn't put him in boxing class to make it a career for him. She did it to create a highly skilled fighter on the streets. She knew one day the lessons he learned would be used in a life or death situation.

Linda took Malik to the pool hall on Seventh and T Streets, Northwest—what she called the gangster's academy. The pool hall was where one could learn how to be every type of hustler.

Shorty Jeff, the owner, was the first person introduced to Malik. Jeff was a short, chubby guy in his early fifties. Always neatly dressed, he wore expensive diamond rings, but never watches. He used to say there was no need for a watch when getting money was his only goal twenty-four hours a day.

Jeff knew Malik was Michael's son, and he knew that Linda was raising a gangster. He took a liking to Malik because he was eager to learn the tricks of the game, and Jeff wanted to teach him. Although Jeff knew the cops could close down the place if they raided the pool hall and found Malik inside, he still let Malik hang around.

The first thing Jeff taught Malik was how to shoot craps. He taught him everything from pad rolling to switching dice. Malik became good at shooting craps, but he failed at his talk game.

Linda then introduced Malik to Buttons, the pimp. Buttons was the biggest and slickest pimp in D.C. He often played pool with Butter while waiting for his hoes to come pay him. Linda always liked Buttons, but she never wanted to deal with him. Buttons was too slick for his own blood.

Linda wasn't the one to answer to a pimp. She'd already been through that with Butter long ago. Linda was her own person and had two whores in her stable that were bringing in at least a thousand dollars a day. Other pimps hated her, but Buttons respected her.

"Hey, Buttons, can I see you for a minute?" Linda asked, walking over to his table.

"Yeah. Whazzup, baby girl?"

"Look, I've known you for a long time now, and as long as I've known you I've never asked you for nothing."

"So what's your angle?" asked Buttons, crossing his leg and looking at her curiously.

"Well, see that little boy over there talking to Shorty Jeff?" She pointed at Malik.

"Yeah, I saw him in the back last night shootin' craps. He had a nice shoot, too."

"Yeah, I know. That's my nephew, and I wanna teach him some things 'bout this game. Will you help me?" she asked, tilting her head.

"What you tryna do? Raise a pimp?"

"Nah. I just want you to spend some time with him for me. Give him that gift of gab. He needs a talk game to go with that shot he got."

"Well, baby girl, if I do that for you, what you gonna do for me? You know I'm a pimp, and don't nothing come for free in this profession."

"A'ight, Buttons, how much?"

"Who said I want some money?" Buttons replied with a slight grin.

Linda jerked back and looked Buttons directly in the eyes. "Now, I know you don't want no pussy."

"Baby girl, what's the sense in getting a piece of pussy if it can't make no money for you, huh? And you and I both know you ain't tryna be my ho."

"Well, what is it you want then?"

"I want an investment. I want one of your whores, preferably the Chinese one."

"Buttons, I can't just give up my girl like that."

"Why can't you, madam? Besides, the game I'm a give that youngster will be a future fortune that will last a lifetime. He ain't gonna get that from nowhere but a nigga like me. Last time I checked, there ain't no nigga out here like me yet."

Linda knew Buttons was speaking the truth. Buttons was the smoothest nigga she'd ever met, and she wanted Malik to inherit some of that game.

"A'ight, I'll talk to China. But if she don't wanna roll wit' you—"

"Don't worry 'bout that. Leave that part up to me."

"Okay, then we got a deal?"

"Done, baby girl."

Over the next six months, Buttons spent his evenings giving Malik every part of the game he needed. He took Malik down to the track and exposed him to a life that would later be either a blessing or a curse. He taught Malik how to talk his way out of situations and how to get a virgin in bed on the first night they met.

Buttons taught Malik the con game, the way he should conduct himself around other gangsters, how to observe other people's character and appeal to their intellect, and how to stroke egos before making his move. Everything Buttons taught, Malik sucked up and came home to practice on Linda.

Malik was growing into a handsome young man. He had curly hair like his father and a smooth peanut-butter complexion. At fourteen, he was a little less than six-feet tall and held himself like a man. Around this time, Malik started hanging with his new friend, Louie, who was four years older and had a reputation for killing. He was also the one who had Seventh and T Streets locked down with scramble dope that they called 'bam'. Louie took a liking to Malik after seeing him knock out the neighborhood bully at Kennedy playground. Louie couldn't believe how well Malik put his punches together.

"Hey, youngin'. Come here for a minute," he called to Malik.

Malik looked back at Louie. "My name's Malik."

"Well then, Malik, come over here. My name's Louie. Let me holla at you."

Malik went over to Louie. "What's up?"

"You're Linda's nephew, right?"

"Yeah."

"Well, since you're out here knocking niggas out like Marvin Hagler, why ain't you in the ring?"

"I ain't tryna box. I'm only fourteen, and a nigga ain't makin' no money boxing at fourteen. They just doing it for fun. I ain't out here to have fun. I need money."

Louie smiled. "I hear you. So you sayin' you need money, huh?"

"Yeah, why? You got a job for me?"

"Maybe, maybe not. I don't know if you ready for the type of shit I'm into."

"Man, slim, I'm ready for whatever. Maybe you ain't hear me clearly. I need money."

"What kinda money you talkin' 'bout?"

"I'm tryna be the biggest nigga out here. I wanna get loot, lots of loot, and retire like the legendary Big Luke."

"You know Big Luke?"

"Nah, but my father did," Malik replied.

"Who's your father?" Louie asked.

Malik looked down at the pavement before answering in a low tone. "My father's dead. His name was Michael Perry."

"What? You talking 'bout Mike P from Southeast?"

"Yeah, that's my pops. You knew him?"

"Nah, but I heard of him. His man Black Sam used to come 'round here and gamble with the big boys."

"You know my uncle Sam?"

"Sam's your uncle?"

"Yeah, that's my uncle, but I can't find him. I think he's locked up or something."

"I dunno. He might be, 'cause I ain't seen him too much myself. Anyway, back to our conversation. You say you tryna make some money. You know anything 'bout blow?"

"Nah, not really, but I learn quick."

"Okay then, we gonna do it like this. You run with me for a couple weeks. I'm a give you the game, and then you decide if you wanna keep hustling."

"A'ight. Thanks."

"Yeah, no problem."

The first two weeks, Louie taught Malik how to bag up the blow and the perfect times to move it. The rest was up to Malik. He was a natural. He out-talked and out-hustled everyone on the strip. He had so much clientele that the other workers would wait until he finished just so they could sell their shit.

Malik rose up in the dope game faster than Louie expected. After a few months, Malik started buying from Louie himself, and Malik became the youngest hustler on Seventh and T Streets to go into business for himself.

Chapter 13

-PRECIOUS JEWEL-

When Malik turned fifteen, Linda gave him two presents. On his birthday, he woke up early, went into Linda's room, and sat on the end of her bed. Often, this was where they had their family meetings. Malik never held anything back from Linda. Whatever she asked him, he told, even if he felt ashamed.

Linda, on the other hand, was truthful with Malik, but held back one thing. She promised herself that at the right time she would tell him who killed his parents. Every time he asked about his parents' homicide, she'd give him a bit of street knowledge that would stick with him forever.

"Good morning, Aunt Linda."

Linda woke up and sat up in her bed looking at the young, handsome Malik. "Good morning, baby. Matter of fact, happy birthday! Look at you. You're starting to look more and more like your daddy."

"I know." Malik paused. "Ay, Aunt Linda, I got a question."

"What is it?"

"It's the same question I've been asking ever since you took me in."

"Well then, you already know what my answer is."

"I think a nigga's old enough now to know what happened."

"Yeah, you're old enough to know, but too young to handle it. All I can say is that no matter what happened, a valuable lesson was learned."

"I know. You told me a thousand times never trust no one, even you."

"That's right, Malik, even me. No one in this world is to be trusted. No one."

"I hear you. But it ain't that easy not trusting you. You're my only family."

"You're my only family too. All we got is each other. But still, sometimes it's family that will be the ones to do you in. Remember that, Malik. Always remember that."

"I will."

"Anyway, I got you a present."

"What is it?"

"Hold on." Linda went into her closet, pulled out something wrapped in a towel, and laid it on the bed. "I was waiting for the right time to give this to you. I always thought I'd give it to you on your eighteenth birthday, but by the way you've grown, it's a must that you get it now."

"What is it?" he asked with wide eyes and a grin.

Linda opened the towel and showed Malik a shiny, nickel-plated, sixteen shot Taurus 9-millimeter with a black rubber grip. Malik's eyes lit up like Christmas lights.

"Damn, where did you get that?"

"It used to be your father's gun. I just wish he had it on him the day he and your mom were killed."

94

PRINCE OF THE CITY

When Linda talked to Malik about his parents, she held back nothing. She let Malik know that his father was a true gangster. Whenever she looked at Malik, he reminded her of Michael.

"I know your lil ass already got a gun, 'cause I found it one day tucked inside your Timberlands when I was cleaning."

Malik looked ashamed. He was embarrassed that Linda found out about his .22 caliber pistol hidden in the house.

"I was gonna tell you about the gun, but—"

"But what? You didn't tell me 'cause you couldn't trust me?"

"Nah, that ain't it."

"It better be it. Well anyway, that lil gun you got ain't big enough for these streets. You need a real gun, something that'll keep them niggas in check. Malik, do you know how to use this?"

"Yeah. Come on. You know I've been out here in these streets since I was ten."

"What I'm saying to you is that this ain't no toy. Use it for your protection and use it wisely."

"I understand."

"I know you do." Linda then rolled a joint, took two long puffs, and passed it to Malik. Malik smoked weed, but he never smoked in front of Linda. He had too much respect for her.

"Here."

"Nah, no thanks."

"Boy, your ass better take this joint. You think I don't know your ass out there smoking? If anything, you should be in the house whenever you do it. This is where you safe."

Malik took the joint from Linda and puffed two long hails. "Hey, Aunt Linda?"

"What's up, Malik?"

"You know I love you, right?"

"And you know I love you too."

"Yeah, I know. And as soon as I make enough money, we're getting outta this place."

"Malik, your money is your money. I got enough money right now that could get us outta this place. But to be honest I love it here. I love the streets and the excitement. I love being ghetto fabulous. That's just me, baby. That's how I came up, and that's the only thing that separated me from your mother. She was the one to have what she wanted in life and be happy. Me, on the other hand, there was never enough for me to be happy. I just love what I do, and I ain't ashamed of it."

Malik knew that Linda came up hard since they often talked about her childhood.

"I gotta go take care of some business. I want you to be here by the time I get back. Okay?" Linda said to Malik. She went to her drawer and gathered the things she'd need after she showered.

"A'ight, but how long you gonna be, 'cause you know I gotta go collect my money from my workers?"

"What? You got workers now?"

"Yeah," he replied, proudly poking his chest out.

"Damn, boy, you're movin' up. I knew you were on your own, but I didn't know you had workers yet."

"Had 'em for two weeks now."

"Are they loyal?"

"As far as I know, they are."

"Good then, 'cause I'ma introduce you to a better connect, and you're gonna need them workers for the shit this nigga got."

"A'ight, that'll be good."

"Well, I shouldn't be that long. If your workers are loyal, they'll wait."

"Okay, I'll be here."

Linda went to the closet, took out an outfit, and laid it on her bed. Then she headed toward the door.

"Oh, hey Aunt Linda. Hold up for a minute."

"What is it?" She turned to look back at Malik.

"Who's this connect you're gonna introduce me to?"

"His name is Sonny James. He used to deal with your father. He's a good man. We'll talk about this later."

"Okay," he said as she made her exit and went into the bathroom to shower.

Forty-five minutes later, Malik watched Linda get into her green convertible BMW from the bedroom window. Tall, light-skinned, and built like an amazon, Linda was a beautiful woman and men still considered her a dime piece.

After watching Linda leave, Malik went in his room and pulled out all the money he'd made. All together, he counted $8,300. Not bad for a fifteen-year-old kid raised by a high-class whore with bitches in her stable, he'd thought. After he counted all the money, he went into Linda's room, took his gun off the bed, took the clip out, and ran his fingers up and down the barrel in amazement. "Damn, this was my father's gun. This is a pretty muthafucka too. I wonder if he had a name for it." Malik admired his new piece. He looked at it as a treasured heirloom being passed down from father to son.

"Damn, you pretty," he said to the gun. "I bet you been around a long time. You still fresh though, like brand-new. My pops treated you good. From the looks of you, he had to. Well now, Mr. Shiny Thing. I'm a give you a name. From this day

97

JASON POOLE

on, you are now Prince. Since you're the prince, then I'm the king. The prince does whatever the king says. So when I call on you, you better be ready. Okay?" Malik put the clip back in the gun and put it in his room, along with the money. He decided to shower, and afterward he put on the Polo robe Linda bought him. He then sat in the living room smoking a perfectly rolled blunt. Malik was so high that he just lay back and drifted off while listening to Marvin Gaye's hit "Trouble Man."

"I came up hard, baby . . ."

* * * * * * *

Malik instantly jumped up as Linda and Peaches came into the house. "Boy, what's wrong with you? Why you so jumpy?" Linda asked.

"I just dozed off for a minute listening to your CD. Next thing I hear is someone coming in the door."

Peaches giggled while Linda looked at Malik like he was crazy. "Boy, your ass ain't doze off. You were just high as a muthafucka in here. Stuck like Chuck," Linda said as she and Peaches cracked up laughing.

"That must have been some good-ass weed, Malik. You got some more?" Peaches asked.

"Nah, I got it from my favorite aunt."

"What you mean, your favorite aunt? Boy, I'm your only aunt."

"And you're the only aunt I'ma ever love."

"See, you been 'round Buttons too long. Always know what to say at the right time. Go in my room, Peaches. There should be something on my nightstand if Smokey here ain't punish it all."

As Peaches went into the bedroom, Malik watched her every move. He'd always adored Peaches. She was the

98

baddest bitch he knew. Short, stacked like a stallion with long hair and thick-ass lips. Her skin tone was high yellow, which earned her the nickname Peaches. Since Linda gave China to Buttons, Peaches was the only ho left on her team. Whenever Linda brought her around, Malik would always throw hints at her.

"Damn, Peaches, when you gonna get with a young nigga like myself?"

"Malik, you ain't ready for this yet. But when you get ready, I'll be here to give it to your lil fine ass, free of charge."

Peaches was nineteen, but carried herself like a vet. She was Linda's protégé. Linda gave her the game when she was sixteen, and Peaches never looked back. At nineteen, Peaches owned a Lexus ES, a condominium on New Jersey Avenue, and a wardrobe made up of all the top designers. Her plan was to save enough money so that by the time she turned twenty-one, she could go to school for business management and open a nail and hair salon.

When Peaches went into the back, Linda pulled out a small, gift-wrapped box and handed it to Malik.

"Here, boy."

"What's this?"

"It's your other present, but don't open it now. Wait till I leave."

"Where are you going?"

"I gotta see Sonny James and try to get you that connect."

At that, Malik remembered he was supposed to meet Louie. "Oh shit!" he said, checking his pager. Louie had paged him about ten times waiting on Malik to pick up his last ounce of blow.

"What happened?" Linda said.

Malik looked at the digital clock on top of the TV. He had paged Louie the night before and told him he needed to re-up. Louie was reluctant to sell to him because it was his last ounce, but after Malik put the talk game down and stroked his ego, Louie easily gave in to the fifteen-year-old slickster.

"I was supposed to meet Louie at eleven o'clock to cop an ounce. He probably been looking for me all day."

"Well, it's almost one o'clock now. Don't you think you're a little too late? Besides, you don't need to spend your money on that bullshit anyway. You're about to meet a real connect. In a minute, you'll be the one serving ounces to Louie."

Malik smiled at the thought of having a good connect. "Yeah, you're right, Aunt Linda. Louie probably gave it to one of his workers by now anyway."

"Good then. Now you can stay here and enjoy your present."

"What is it?"

"Don't open it yet, Malik. Wait till I leave. I'm sure you're gonna like it."

Linda went into the room with Peaches and smoked a joint. Then she came out and headed for the door.

"Malik, Peaches is gonna stay here while I'm gone. I should be back within an hour or so."

"Okay."

"See you later. And don't open that box until I'm all the way gone."

"A'ight, I got you."

Malik watched Linda make her exit and then he got up to check out his present.

* * * * * * *

As Louie paced up and down Seventh Street for almost two hours, while looking at his watch and turning down his workers, his frustration built toward Malik.

"Man, where in the fuck is this lil nigga at?" he said to himself. Louie then called over to one of his loyal dope fiends who was working the block and asked in an angry tone, "Hey Booga, have you seen Malik?"Hey Booga, have you seen Malik?"

"Nah, Louie, not yet. He told me last night to be here at eleven o'clock. I don't know where he at. Shit, I hope nothing happened to him."

"Nah, ain't nothing happened to him. His lil ass just think a nigga is supposed to wait. Look here.When you see him, tell him I said he missed out. And the next time he do something like this, I'm a smack the living shit outta him."

"A'ight, I'll tell him."

Louie headed down to the end of Seventh and T where his 735i BMW was parked. When he got within five feet of his car, three unmarked cars pulled up and detectives jumped out. The main detective on the jump-out squad was Cowboy, who pointed his 9-millimeter directly in Louie's face.

"Go ahead, nigga! Try and run so I can bust a cap in your ass."

Louie thought for a second. He knew Cowboy wasn't bullshitting. Cowboy always wanted to get Louie, but could never catch him. Louie was too smart for Cowboy. He knew the days and times Cowboy worked, and he made sure that from noon until eight on Tuesdays and Thursdays, he was nowhere near Seventh and T. Today, for his young protégé, Malik, Louie figured he could serve Malik before Cowboy's shift, and then roll out until later that day. Unfortunately, Malik never showed and now Louie was caught.

"Get your ass on the ground!"

Louie did what Cowboy commanded.

"You got anything in your pockets?"

When Louie didn't answer, Cowboy searched him and found the ounce of dope, a fully loaded Glock 9-millimeter, and a fat-ass knot of Ben Franklins.

Chapter 14

-WHAT A BIRTHDAY-

About five minutes after Linda left, Peaches yelled for Malik from the back.

"Hey, Malik?"

"Yeah, what's up?" he said loud enough for her to hear.

"Come here for a second. I need you to help me with something. And bring your gift."

Malik picked up the gift-wrapped box and went into the bedroom. His eyes lit up at the sight of Peaches's naked body.

"Got damn, Peaches! You phat as a muthafucka."

Peaches's body was perfect. Flawless skin, erect nipples, and her pussy was neatly shaved. Her ass looked as smooth as silk. She stood there completely naked except the red pumps donning her feet. They made her look like a centerfold model torn directly out of the pages of Playboy magazine.

"Go 'head, Malik. Open your present," Peaches stated.

Malik opened his gift and smiled at the box of Trojan rubbers.

"Happy birthday, Malik. Are you ready for your present?" she asked, posing.

"I've been ready a long time."

"Good then, I guess you won't be needing this robe no more." Peaches gently untied Malik's robe, pulled it off, and kneeled down to place his long, swollen dick inside her wet, warm mouth. She didn't bother to use a condom like she'd done with her tricks. This was something special, something she always wanted, and she knew that when the time presented itself that she was going to give Malik her all. Peaches started sucking Malik's dick like the pro that she was. She sucked and jerked at the same time while licking up and down from his balls back to the head.

Although Malik wasn't a virgin, he'd never gotten his dick sucked as well as Peaches was sucking it. She then placed him on the bed and continued to suck his dick while playing with her pussy at the same time.

"Damn Malik, if I would've known you was this healthy, I would've given you some a long time ago."

Malik didn't say a word. He just sat back and enjoyed the ride. It was a totally new experience for him. Peaches was freaking him out. She moaned as if sucking his dick was giving them both the same pleasure. Malik couldn't hold back anymore. The feeling of getting his dick sucked so well excited him even more.

"Damn Peaches, that feels good."

"I know, baby, and it's all for you. I'm your bitch for today, and you can do whatever you want to me." Peaches continued sucking while Malik played with her pussy, fingering her and rubbing her clit. He noticed the more he rubbed her clit, the more she moaned. Her body moved to the rhythm of his fingers until she couldn't take it anymore.

"Daddy, fuck me please. Please, daddy. I want this big, long dick in my pussy. Come on, daddy, fuck me."

Malik pulled Peaches on top while she eagerly grabbed his dick and guided it into her pussy. She eased down the shaft of his dick slowly, taking in every inch and adjusting to his size. "Oh my God, daddy! This dick is so big." Peaches moved her hips back and forth, rubbing her clit up against Malik's pubic hairs to cause friction. Malik had one hand on her ass and the other caressing her tits. Their rhythm became one as they moved back and forth, up and down. The faster they fucked, the louder Peaches cried. "Oh my God, daddy! Damn, this dick is good. Oh yes, daddy. Fuck me, daddy. You feel so good in this pussy. You can get this pussy anytime you want. Damn! Oh my God!"

The louder her moans became, the more Malik grabbed her ass, pulling her up and down on his dick. "Oh shit, daddy! I'm about to come, daddy. I'm about to come. Come with me, daddy. Oh, yes! Oh yes . . . yes . . . yes!"

As Peaches came all over Malik's dick, he came simultaneously.

"Damn, daddy, I can feel your dick pulsating in this pussy."

After they both finished coming, Peaches lay on Malik's chest and caressed his nipples. "Damn Malik, that was so good. Where did you learn to fuck like that?"

"I wanted to do this to you for a long time."

"Boy, if I would've known it was like this, I would've been gave it to you."

"Well, now you know," Malik replied, and then got up and put on another rubber. "Now get up and turn around. I want to hit it doggie style."

"Malik, be easy with this."

"Shut up, bitch, and do what I say!"

"Okay, daddy."

Malik slid his dick in Peaches's wet pussy, and within seconds, Peaches screamed out a long, loud cry. "Oohhh daddy, that hurts."

Malik started fucking her faster. "Shut up bitch and take this dick."

"Okay daddy. I'm a take it."

As Malik pounded her pussy, their rhythm became one again. Peaches's pussy was so wet the juices were dripping off Malik's balls.

"Oh yes, daddy, that's right. Pound this pussy. That's right, daddy. I'm your bitch. Now fuck this pussy." Peaches spread her cheeks apart as wide as she could. "You see that, daddy? You see that big dick going in and out of this pussy?"

Malik continued pounding harder and faster.

"That's right, daddy. Oooh, fuck me. Fuck this pussy. This is your pussy, daddy. Fuck me. I'm your bitch."

The harder Malik fucked, the more Peaches backed her ass up on his dick, taking in every inch.

"Oh daddy, what are you doing? Why are you fucking me like this? Damn, it feels so good, daddy. You're fucking the hell outta me. Can you fuck me all the time? Please, daddy . . ." At the sound of Peaches asking him to fuck her all the time, Malik pounded so hard that he exploded again just as Peaches did. Spent, Malik lay on his back as his chest quickly rose and fell with each breath. Peaches lay beside him and wrapped her arms around Malik, holding him close.

"Malik. Listen, and please don't take this the wrong way. I wanna be your girl, not just because you fucked me good, but because I see something in you I don't normally see in other niggas."

Amazed by her comments, Malik turned his head to face Peaches. He seemed confused because she never showed these type of actions in anyway other than the occasional flirt. "What you tryna say, Peaches?" he asked, almost laughing.

"Look. I'm tryna get my shit together, and the only way I'ma be able to get out these streets is by the will of a man. I mean, I can do this shit on my own, but I need a man to push me to my limits."

Malik hunched his shoulders, still in disbelief. "Peaches I just turned fifteen, and you telling me you need a man. Come on, boo stop the games." Malik chuckled and sat up on the bed.

"I'm only three years older. Ain't much difference. And besides, you know the saying, age ain't nuthin' but a number," Peaches responded. But this time there was something different in her delievery. It seemed more sincere, and Malik noticed when he saw the tears developing in her eyes.

Malik wiped away her tears. "Now Peaches, how am I supposed to make a ho into a housewife?"

"I'll do whatever you want. You and I can even go into business together."

"What! I ain't no pimp. I don't need a bitch to make my money. I make my own bank. Besides, Linda would whip your ass if she heard what you were saying."

"Fuck that. Linda don't run me. I'm my own bitch. We just do business together. For you, I'm willing to stop, even if it costs me my life. Malik, you don't understand. I need you. I need a nigga with that Boss potential."

Malik looked at Peaches as if she was crazy. This shit was confusing him. All he did was fuck her good, and now she wanted him to save her life.

"C'mon, Peaches. That weed got you trippin'."

"I ain't trippin'. You just don't know that if you throw me away, you'll be missing out on a good bitch, and a loyal bitch at that."

"Yeah, whatever. Just put your clothes back on. Linda should be coming back anyway." Peaches put on her clothes, but she couldn't stop the tears from flowing.

When Linda returned, she didn't use her key. Instead, she knocked to make sure they were finished.

"That's Linda now. Wipe them tears, girl."

"Shut up, Malik. You make me sick."

"Damn, just a minute ago you wanted me to take you away from this shit," he said while shaking his head as he went to open the door.

Linda walked in with a big smile.

"Did you like your birthday gift, Malik?"

"I loved it, Aunt Linda."

Peaches headed toward the door with her head lowered. Before leaving, she turned and said, "Malik, you couldn't have loved your gift. You only liked it for the moment."

Linda looked at Peaches and then at Malik. "Is everything okay here?"

"Yeah, everything's fine," Malik answered.

"No it ain't. Linda, let's go. I'll tell you about it," Peaches said.

"Malik, did you behave yourself?"

"Yes, I did. Did you talk to Sonny James?" he asked.

"Yes, but first, I wanna know what went on in here," Linda replied.

"Come on, let's just go," Peaches told her.

Malik just looked at Linda and threw his hands in the air.

"I'll see you when I get back. And don't leave."

"Damn! What? I'm on punishment now?"

"Boy, don't get smart with me," Linda said in a firm tone.

"A'ight, I ain't going nowhere."

"Good 'cause when I come back we need to talk," she told him while leaving.

The moment Linda left, Malik sat back and shook his head in disbelief. "Damn, what a birthday," he said, throwing his hands in the air.

Chapter 15

-A HUSTLER'S AMBITION-

While waiting for Linda to come back, Malik called all the numbers on his pager. That was when he learned from talking to one of his workers named Booga, that Louie got locked up earlier on Seventh and T Streets.

Damn, I hope the nigga aint have shit on him. "Ay, Booga, did he get caught with anything?"

"I dunno. They had me laid down in the alley. They did impound his car, so he might have had something in that joint."

"I hope Louie ain't that dumb, riding around dirty in a luxury car."

"I don't think so, but I can tell you one thing."

"What's that?"

"Man, Louie was out here lookin' for you 'bout two hours. He was mad as shit too."

"Okay. Thanks."

"Man, when you gonna come out here and put some work out? Ain't nobody got nothin', and this joint is jumpin' like crazy."

"I'll be out there later on with some different shit. Tell everybody I'm giving out testers to the first fifty customers."

"A'ight, I'll do that."

"Good then. Did Louie say he had something for me?"

"Nah. You know Louie is secretive. You might be with him all day and don't even know he's strapped with a machine gun."

Malik laughed. "Yeah, you're right. I'll see you later. In the meantime, while you're out there, try and find out if Louie got caught with anything on him."

"A'ight. You just hurry up and get out here. A nigga's ill. We dope fiends, remember?"

"I got you," Malik replied while laughing. He ended the call, somewhat worried about Louie.

Malik took another shower and then dressed in his new gray and blue Polo sweat suit with a fresh pair of 996 New Balance running shoes. He also wore a medium-sized pinky diamond ring with a matching fourteen-karat gold watch, and a bracelet by Raymond Wiel.

Malik was a clothes and jewelry freak. He loved to look fly all the time and made sure he was fresh every day before he walked out the door. Although he was only fifteen, he carried himself like he was twenty-five.

All the major players in the pool hall respected and liked young Malik. He had an aura, and the women loved him just like they loved his father. Most of the women were older, but still tried to get with him early because they saw a future king rising to his throne.

Malik was aggressively gentle, often having his way with anyone he wanted. Those who did business with him liked his forwardness, and those who didn't, emulated his style. Malik Perry was the new up and coming hustler.

Linda returned home after dropping Peaches off. A tall, slender man with a grayish, perfectly trimmed beard, who was neatly dressed in blue slacks and a blue and gray Versace silk shirt accompanied her.

Malik wondered who this man could be. He knew Linda never brought any of her tricks home, and she wasn't one to have a pimp. The only male Malik had ever seen Linda with was Butter, and for the past two years, he had been out of sight. They had broken up when Linda moved out on her own. Since then, the only time Malik saw Butter was at the pool hall.

As Linda introduced Malik to the man, Malik stood up straight, showing the much older man that he was fearless.

"Malik, this is Sonny James. Sonny, this is my nephew."

As Sonny reached out to shake Malik's hand, he noticed something. There was a feeling to Malik's shake that felt familiar. Malik pressed his hand hard and firm while looking Sonny straight in the eyes.

"Pleased to meet you, Malik."

"Same here, Sonny."

"Have a seat, Sonny. Can I get you something to drink?" Linda asked.

"No thanks. I'm fine. Just let me have a minute alone with Malik."

"Okay, but if you two need me for anything, I'll be in my room."

Sonny grabbed a chair, flipped it around, and sat with his arms folded over the back. "So, Malik, Linda tells me that you're a very smart youngin'. Is that so?"

"I guess there's only one way for you to find out." Malik replied while sitting in a chair opposite of Sonny. His arms folded and and leg crossed as if he was already a seasoned hustler.

Sonny smiled at the young boy's perfect answer. "You know, your father and I were good associates, and he and my brother Slim were good friends in prison."

"So I guess that means me and you could be associates, too, but I would like to make it known that I am my own man. Although I admire, respect, and love my pops, I never want to ride on his coattails. Whatever I accomplish with you, I want it to be for myself, not because I'm Michael Perry's son. I don't need those types of favors."

Sonny nodded. He respected and understood Malik's position. In fact, Michael would have said the same thing.

"I understand. Business is business. That's what I like. However, I do owe your father that much respect not to see you out here scrambling for your eggs. So what I'm gonna do is work with you on a business level that could either get you rich, in jail, or dead. It's up to you to take advantage of it."

"I will. Indeed, I will. So what them thangs going for?"

"It all depends on what you want. I got coke and dope. And believe me when I tell you I got the top-of-the-line shit."

Malik sat back and thought for a second. Often, when customers asked if any coke was out, someone would direct the traffic down to Ninth Street, where Sticks and Keith hustled fifties of coke. Malik weighed his options in his head. If I get some coke, then I could take all of Ninth Street's business. Perhaps move up to kilos and serve everybody on this side of town. But if I did that, then the dope fiends would have to go somewhere else to cop. Shit, it's 1993, and coke is booming. Heroin is declining, for real. A nigga's getting tired of having to keep waking up early in the morning just to get

113

that rush. I can pass out work, sit back and collect without having to risk being locked up or robbed by some bitch-ass nigga who can't get out here and get his own.

"Okay Sonny. What would you sell me a half kilo of yay for?"

"The only way I sell coke is already cooked up, and on a scale of one to ten, my shit is an eleven—straight butta."

"Damn Sonny. I understand your shit is butta, but you can't give it to me in powder?"

"Nah, not at this moment. Anyway, I'm not in a position to do that yet. But I'll tell you what I can do."

"What's that?"

"I can give it to you for a low number."

"How low?"

"Like eighteen a key. And the more we do business, the more the price drops."

"Damn, eighteen sounds good. The going rate right now is twenty-two a key. I want to get a half a brick, and if your shit is butta like you say, then we'll be in business for a long time."

"Here's my pager number. Call me when you want it."

"Shit, I want it now."

"Right now?"

"Yeah, the sooner the better."

"A'ight, young nigga. I see that you about money just like your father was. I'll be back in twenty minutes."

When Sonny left, Linda came out of the back room.

"So how'd it go?" she asked.

"It went good, Aunt Linda, but I think Sonny is tryna wing me out of a few Gs."

"Why you say that?"

"'Cause he won't sell me no powder."

"What's the difference between rock and powder?"

PRINCE OF THE CITY

"See, he probably gets a key of powder for like seventeen or eighteen. He then cooks it up and adds some shit to it, like baking soda so it can fluff up. By the time he finishes it, he got like a key and a half. So, he sells the key and keeps a free half."

"So, if you don't get the powder, you're missing out on a ten-thousand-dollar profit."

"Yeah, but it's cool though, 'cause it's hard to get powder right now. Anyway, I just need to fuck with him for a minute till I make enough money to meet one of them out-of-town connects."

"Sounds like you know where your ass is at, Malik."

"Aunt Linda, look at me. I was born the son of a gangster and raised the nephew of a ho who taught me how to survive these streets. What you expect?"

"Shut up, boy, with your smart-ass mouth."

They both laughed.

"Hey, I need a favor," Malik said to Linda.

"What is it?"

"Sonny is gonna sell me a half key for nine thousand. All I got is eighty-three hundred. Can you loan me seven?"

"Yeah, hold on," Linda said as she reached into her pocket and pulled out a knot of Ben Franklins. She counted out seven crisp one-hundred-dollar bills. "Here. Now let's make a toast to your new investment." Linda popped a bottle of Demi-sec Moet and poured two glasses. As they held their glasses in the air to toast, Linda looked into Malik's eyes.

"Here's to a young prince on the rise to his throne. I love you, Malik."

"I love you too, Aunt Linda."

"You're about to make a lot of money."

115

Malik looked toward the sky as if he were talking to his parents. "Yeah, I know. Just picture me rollin'."

They both laughed. "I'll drink to that one, Malik."

Chapter 16

-STRAIGHT UP MENACE-

Within two months, Malik turned Seventh and T into a twenty-four-hour coke strip. Crackheads came from all over to get a taste of the butter popcorn Malik had. By now Malik was copping at least a brick and a half from Sonny James every week. His strip sold nothing but twenty rocks the size of fifties. The rocks were so big that the crackheads nicknamed Seventh and T Streets the Bowling Alley.

Malik also sold wholesale to the young hustlers around the way. He had niggas on Fifth and Sixth buying half ounces daily. He also had a few youngin's around LeDroit Park buying ounces and a few customers on Fourth and 'N' Streets. The Bowling Alley was his most profitable spot. There, Malik would break down an eighth of a kilo in all twenties and not leave the block until every crumb was gone. He relentlessly moved his package nonstop. The businessmen at the bowling alley moved so fast that Linda would stop by in the middle of the day and pick up a majority of Malik's money, so she could place it in the safe back at the house.

117

JASON POOLE

As Malik approached his sixteenth birthday, he was making so much money that he felt he had to move out of Linda's apartment. So he rented an apartment on Kenyon Street, right above the Madness Shop, which was considered D.C.'s first urban landmark for hustlers. A clothing store located off Georgia Avenue that catered to the hustler's lifestyle and owned by some well-known old timers that everyone respected. Linda knew the owner of the Madness Shop, who was also the owner of the building, and she rented Malik's apartment under her name. The location was convenient since Malik was only five minutes away from Seventh Street.

His apartment was lavish. The floors were hardwood and the bathroom was marble. The windows faced both Kenyon Street and Georgia Avenue. Sometimes Malik would look out the window on the Georgia Avenue side and watch the hustlers run in and out of the Madness Shop. He admired the old heads' style. Although they didn't drive luxury cars, he could tell by their timepieces that they were holding stacks of cash, something he learned from Buttons.

Buttons used to say, "Malik, you can count a nigga's bank by just looking at him. The ones with the big cars are usually the broke ones, and the ones with the average cars and clothes got a mini armored bank truck sittin' in the backyard. You can always tell if a nigga is holdin' by the timepiece he wears. The ones wearing a flashy Rolex with all the diamonds are just for show. The guy most likely spent his last dime on it, but the ones who wear Patek Philippe or plain looking Cartier got it. You know they got it because they never let it show. They're in it for the fortune, not the fame."

Malik fell in love with the game. He wanted the fame and fortune. He saw how the females would pull up in front of the Madness Shop and talk to the old timers. Every last one of them was a dime piece too. There wasn't a doubt in Malik's mind that he was going to make it big. He knew it, not because he wanted it, but because it was in his blood. After all, he was Mike Perry's son, the man who controlled Southeast at one time.

On Malik's sixteenth birthday, Linda knocked on his door early in the morning. When he didn't answer, she opened the door with her spare key and entered the not-so-clean apartment.

"This damn boy still don't clean up behind himself. He needs a maid or a girlfriend. Look at this shit! Dirty dishes and clothes everywhere. Looks like he ain't cleaned this place in weeks."

Linda went into Malik's bedroom, and for a few seconds, she just sat there looking at him while he slept. Look at you, Malik. I remember when you were born. You were so handsome and innocent, like an angel. No one would ever understand the way you turned out, not even you. Then she looked up at the sky, as if she were talking to Connie and Michael. I'm sorry I raised him like this, but please understand this is all I know. God, whatever Malik does to deserve a place in hell, I take full responsibility. I will gladly take his place.

Malik twitched and instantly reached for his 9-millimeter pistol when he realized someone was in the room with him.

"Malik! Malik! It's me. Boy, look at you. It's too late for that. If I was someone coming to kill you, your ass would've been dead already."

Malik wiped the sleep from his eyes. "Damn, Aunt Linda, how long you been in here?"

"Too damn long. And why are you sleeping so hard? What you do last night? Get some pussy?"

"Come on, Aunt Linda, I get too much pussy."

"What I tell you about that, Malik?"

"Never get attached to pussy, no matter how good it is. Pussy is the ruler of a nigga's emotions. When you think with your dick, most likely you end up getting your wig split."

"So I see you still remember the Golden Rule."

"How could I forget? We've been rehearsing this ever since I was ten years old."

"That's right. And you better keep rehearsing it till the day you die."

"I will. I will."

"And why isn't this place cleaned up? While you're up in here getting all this pussy, you better put them lil bitches to work. Make them clean this muthafucka from top to bottom."

"Shit, I don't want those bitches in here long enough to take a piss. After I'm done handling my business, I put those bitches out."

Linda laughed. "Well, anyway, happy birthday!"

"You came all the way over here for that? You could've called and let me stay sleep."

"Shut up, boy! Get yourself dressed. I'm a take you out to breakfast."

Malik got up, took a shower, and put on his brand-new brown and white Iceberg sweater that had a Snoopy cartoon character on it. He also wore a pair of lightly faded Iceberg jeans, one size too big to give a slight sag fit, and a pair of butter Timberlands. To complement his outfit, Malik wore a three-carat diamond stud in his ear, a Movado watch, and a gold bracelet.

Over the past year, Malik had let his hair grow into a good grain of dark curls that formed a perfect bush. He wore cornrows, eight straight back. Malik's hair was so long and thick that he had to go to the hairdresser to get it done because most girls he dealt with didn't want to take the time to do it. Still, they loved to run their fingers through it.

After Malik was dressed and ready to go, he looked around at how Linda had cleaned up and placed his dishes in the dishwasher.

"Thanks, Aunt Linda."

"For what? Boy, I've been cleaning up behind your ass for sixteen years, and now, all of a sudden you're thanking me? What happened to the thanks for all those years I changed your shitty-ass diapers and washed your pissy underwear, huh?"

Malik just smiled. "You know I love and appreciate everything you've ever done for me."

"I know, Malik, I know. Come here, baby. Give me a hug." Linda embraced her nephew. She missed Malik. Ever since he'd gotten his own place, she was miserable without him. No more long talks, laughs, and stories about his parents. No more giving him the rules of the game. During the time he was with her, he'd learned so much that there was nothing left to give him. Sometimes they talked on the phone, but not long due to both of their professions. Whenever Linda had a chance to be with Malik alone, she took advantage of the opportunity, for he was all she had.

As Malik and Linda headed toward her BMW that was parked in front of the store, they passed a short, stocky, older guy who looked like he worked out on a daily basis.

"Hey Linda. What's up, boo? I ain't seen you in a long time."

"Oh! Hey Lee. How are you doing, baby?" Linda asked, smiling at the man.

"I'm fine. Still out here doing my thing on the low. You know me. What about you? Are you still with Butter?

Linda dropped the smile and looked at him as if he should have known better. "Me and Butter ain't been together in years. I'm on my own. Been there, done that. You ain't heard?"

"Yeah baby, I heard. I just thought I'd throw that out there to make your day."

"Lee, your ass is still crazy." They both laughed.

"Take care of yourself, Linda. It was nice seeing you."

"You too, Lee."

"Oh, Linda?"

"What's up, Lee?"

"Damn baby, you still look good!"

Linda burst into laughter. "Bye Lee, with your silly ass."

"Bye-bye, baby girl."

Malik was waiting for Linda to get in the car, and as soon as she did, he made his move. "Do you know that dude?"

"Yeah, that's Lee. He's been doing his thang for a long-ass time and ain't ever gone to jail."

"Oh yeah? What he moving?" Malik asked.

"Last time I heard, he was chillin' because some dudes he was hitting off with keys had gotten locked up by Feds, and you know what they say about Feds, Malik."

"Nah, Aunt Linda, help me out."

"Well, for some reason when a nigga gets locked up by the FBI, a whole lot of other niggas get locked up right behind him. Now, either the nigga who got locked up happened to sell his soul and snitched, or the FBI got lucky and caught their man on a humble. From years of being in the streets, I've never seen the FBI get that lucky to catch niggas on a humble. Most of the time when niggas get locked up, they don't find out until right before the trial that their main man snitched on them."

"Damn, that's fucked up."

"Yeah, I know. That's one of the reasons why I stress to you not to trust anyone, Malik, and I mean no one."

"I feel you. Well, do you think that dude Lee is back in action yet?"

"I dunno. Why do you ask?"

"'Cause I want you to introduce me to him. I got a feeling that nigga's hustling, 'cause I see him coming to the shop a lot talking to the niggas who live next door to me. Believe me, Aunt Linda, when I tell you them niggas next door are hustling. I mean, they're hustling real good."

"You must be talking about Fat Troy and them Edgewood dudes. Well, if they hustling so good, why don't you cut into one of 'em and try to get down?"

"'Cause, I don't wanna deal with them. I wanna fuck with the source. And I know that nigga Lee is the source. He be pushing 500SLs, Range Rovers, and all that big shit."

"Okay, Malik, I'll talk to him, but I can't make any promises," Linda said as she pulled off.

Linda took Malik to Copeland's Restaurant in Alexandria, Virginia, fifteen minutes away from the D.C. line. Malik ordered steak and eggs, while Linda ordered a cup of French coffee and a blueberry bagel.

"Damn, Aunt Linda, you need to order some food. A cup of coffee and a plain-ass doughnut ain't gonna get you full."

Linda laughed. "Boy, this ain't no doughnut. It's a fat-free bagel. Besides, I'm okay. I don't need all that heavy shit on my stomach. I gotta watch my figure. You know I'm getting up in age. I'm almost thirty-two-years-old."

"Yeah, but you look twenty-two."

"That's because I know what to eat and when to eat."

"Nah, that ain't it. You just look naturally pretty. I bet in ten more years you'll still look the same. Look at yourself. There are bitches out here ten years younger than you and can't even stand next to you. Face it, Aunt Linda. You are just a bad muthafucka, a straight dime piece. On top of that, you got more game than the Washington Redskins."

Linda laughed. "Boy, you're crazy. But you do know how to make me feel good. By the way, Malik, do you know how Peaches feels about you?"

"Man, Peaches is kinda crazy."

"No she isn't. She's just open when it comes to something she wants. She sees that you both are cut from the same cloth. She's been through a lot, and you're the only man that ever made her have an orgasm."

"Get the hell outta here with that!"

"No, I'm serious. The men that Peaches has been with could never satisfy her. She only does it for the money. In fact, she hates it so much that after every client, she takes a long bath in alcohol just to get the filth off. You see, Malik, Peaches isn't like me. She hates what she has to do. She only does it to get ahead in life, and in another year or so, she's quitting and going to school."

"Why are you telling me this?"

"Because if there's any woman I want to see you with, it would be her. She genuinely loves you, for real. Plus, she's loyal. I can't say too much about being strictly faithful, because everybody got skeletons in their closet and no one is to be trusted. But I can say this. If she's down with you, she's down till the bloody end."

"Well, I don't need a girl right now. Especially at the rate I'm going. They'll only slow me down. You're the only female I need in my life, and that's enough."

Linda smiled. "I hear you. You're so mature with your decisions. I admire that in you. Remember this, though. Peaches is good for you, and that's my advice."

"Thank you for the advice, but no thank you. But I'll still have sex with Peaches whenever the time presents itself."

"Shut up, boy, with your nasty self."

"Oh, Aunt Linda?" Malik said, putting down his fork to talk.

"Yeah, what's up?"

"What would you say if I told you I wanted to buy a car?"

"Well first, I'd say how you gonna drive it when you don't have a license?"

With that, Malik reached into his pocket, pulled out a fresh driver's license, and shoved it in Linda's face. "Bam!"

"When did you get this? And how?"

"I got a few connects. You know you ain't the only one who makes all the moves. I've been messing with this broad who works down at the DMV. She got all my info and did it in one day. All I had to do was go there and take the picture."

"Let me see it," Linda said, reaching for it. "Damn Malik. It's legit too."

"I know."

"Well, if you want to buy a car, I can't argue with you on that. But do you have enough money to get what you want?"

"Well, right now I got like fifty thousand saved up, plus half a kilo. I can stand to spend somewhere around thirty thousand and still cop me a brick."

125

"Okay, but when you buy a car you gotta get insurance and all that other shit."

"Yeah, I got all that covered with the broad at Motor Vehicles."

"What kind of car are you looking to get?"

"I want something ain't nobody got."

"Ain't too much you gonna get with only thirty-something thousand, Malik. Everybody uptown is pushing shit that cost fifty or better."

"I know, but look at me, Aunt Linda. I'm only sixteen. I'd look crazy buying a Ferrari." They both laughed. "One day, I will though," he added.

"I'm sure you will. Anyway, I can take you to a good car dealer right up the street from here where I bought my BMW."

"Are you gonna co-sign for me?"

"Naw baby, you don't need a co-signer. All you need is money. Those muthafuckas are all crooked."

Linda and Malik pulled into Eagle Motors in Arlington, Virginia. As soon as she parked, a salesman she knew walked straight up to her. He was a short Arab-looking guy named Andy.

"Hello Linda. How are you?" he asked in his foreign accent. "I haven't seen you in a while. Still driving that BMW, huh?"

"Yeah Andy. I love my car."

"So what brings you here today?"

"Andy, this is my nephew, Malik. He's interested in buying a car."

"Well first, what kind of purchase you have?"

"Cash, Andy, always cash."

"Good. Let me show you some nice cars." Andy led Linda and Malik to the luxury cars lined up in front of the lot. "How

126

much do you plan to spend and what kind of car do you have in mind, sir?"

"I want luxury with speed. Something medium-sized and sporty, but not too sporty."

"Sounds to me like you want a BMW 735i. Here's one right over here." Andy opened the door to the silver BMW with light gray leather and wood grain. "This here is a grown man's car. It's fast, soft, heavy, and handles like a race car. It hugs every corner."

"How much is it?"

"Seventy thousand, but since you're Linda's nephew, I'll give it to you for sixty-five."

"Ah, hold up, Andy. He wants something in the fifty thousand price range or possibly a little lower," Linda said.

"Oh, I see. Well, we got a Lexus LS400 over here for forty-seven."

"Nah, too many people got them joints," Malik replied.

"Well, how about the Infiniti Q45?"

"Nah, they're all over the city too."

"Hold on for a second. I have something around back that just came in this morning. You'll love it. Believe me, sir. No one has this yet. I bought it off the showroom floor myself. Come with me."

When Linda and Malik went around back, both their mouths fell open. "Damn, that's a pretty-ass car," Linda admitted.

"I know. This muthafucka is nice. It looks expensive though. I know I ain't got enough for this joint." Malik then walked over to the car in amazement, placed his finger on the paint and traced as if he were running his fingers through a cat's fur.

JASON POOLE

"Do you really like it?" Linda asked.

"Man, I'm in love with it." He said opening the door to inhale the smell of soft leather.

"Well, I tell you what. I'll give you fifteen thousand to add to your thirty."

"Nah, keep your money."

"Boy, you better take it. Anyway, that's nothing to what I'm holdin'. That shit won't even knock the dust off my money."

"You got it like that, huh?"

"Let's just say I got enough to give you fifteen and not squawk about it. And what is this anyway?" she asked, turning her attention to the salesman.

"It's the new Cadillac STS. It's top of the line. It comes with wood grain, Coach leather seats, CD player, chrome rims, Vogue tires, and every other feature the Lexus, BMW, or Mercedes has," Andy replied.

"Damn, this is a bad muthafucka." Malik stepped back to admire his soon-to-be wife. She was dark cranberry with cream interior. "How much?"

"For you, Malik, forty-two five. No less. That's the best I can do. It's a steal, and if you ask me, it's like giving it away. It normally runs no less than forty-nine. But since Linda and I have been doing business for so long, I'm willing to sacrifice."

Malik looked at Linda. "Boy, this nigga got game, huh?"

"This is his hustle, Malik. You either accept or reject it. But whatever you do, just respect it."

"Well, Andy, I want it. I'll be back in about an hour to pick it up, so you can go ahead and start the paperwork."

"Good, Malik. I like doing business with you. Just hurry back with the money."

"I will."

128

"Now, Ms. Linda, would you like to purchase something nice?"

"Nah. You got enough of my money already. You should be giving me something for free."

"No, no, no, Linda. I'm sorry, I can't do that. But I'll tell you what. I can make you a good deal."

Linda and Malik laughed. "Bye, Andy."

"Bye, you two. Now hurry back with my money before I put another For Sale sign on this car."

Malik mumbled to Linda, "If he does that, I'll personally peel his cap back."

Chapter 17

-A GANGSTA'S BLOODLINE-

The next morning, Malik got up early. He had to make two runs. First, he dropped off his car to get his windows lightly tinted. Malik's car was too pretty and smooth not to have tinted windows. Second, he paged Sonny James to cop another kilo. The money Linda gave Malik really helped him out. He was able to buy his car and still cop what he wanted. Although Malik had a strong feeling about meeting Lee, he still kept his money in motion. That way, he could pay all his bills and spend whatever he wanted on clothes.

Ring!

"Hello? Did somebody page this number?"

"Yeah Sonny. It's Malik. You forgot my code?"

"Nah, I just ain't ever seen this number come up on my pager before."

"Oh, that's because I'm at the auto shop getting my windows tinted."

"You bought a car?"

"Yeah, you know I had to do something nice for myself."

"What kind of car did you get?"

"A Caddy."

"What, nigga! You're only sixteen. What you know about a Caddy?"

"I know my pops had one when he was sixteen, so I guess you can say like father like son. You know gangsta shit runs through my blood."

"Yeah, whatever. But I think your pops came up a lil harder than you. Niggas down Lorton still telling stories 'bout Mike P."

"Yeah, I know. But anyway, I'm tryna get down ASAP. What's up?"

"I ain't got a problem with that, but I do need to talk to you in private. I heard some things that you and I need to discuss now." From the sound of Sonny's voice, Malik knew it was something serious. Instantly, butterflies nested in his stomach.

"Well, my car is finished, so where do you want to meet?" he asked.

Malik spoke with clarity to camouflauge his uneasiness. "Meet me on Seventh Street in front of the pool hall."

"Okay, I'll be there in about fifteen minutes."

Malik got in his car and drove down Seventh Street. Before he went into the pool hall, though, he stopped by Linda's apartment to get his piece. He knocked on the door. Even though he didn't see Linda's car out front, he still wanted to make sure no one was there before he used his key.

Malik went to his old bedroom. He had been gone for over a year, but everything in his room was the same. Linda left it untouched. Malik went straight to his safe and pulled out his 9-millimeter, Prince. He was always taught to trust no one, and from the eerie feeling he had, he made sure he held on to that principle.

"Now Prince, I don't know what Sonny is up to, but just in case he thinks he's gonna pull a funny move, I'm a peel his fuckin' cap back."

Before leaving back out, Malik changed into a black Hugo Boss sweat suit, a black pair of Charles Barkley Nikes, and a black and gray LA Raiders fitted cap. He then headed out the door, leaving his car parked around back. He walked up Seventh Street where Sonny was parked in his black, big-body Mercedes. Malik noticed that Sonny wasn't in front of the pool hall. Instead, his car was parked in the alley. He could tell someone was in it, but the tinted windows were so dark he couldn't tell who. He played it off like he didn't notice that someone was in the car and continued to walk past.

Beep, Beep!

At the sound of the horn, Malik turned toward the Benz as if he were surprised someone was in it. He then walked to the passenger side and proceeded to get in, but someone was already in there with Sonny, so Malik walked to the back. However, the person in the passenger side got out. "Malik, you can sit up front," the dark-skinned man said, happily giving up his seat.

"Smitty?"

Smitty was Louie's right-hand man. Smitty had just come from Lorton, and from the looks of it, he wanted his strip back. It was rumored that he'd do whatever to get it back. Malik had heard stories about Smitty from Louie.

Smitty was a cold-hearted killer, but real smooth about it. Most of his kills were so smooth that everybody thought Louie was the one doing all the killing. That's how Louie got his reputation. Smitty was killing everything that moved, and Louie was catching all the heat, but in return was receiving all the benefits. Louie instilled fear on Seventh Street, and everybody in the game fell victim to that fear, even Sonny James.

"Go 'head and get in," Smitty said.

Malik got in and closed the door while Smitty got into the backseat. "So what's up, Sonny? What is it that you needed to discuss with me so urgently?" Malik studied Sonny's every move. Both his hands stayed on the steering wheel while he looked forward. When Malik first got in the car, he sat halfway in the seat so he'd be in a position to see Sonny face-to-face and Smitty through his peripheral vision.

"Well, you know Smitty here, don't you?'

"No, not really, but I've heard of him through Louie."

"I don't actually know you either, but I too, have heard of you through Louie," Smitty said.

Smitty held out his hand to greet the young, brave hustler. Malik didn't press Smitty's palm though. Instead, he tilted his hat to Smitty, which was noticed in the gangster world as a sign of respect. Smitty pulled his hand back, sat back in the seat, and admired the strength he saw in the young nigga.

"Well, Malik, the subject of this meeting is you," Sonny said.

"Me?"

"Yes, you."

"Well, give it to me in the raw."

"Okay then. Smitty here just came home from Lorton, and while he was there, Louie came in with a fresh ten to thirty years thanks to you."

"What the fuck you mean 'thanks to me?' I ain't turn in Louie." Instantly, Malik was offended.

"You may not have turned him in, but he believes you set him up," Sonny explained.

133

"That's crazy, man. Why the fuck would I do some shit like that?"

"That's what we want to know, Malik," Smitty said.

"Louie says you were supposed to meet him on Seventh and T at eleven o'clock to cop an ounce. He says you were real eager to cop his last ounce and that you damn near begged him to sell it to you."

"Yeah, that's true. But I ain't set him up though."

"Let me finish talking before you start defending yourself. Now Louie says you always talked about turning this joint over to a coke strip, and that every time you suggested something about doing it, he declined and told you no. On the other hand, you had a vision. You always thought that coke would move better in this spot being that there's too many dope strips nearby. So one day you call him, and he agrees to meet you at eleven o'clock, hours before the jump-outs come. He says he kept paging you, but you never called back. He waited almost two hours for you. Then he finally gave up and headed on his way, but for some strange reason, the same jump-out, Cowboy, who been tryna lock Louie up for years, gets him with the ounce of raw dope, a gun, and about nine thousand dollars. Louie got ten to thirty years behind that shit, Malik, and we're sitting here wondering why is it so obvious that Seventh and T is all of a sudden a coke strip being heavily run by you?"

Malik kept his eyes on both men, but mainly on Smitty. Sonny James never looked Malik in the eyes. That was a dead giveaway, because every time he and Sonny did business together, he always looked Malik in the eyes. Therefore, he kept his focus on Smitty for any sudden movement, but looked at Sonny for any signal.

"Now, Sonny, you know me. You knew my father."

PRINCE OF THE CITY

"Hold up, Malik. When I first met you, you acted like a man. You told me that you never wanted to ride on your father's coattail. So this ain't the time to be bringing up his name."

"Then let me give it to you like this. I was always taught by a whore that a man knows nothing by being told. Now, he may believe what someone says, but unless he investigates it himself, he still doesn't know. There are always two sides to a story. Now, it's up to you to hear me out."

"Hear you out? Why the fuck should we hear you out? I've known Louie since he was a kid. He used to take out my mother's trash. Smitty here has been with Louie his whole life. Nigga, the only thing we know 'bout you is that your father was getting money in Southeast and ended up getting whacked along with his wife, and you were raised by a dick-sucking whore. So what the fuck we need to hear you out for, huh?"

As Sonny was talking, Malik's heart began to race. He knew his fate was calling him. He knew in a matter of seconds a signal would be made, and his brains would be sitting on top of Sonny's dashboard. Malik held his hand close to his waist, where Prince was patiently waiting for his call. When Smitty looked outside through the tinted glass, Malik knew he was looking for potential witnesses to the crime he was about to commit.

"Man, I ain't no rat. I understand Louie's pain, but the picture here has been painted all wrong. It's only right you hear me out."

For the first time, Sonny finally moved. When Sonny looked into his rearview mirror at Smitty, Malik knew it was his time to die. This was the signal that would send him to his resting place. Through his peripheral vision, Malik saw Smitty

135

reaching for his gun. Instantly, Malik pointed his finger toward the driver's side window.

"Police is coming!"

Both Smitty and Sonny frantically looked in that direction, falling for the oldest trick in the book that ultimately was their most fatal mistake. Malik shot Smitty first. He quickly placed his gun up to Smitty's temple and pulled the trigger.

Boom!

The impact of the bullet jerked Smitty's head, and brain matter covered the backseat of Sonny's Benz. Malik then turned his gun on Sonny.

"Now, hold on, Malik. Don't kill me. Please don't kill me." Sonny begged like a coward.

"You sat here and tried to trick me out of my life. You talked shit about my parents as if they were nothing. You disrespected my aunt and questioned my loyalty as a man. Sonny, I was always taught never to trust anyone, and that's the reason I brought my friend here to meet you."

"What the fuck are you saying, Malik?"

"Sonny, meet Prince. Prince, this is Sonny"—and with that, Malik pulled the trigger.

Boom!

Malik caught Sonny right between the eyes. Blood covered the tinted windows, while Sonny's face was stuck to the glass. It sort of reminded Malik of his favorite movie, Scarface, when Tony Montana killed Sosa's associate while driving so he wouldn't detonate the bomb.

Malik quickly got out of the car and looked around for potential witnesses. No one was out there. It was too early in the morning. As Malik walked out of the alley, he pulled down his cap and moved in a quick but unpanicked stride. Out the corner of his eye, he could see Booga at the end of T Street, hoping he went unnoticed. Malik hit the corner of Seventh and jogged to where his car was parked.

Malik got into his Cadillac and took a deep breath. It was his first kill and his next step on the ladder to being king. He knew that what he'd just done was justified, but he also knew there was no way Louie would understand. Malik had crossed the point of no return. He'd killed Louie's best friend, and one of Seventh Street's oldest pioneers, Sonny James. So many things raced through Malik's mind as he sat behind the tinted windows of his car rolling a blunt. He wondered if Booga saw him. He wondered if anyone found out what he'd done, and whether it would put Linda in danger. Malik decided he had to tell Linda what happened, but only if she asked.

Malik placed Prince on his lap, started his car, and pushed number three on his CD player. Within seconds, MC Eight's song "Straight up Menace" blasted through the speakers.

"A fucked-up childhood is the reason why I am . . . got me in a state where I don't give a damn."

That first verse stuck in Malik's mind like glue, as he fired up his blunt and took a long pull before heading back to his apartment on Georgia Avenue.

Chapter 18

-GANGSTER PARTY-

After laying the lick down on Smitty and Sonny James, Malik laid low for a minute so everything could die down. His money was getting shorter and shorter. The Bowling Alley was turning into a ghost town, and the pool hall was shut down due to the intense investigation of the double homicide.

During the weeks following the murders, the police found Booga in the same alley with two gunshots to the head. Malik wondered if Smitty and Sonny's people thought Booga had something to do with the murders. Or maybe Booga pulled a move on somebody and didn't pay. No matter what happened, Malik was still relieved that Booga was dead because he would have been the only witness.

Malik sat in his apartment window admiring his car, which stood out amongst the BMWs, Benzes, and Lexuses. As Malik watched how people admired his new car, a pearl-white convertible 500SL Mercedes pulled up and Lee got out. He took a look at Malik's Caddy before going over to the crew of young hustlers who lived next door to Malik.

"Hey now. Which one of you young niggas is the proud owner of that pretty muthafucka?"

138

The three young hustlers laughed. "That is a bad muthafucka, Lee, but sadly, that joint ain't any of ours," one of the youngsters replied.

"That joint is officially a bitch catcher. I think it's the lil dude who stays next to our apartment," another youngster said.

As everyone looked at Malik's prize, the owner of the Madness Shop came out. "Hey, Lee, that's a pretty car, ain't it?"

"Yeah, but whose is it though?"

"Oh, that's Linda's nephew's car."

"What? Linda? Butter's Linda?"

"Yeah, her nephew lives upstairs. Young dude is real smooth. Stays by himself and keeps a rack of bad bitches with him. Every time I see him, he got a nice dime piece coming in and out of his apartment."

"You talking 'bout the lil light-skinned dude with long cornrows in his hair?" Lee asked.

"Yeah, that's him. That's Linda's nephew."

"I did see him with her the other day."

"Linda still looks good, don't she?" the owner asked.

"Hell yeah, man. She looks good as a muthafucka. To be honest with you, I wouldn't mind tryna get with her."

Immediately, Malik picked up the phone and called Linda's cell.

"Hello?"

"Hey Aunt Linda, what's up?"

"Ain't nothing, baby. What's up?"

"Where you at?"

"Me and Peaches are riding up Georgia Avenue. We was gonna stop by your place. Why? Is something wrong?"

"Nah, ain't nothing wrong. So far, everything is going good. I need you to do me a favor though."

"What is it, boy?" Linda asked.

"I can see you out my window pulling up. The dude Lee is out front. Can you holla at him for me now?"

Linda pulled up behind Malik's car while still on the phone with him.

"Boy, that's what you called me for?"

"Yeah. Now's the perfect time. Plus I know he'll do it."

"How do you know what somebody else is gonna do? Are you psychic now?"

"Nah, I ain't psychic, but I did overhear him talking about how good you still look. Plus, he said he wanted to get with you."

"Malik, stop lying."

"Nah, I'm serious. I know this nigga will fuck with me just for the simple fact that he likes you."

"Well, he probably does like me and wants to fuck the shit outta me. But I ain't giving him no pussy just to get you a connect."

"Aunt Linda, I'm your nephew. I'm not tryna pimp you."

"I know. I'm just joking with you. Besides, if he did want some pussy, I would give it to him just so you could get the connect. You know why, Malik?"

"Why, Aunt Linda?"

"Because I love you, and I know it would benefit you in the long run."

"Hey."

"What, boy?"

"I love you."

"Yeah, whatever. Peaches is in the car with me. You wanna speak to her?"

"Sure," he replied.

"Hey, Peaches, what's up?" he asked once she said hello.

"You and me, that's what's up."

"Oh yeah? Well, tell you what. Why don't you come upstairs and braid my hair for me?"

"No. Why don't I come upstairs and you fuck my brains out?"

"Damn Peaches, ain't no shame in your game, huh?"

"Not when it comes to you, Malik."

"Well, in that case, why don't you bring your fine ass on up here?"

After they hung up, Linda and Peaches got out the car, and every nigga out there tried their hand, especially the young ones.

"Damn, baby, can I please have a minute with you?"

"Who you talking to?" Linda asked.

"I'm talking to both of y'all," the youngster responded.

"Well baby, I'm here on some business right now, but maybe some other time," Linda replied.

"And I'm happily engaged," Peaches said as she walked past the crowd of gawking men.

"Have you ever considered having an affair?" another youngster asked.

"Never in a million years," Peaches replied before entering Malik's building.

"Hey Lee. Can I talk to you in private?" Linda asked, walking toward him while he leaned against his Benz.

"Yeah, what's up, baby girl?"

Linda and Lee began walking down Georgia Avenue together to discuss Malik's future.

* * * * * * *

Malik and Peaches were in a session of lovemaking. This time, Malik was the aggressor. He placed Peaches on his living room floor and romantically kissed her from head to toe. He viciously made love to Peaches in every way possible, giving her the best experience she'd ever had.

After they made love, Peaches washed Malik's hair and braided it into cornrows. For every cornrow she braided, Malik had to give her a kiss. Peaches was falling in love with Malik while Malik was falling in love with money.

Malik jumped up as soon as Linda stepped inside the apartment. "What'd he say? What'd he say?"

"Damn, boy, sit your pressed ass down," Linda said, laughing at Malik's desire to get paid.

"Come on, Aunt Linda. What did he say?"

"Well, first of all, don't you wanna thank me?"

Malik grabbed Linda and gave her his tightest hug. "I knew you could do it! I knew it." He kissed Linda on both cheeks. "You're the best aunt in the whole wide world."

"Yeah Malik, that only worked when you were ten years old. Now, look here. Lee is a very serious dude. If you deal with him, be straight up and don't accept nothing you can't handle, 'cause believe me, he's gonna be tryna drop a lot of shit on you."

"I can handle everything from this point. When do we meet?"

"As soon as we leave he's coming up here to talk to you."

"Good then."

"By the way, what were y'all up in here doing?"

"None of your business, Ms. Nosey," Peaches said.

"Well, since it ain't none of my business, let me go on. Malik, I gotta make a run. Call me later and tell me how it goes with Lee. Okay?"

"A'ight," he said and then kissed his aunt on the cheek.

PRINCE OF THE CITY

As they were on their way out the door, Peaches whispered in Malik's ear, "I wanna tell you something, even though I know you don't wanna hear it."

"What's that?"

"I love you, Malik Perry." Then she planted a wet kiss on his cheek before leaving.

Malik didn't answer Peaches. All he was worried about was his meeting with Lee.

* * * * * * *

The first thing Lee told Malik was to go down to Strictly Business, a few doors down, and purchase a cellular phone and a Sky pager to be used strictly for business. He also taught Malik the whip game, which was how to whip up coke and make extras off each brick he cooked. The same thing Sonny James had done to him.

Within two months, Malik was copping three bricks of powder and getting two fronted to him. He was paying seventeen thousand a key, the lowest number he'd heard of in the city for some of the purest white, fish scale, Grade A cocaine.

Malik was mesmerized at how real bricks of cocaine looked. He wondered why they would compress it, wrap it in a rubber inner tube, and heavily duct tape it. Shit, they probably package it like this just in case they gotta drop it in the water when the Feds get close. Damn, them Columbians don't take no losses. He also wondered why each brick had a scorpion stamp printed on it. Maybe this is to guarantee their customers that all these bricks come from the same source and are not tampered. Damn, now that's how you conduct business. Lee is probably getting like two hundred of these thangs and moving them like ice-cold water on a hot-ass sunny day.

Lee gave Malik five bricks each time and always told him if he needed more, there were plenty. Malik was steadily moving up in the game. By the time he was on his third kilo, all of his previous customers moved up from buying ounces to getting quarter and half keys twice a week.

Malik was strictly moving weight. He had all his previous customers from LeDroit Park, Ninth, Sixth, and 'S' Streets, New York Avenue, and Edgewood Terrace. He even had a new customer from the Southeast side around Fourth Street, who copped at least a brick a week. Rock was Malik's best customer. They developed a friendship over the months, and sometimes Rock would come uptown and kick it with him.

However, Malik stayed away from Southeast. He had his own reasons, which no one knew but him. The only time Malik would even cross the bridge to the south side was after he had counted up all his money for the day, which was around midnight.

Malik would buy a bottle of XO Remy Martin, roll a blunt, get in his Caddy, and ride out to Wingate Condominiums. He'd park his car in the back parking lot and look up to the tenth floor balcony where his father used to look out over Southeast. Malik would think of his parents while Tupac's "Dear Mama" blared from the speakers. As he sank into Tupac's lyrics, a river of tears would run down his face. It was the only time Malik expressed his pain. This was where he found peace, where he talked to his parents, where he cried out and felt his parents were listening.

It was Malik's cemetery for his mother and father, the king and queen.

Chapter 19

-GANGSTA'S BALL-

Six months later . . .

Malik was way ahead of the game at seventeen. Lee gave him the chance to see what it felt like to get money and have fun at the same time. He invited Malik to attend a hair show he threw in Atlantic City. It would be Malik's most memorable moment that glorified the game.

"Hey, Malik, you coming to my hair show?"

"Yeah, I'm coming, but I don't know what to wear to that type of event."

"Whatever you wear, make sure it's proper attire, young nigga."

"What you mean by proper attire?"

"I'm talking slick shit. That Versace or Armani shit. No sweat suits and tennis shoes."

"Okay then. You want a nigga to put it on, huh?"

"Yeah, this is a real event. This is a gangsta's affair, nothing but bad bitches and niggas with bank. When you come to a joint like this, you gotta represent. You gotta put it on and have some serious pieces on your arm."

"Oh yeah? It's like that?"

"Yeah. A real live Gangstas' Ball where niggas meet bad bitches who have they own houses, cars, and businesses. Niggas find ways to make money with each other."

"I'm a'ight on the clientele tip. I ain't tryna meet no new friends, but I will come for the bitches though. A nigga needs some different pussy every now and then."

Lee laughed. "Yeah, young nigga, I know what you mean."

"Why you wait so late to tell me 'bout the party?"

"I been told your ass about this event, but you were too busy chasing that paper and slamming your dick up in that fine-ass broad that be with your aunt Linda."

"Oh, you talkin' 'bout Peaches."

"Peaches, Plum, Apples, Grapes, whatever you wanna call her. I tell you, Malik, that's a bad-ass broad you got there."

"She a'ight, but she ain't my girl. A nigga like me ain't got time to be having no girl. I'm an entrepreneur. I just get money and fuck bad bitches."

"I hear you, young nigga. That's right. Just stay focused on getting that bank right."

"So where's my ticket at?"

"Nigga, you don't need a ticket. You're rollin' with me. You VIP."

Malik laughed. "Yeah. Well, I hope you can get me some VIP pussy."

"That's nothing. You gonna do that yourself. Just watch how those bitches be tryna get at you."

"We'll see. In the meantime, I'm a go get my hair braided and do a lil shopping for tomorrow."

"A'ight then. I'll see you later."

"A'ight. Later."

After Malik got his hair braided by his favorite stylist, Tracy, he drove up Wisconsin Avenue to the Versace boutique and picked out the nicest suit the store had. The salesperson told him that only ten of the suits were made and every Versace boutique only carried one.

Malik tried it on and loved it. It fit him perfectly. The suit was dark blue with Medusa head buttons. Malik also purchased a pair of Versace slip-ons.

To top off the outfit, Malik was going to wear his three-point-five-carat diamond earring and Presidential Rolex. Not too many niggas could rock a three-thousand-dollar Versace suit with cornrows and make it look official, but Malik somehow pulled it off.

Lee's party was the talk of D.C. Everybody who was somebody was buying tickets and making lavish shopping sprees to be part of the big event. It was the Grammy's for major niggas and bad bitches, and Malik planned to make his best impression at his first real party.

While most who attended the event drove their exotic cars to Atlantic City, which was a two-hour drive, Lee and Malik were escorted in the casino's private limo. Lee was doing the Taj Mahal a favor by having his party there, and the manager insisted Lee and his guest be treated with the best luxuries the hotel had to offer.

Malik and Lee were given the penthouse suite. As they entered the room, Malik couldn't believe his eyes. It was the type of shit he'd only seen on TV. He never thought he'd be a guest in a hotel room like this, nor treated the same as famous stars and entertainers.

After settling down, Lee and Malik went into their separate rooms and began getting ready for the party, which had already begun.

Forty minutes later, Lee arrived in Malik's room wearing a tailor-made gray silk suit with a pair of gray gators. "Damn Lee, what the fuck you got on? That shit's fly," Malik said, checking out Lee's suit.

"This that Everett Hall shit, personally tailored. They make clothes for famous muthafuckas," he replied while posing.

"How much it run you?"

"This one here cost me like sixty-two hundred."

"What?" Malik's eyes widened. "Damn, nigga, I'm scared to ask how much those shoes cost."

"Well, for your info, young nigga, these come from a store in B-More called Total Male, and they ran me like thirty-five hundred," Lee said, smiling.

"Got damn! You're wearing a down payment on a townhouse."

They both laughed.

"My suit only cost three thousand, and from the looks of you, I'm scared to wear it," Malik said, knowing deep down inside that his suit looked just as nice.

"Yeah, but you're wearing that muthafucka like it cost a million. You look good, young nigga. You're shining like a star. On top of that, you got the cornrows in tight. I ain't never seen a nigga put on a suit and rock cornrows and make the shit look fly. You know you 'bout to make a fashion statement," Lee said, admiring his young protégé.

"There's a first time for everything. Now, pop that bottle of Cristal you got over there."

They both made a loyal toast and drank to their newfound friendship. Lee was the closest father figure Malik would ever have, and Malik loved and valued every moment they spent together. Malik was given his game by a woman and enhanced by a man. That man was Lee, a nigga who gave Malik a chance. For that alone, Lee had Malik's loyalty forever.

As soon as they got off the elevator and proceeded toward the long line of people trying to get into the show, females were constantly looking and whispering as if they were stars. Peaches and Tracy smiled at each other after overhearing the females talking about Malik. As much as Peaches wanted to turn around and tell them the man they were talking about was the love of her life, she couldn't. So instead, she just listened to their flattery, knowing deep down inside that they would never experience the passionate lovemaking with the young nigga.

Malik and Lee walked straight past the crowd and were led into the party by a burly, well-dressed bouncer. Once they entered the party, gangsters came up with bottles of champagne and women brushed past each other to get a glimpse of the man throwing the party and his young protégé.

Malik and Lee were seated in the VIP section along with some of D.C.'s major players, the real big boys, those who sold bricks and those who got paid heavily to kill.

Each one of the gangsters paid their respects to one another with a strong embrace and a tight handshake. At one table was the young nigga who lived next door to Malik. Fat Troy and his crew had bitches practically trying to suck their dicks in VIP. Seated at another table was the OG named 'O', who was accompanied by the dude Pretty Rick from Kennedy Street. And deep in the corner with some of D.C.'s baddest dime pieces was Malik's man from Southeast, Rock. All of Rock's women were bad, but none of them could fuck with Peaches.

Lee was the first to see Peaches walking around the party. After excusing himself from Malik and two fine-ass divas, he proceeded toward her.

"Hey, where are you going?" Malik asked Lee.

"I see somebody I know. I'll be back. Enjoy yourself."

"Don't worry about him. We'll keep you company," one of the females said as she placed her hand on Malik's dick under the table.

While Malik was busy with the two women, Lee was trying his hand with Peaches. "Ah, excuse me, miss. Can I have a word with you?"

Peaches turned in Lee's direction. "Are you talking to me?"

"Yeah, boo. I've been tryna get at you ever since I saw you on Georgia Avenue."

"Your name is Lee, right?"

"Yeah boo, I'm Lee," he responded proudly. Lee actually thought because of his status that Peaches would be interested in him.

"Well, Lee, I don't mean to be rude or anything, but you know me and Malik—"

"Look, whatever you and Malik do is between you two. I'm just tryna show you something worth your while."

"Well, what's up with you and my girl Linda?" Peaches asked curiously.

"You know me and Linda cool. You also know Linda could never be a nigga's woman, not in her profession." At that very moment Peaches became offended.

"And how do you know I ain't in the same profession?" she asked in a defensive tone.

"'Cause baby, if you was, a nigga would've been pulled you out and made you his wife." He then tried reaching for her hand, hoping she'd fall for his charm.

PRINCE OF THE CITY

Peaches smiled and thought, I wish Malik thought the same way. "Lee, I'm sorry. To be honest, I'm totally in love with Malik." She pulled her hand back from his.

"Malik is young, sweetheart. What can he do with a woman like you?"

"Do you really want me to answer that?"

"Yeah, 'cause a nigga like me need to know."

"Well, for your information, Malik makes me have multiple orgasms even when he doesn't touch me."

"Damn! Malik must be a bad muthafucka."

"No, he's a good Peaches fucker."

"I hear you, boo. But if you ever decide to stomp with a big dog, let me know."

"No thank you. Malik's enough."

* * * * * * *

Malik was in the elevator going up to his suite with two gorgeous divas, Monica and TJ. While Monica caressed Malik's dick, TJ was rubbing her hand over Monica's breasts. As soon as they got in the room, Malik popped a bottle of champagne and rolled a thick blunt of that sticky green. Then he sat on the sofa smoking his blunt while Monica played with his dick and talked dirty in his ear.

"You want me to suck this dick, don't you? You wanna see me swallow your whole dick, don't you?"

Malik just laid back smoking and drinking while TJ unbuttoned his shirt and began licking his chest.

"Hey Malik, you got any music?" TJ asked.

"Yeah, over there." He pointed. "Just press play. There's a CD already in there."

151

TJ got up off the sofa and went into the bedroom for a few seconds. She then hollered out to Monica to turn on the music. Monica pressed play and jumped back on the sofa to continue playing with Malik's dick.

As soon as the music blared from the speakers, TJ walked back into the room butt-ass naked with heels on and danced in front of Monica and Malik to Tupac's "Gangsta Party."

As TJ bent over and spread her pussy lips open in Malik's face, Monica began sucking his dick, coming up every now and then to ask Malik if he liked what he saw.

"You wanna fuck her pussy, Malik?" Monica asked. "That pussy looks good, don't it? I tell you what. Why don't you watch me eat it first so it'll be wet for you?"

Malik was totally tripped out as he sat and watched Monica eat TJ's pussy from the back.

"Come on, Malik. It's nice and wet for you. Now fuck her while she eats my pussy."

Without saying a word, Malik jumped up and began fucking TJ doggie style, while TJ ate Monica's pussy. The excitement was too much for Malik, and after hearing Monica's loud moans mixed with TJ's hard grunts of satisfaction, he exploded.

Malik then sat back and drank his champagne while he watched Monica and TJ go at it like professional porno chicks. When they got in the sixty-nine position, Malik got hard again and began fucking Monica while she sucked and ate TJ's pussy. The ménage a trois lasted about two hours before Lee came knocking at the door.

Knock, Knock, Knock . . .

Moments later, Malik answered while Monica and TJ stepped out. They both kissed Malik on the cheek and told him they'd had a good time. Lee looked on in amazement as the girls left.

PRINCE OF THE CITY

"Lee, you won't believe what just happened."

"Nigga, please don't lie on your dick and say you fucked both them bitches."

"Like I said, Lee, you won't believe what just happened. Now, let's go back to the party," Malik said as he hugged his friend and smiled.

Malik was in a totally different world. This part of the lifestyle was all new to him, and he was loving every minute of it. The more money he made, the more he became addicted to the lifestyle that could either get him riches, sent to prison, or ultimately killed.

Chapter 20

-HATE ME NOW-

After Atlantic City, Malik was back in action. His clientele grew. Everybody was talking about the young, charismatic gangster who made a serious fashion statement in Atlantic City. Females talked about him in every hair salon, and niggas on every corner constantly asked about the young dude who was getting all the money. Some wanted to get down with him while others plotted to rob him. Niggas were broke and hungry and saw Malik as fat and wealthy.

In the summer of 1995, Malik traded in his Caddy and bought a brand-new silver S500 V12 Mercedes coupe right off the showroom floor. That frustrated niggas, especially the ones over in the Southeast Jungle. For some reason, the hustlers in Southeast thought uptown niggas didn't grind as hard to reach brick status. They thought uptown hustlers were given bricks as graduation presents while they stood on the corner day and night ducking bullets and police. Little did they know, Malik had earned his the hard way just like them, and he was originally from the Southside just like them.

As Malik sat down contemplating an even bigger game plan, his phone rang.

PRINCE OF THE CITY

Ring, ring.

"Hello?"

"Hey, Malik, it's me, Peaches. We need to talk."

"Not right now, Peaches. I'm busy."

"Malik, this is serious. Please baby, we need to talk."

"Are you okay?"

"No, not really. Not until I talk to you."

"Well, what's holding you up? Talk then."

"No, not on the phone. We need to go somewhere private."

"Where you at?"

"I'm at the Embassy Suites on Wisconsin Avenue."

"Damn! What the fuck you doing up there?"

"That's irrelevant right now, Malik."

"Can you meet me somewhere?"

"Yeah."

"It's about eleven o'clock, so we can have lunch. Meet me at Houston's restaurant down Georgetown."

"I should be there in twenty minutes."

"Okay, but if this shit ain't important—"

"This is a life or death situation."

Instantly, Malik's antennas went straight up. "A'ight. Are you sure you okay though? Do I need to bring Prince?"

"Who the fuck is Prince?"

"Nothin', Peaches. Don't worry 'bout it. I'll be there in fifteen." Malik put on his new clothes and grabbed his new gun, which he had also named Prince. After the Sonny James incident, Malik got rid of the original Prince and crowned another in its place. The new Prince was a silver sixteen-shot Smith and Wesson .45 caliber with a black rubber grip.

Malik hopped in his new Benz, placed Prince on his lap, fired up his blunt, and went to meet Peaches.

155

Thirty minutes later, Malik spotted Peaches standing in front of Houston's looking good in her Moschino jean outfit. As Malik pulled up, all you could hear was a song from Biggie's CD thumping its beat throughout the area. When Malik rolled down his window, the first verse of "Juicy" made Peaches smile as she looked at him sitting behind the wheel.

"It was all a dream. I used to read Word Up magazine."

"What's up, Peaches? This joint looks crowded. You wanna go somewhere else and eat?"

"No, not really. This will probably ruin your appetite anyway."

"Well, don't just stand there. Get your ass in, girl."

Peaches got in Malik's car and sank into the soft leather seats.

"Damn, Malik! Now this is a serious-ass car."

"Okay, cut the bullshit, Peaches. What did you call me early in the morning for?"

Peaches turned down the volume on Malik's system. "You're in danger."

"What the fuck you mean I'm in danger?"

"Like I said. You're in danger."

"Explain to me what's up and tell me everything you know."

Malik knew Peaches was serious. At first, he thought she was calling to tell him that Lee was trying to get at her at the party. He already knew that, because Lee told him and he gave him the go ahead. After all, Peaches wasn't his girl and never would be.

"Do you know a guy named Tank from over in Southeast?"

"Nah boo, I don't think so."

"See Malik, you don't even know your own enemies."

"What the fuck are you talking 'bout? I ain't got no beef with nobody but the nigga who killed my parents, and I don't

156

even know who that is. Now, who the fuck is Tank, and why is he my enemy? And how the fuck did you find this out?"

"Calm down," Peaches said, jerking back.

"Maybe I would calm down if you stopped bullshittin' and spit it out."

"Okay, it's like this. Tank is one of my clients, and last night we spent the night together at the Embassy Suites. I picked him up from his friend's barbershop on Martin Luther King Jr. Avenue, and when we woke up, he called his friend to come get him. When his friend came in I went—"

"Hold up, Peaches. What's his friend's name?"

"Will you let me finish first?"

"Go 'head then," Malik said, eager to know more.

"Like I was saying, when his friend came in, I went into the bathroom and was about to take a shower until I heard your name come up. At first I thought I was just hearing things, but being nosey, I ran the shower water so they'd think I was inside, but I pressed my ear against the door."

"So what did you hear?"

"His friend, I think his name is Rock . . ."

"Who? Rock?"

"Yeah. Do you know him?"

"Just keep talking."

"Well, anyway, Tank kept saying, 'I know where that nigga Malik live at. We can get his ass tomorrow. He lives right over the Madness Shop. The nigga's so comfortable he won't even expect it.'"

"And what was the nigga Rock saying?" Malik asked.

"Well, he kept telling Tank, 'We gotta do this right. One slip-up can fuck up the whole move. That nigga keeps a gun on him. Plus, he's always looking over his shoulder. And if any of them old heads find out we robbed and killed that nigga, then our heads are gonna be on the market to the highest bidder.'

"Then Tank said, 'Fuck them uptown niggas. We can rob all they asses.' Then Rock asked Tank how much he thinks you have. And Rock was like, 'Well, I cops at least a brick twice a week, and the nigga wears a Presidential Rolex and drives a brand-new 500 coupe. So no matter what, that lil nigga's holdin' for real. I think he got two hundred fifty stashed in the cut.'

"Then Tank asked, 'What about his man?' And Rock said, 'Who, Lee? Oh slim, that nigga holdin' heavy, and he's easy to snatch, but I don't think he's gonna give it up, 'cause a nigga with that much money already knows a nigga's killin' him once he gives it up.' So Tank replied, 'Man, Rock, I think Lee would give it up. Let's get him first and then Malik.' Rock agreed with Tank and said that they had to go past his house to get his Desert Eagle because he loved smackin' niggas out with that joint. Then they both laughed and started talking about how they were gonna be rich."

After Peaches told Malik everything, his mind raced back to the jewels his father used to drop on him while overlooking the Jungle. Rock was from Fourth Street, and from his father's lessons, Malik knew that Third, Fourth, and Sixth Streets were where the snakes lay.

Michael used to say, "Son, if you lie down with snakes, they gonna bite you, no matter how long they take. You better believe that before you get up they gonna bite."

That jewel kept replaying in Malik's mind.

After Malik left Peaches, he rode down Wisconsin Avenue listening to Biggie Smalls's "Warning," and thinking of a master plan on how to kill Rock and Tank.

"These niggas must be trippin'. They got me fucked up,"

158

Malik said to himself. "How the fuck they think they gonna rob and kill me and get away with it? These niggas don't know I done killed before. My father was a cold, vicious killer. What makes them niggas think I ain't just like him? They don't even understand. I'm the muthafuckin' Prince of Southeast, for real." Malik's anger began to boil. "I'm a smack these niggas' heads off real good." He pulled over and dialed Lee's cell.

Ring, ring, ring, ring, ring, ring.

"Damn, Lee. Come on. Answer your fuckin' phone." After realizing Lee wasn't going to answer his phone, he then paged Lee with the code 911. He knew Lee would call back immediately.

Chapter 21

-KINGPIN-

While Malik was uptown climbing the ladder to success, Black Sam was the reigning king of the Jungle on the Southeast side. Over the years, Black Sam blew up so big that he couldn't even ride around the Jungle without being noticed by everybody.

Black Sam was one of D.C.'s real kingpins. He still operated all of his strips in Southeast, but he also expanded his distribution to cocaine.

After killing Mike and taking over the throne, Sam hired Kojack as his right-hand man. Kojack was the man in Southeast. He had the whole Southside paging him twenty-four hours a day for everything, from drugs to hired murders. All business was conducted through Kojack, while Black Sam took long vacations to Vegas to gamble.

Sam's gambling habit became ridiculous. The more money he made, the more he gambled it away. Sometimes he'd call Kojack and have him send money from the day's profit just so he could have enough for another week of gambling. Black Sam was a real gambler and a wealthy one. While visiting Vegas on the regular, Sam would also visit Chevece Jones, a woman with whom he fell deeply in love.

PRINCE OF THE CITY

Chevece was the wife of the owner of the New York, New York Hotel and Casino in Las Vegas. She was having an affair with Sam out of revenge for what his best friend, Michael Perry, had done to her. Michael had left Chevece for Connie while Chevece was two months pregnant with their child. She moved to New York with her aunt without telling anyone she was pregnant and then traveled to California looking for a new life. Chevece ended up meeting her husband at a dinner party in Hollywood, a white man who never knew about her past and didn't care to know.

Black Sam always wanted Chevece, even when they were in high school. However, he could never have her because his best friend, Michael, loved her.

Sam lived with regret after killing Michael, and he developed an I-don't-give-a-fuck attitude. He began drinking more and snorting coke in an attempt to avoid thoughts of what he had done. Still, every time Sam was with Chevece, he took his frustrations out on her pussy.

"Damn, Sam. Why you be fucking me so hard?" Chevece asked as they were making love.

"'Cause you need to be fucked like that. You ain't nothing but a ho. Besides, I wanted to know what that pussy felt like years ago, but you were in love with Mike."

"Fuck Mike! I wish I never met him. He destroyed my life."

"How the fuck did he destroy your life? Bitch, you're rich. You got a husband that owns a casino. You do what you want. You come and go as you please, and you spend money like it grows on trees. How the fuck can your life be destroyed?"

161

"Fuck you, Sam! For your info, my life is destroyed. I abandoned my child. My husband likes me to fuck him in the ass with a dildo, with his crazy, freaky ass. I don't love him, and fuck the money. The money doesn't even make me happy. I hate my life. I feel like a slave, and Michael is the reason I'm like this. So, fuck Mike, and fuck you too, Sam."

"Hold up, Chevece. You said you abandoned your child. What child?" he asked curiously.

"I don't wanna talk about it. Let's just drop it. Okay?" Chevece tried to walk away but was stopped by Sam's stronghold.

"I will, but only if you drop to your knees and do what you do best."

Enticed by Sam's aggression, Chevece istantly dropped to her knees in submission. Sam smiled as Chevece performed fellatio on him.

Afterward, Black Sam thought about the past, and he wanted to know why Chevece left D.C. After all, she was his fantasy, and any information he could get on her would be useful.

Sam always wanted Chevece. It was one of the things he kept inside that added to his hatred for Michael. Sam envied Michael's relationship with Chevece. To Sam, Chevece was the perfect girl. She was smart, pretty, sexy, and well-rounded in street smarts. Chevece was faithful and loyal. Every quality that Chevece possessed, Sam loved, but Michael never appreciated her. Still, she remained in love with Michael.

"So Chevece, back to what we were talking 'bout earlier. What you mean, 'abandoned your child?' When did you have a child and where is it now?"

"Sam, I told you that I don't wanna talk about it. Now, can you stop, please?" Chevece said as she looked him in the eyes, but then lowered her head.

"Damn bitch, is your life that fucked up? What you do? Kill your kid or something?" he asked with narrowed brows.

"No! Sam, look. I told you—"

Smack! He smacked Chevece so hard that her nose began to bleed.

"Bitch, don't you ever raise your voice to me like that. I ain't your fuckin' husband! Now, sit your ass down and listen. If I ask your ass a question, you better answer." Sam pointed at a chair. Expressionless, Chevece took a seat and wiped away the blood running from her nose with the back of her hand.

She liked when Sam took charge. It turned her on. Her husband wasn't man enough to show her how things were supposed to run. She needed a real man, someone who would lay down the law when needed. Plus, Chevece loved Black Sam's dick.

Chevece chose her words carefully and kept her eyes toward the floor. "Please don't hit me no more, baby. Please. I'll do whatever you want."

Sam took pleasure in smacking Chevece around. It was part of his revenge for all the years she ignored his admiration and affection.

"Bitch, just listen to what I gotta say. I got a plan that can make both of us happy."

"Okay, baby. I'll do whatever you want. Just tell me what it is."

Sam loved it. He knew Chevece wanted to get out of her marriage, and he was her only hope. Chevece was vulnerable and willing to do anything to be with Sam.

"Okay, this is it. We gonna take this white muthafucka for everything he got."

"How we gonna do that? When we got married, he made me sign a prenuptial agreement."

"Do you know where his safe is at?"

"Yes. I know where two of them are, but he only thinks I know about one of them. He keeps the one in his office a secret."

"Do you know the combinations to them?"

"I only know the combination to the one at the house. But I do know where he keeps the extra key for the one in his office."

"Good, baby. Now this is what I want you to do. First, find a lawyer and get the divorce papers together. Then, the day before you have them served to him, we take everything. Now, how much you think is in the safe at home?"

"I know for sure it's two million cash in large bills and about one million in traveler's checks."

"That's a lot of paper. What about the safe in his office?"

"I'm not sure 'cause I've never been in it."

"Fuck it then. It might be some bullshit anyway, like the deed to his hotel and some other business shit."

"Baby, are you gonna take me away from here?" she asked as she then got down on her knees and wrapped her arms around his legs.

Sam took advantage of this opportunity to finesse his way into three million dollars without taking a life or lifting a finger. He pulled Chevece up and held her in his arms close to his chest.

"I'm a take you away from here and treat you like the queen you are. There will be no more pain, I promise. Chevece, with me, you'll be happy." Sam held her tight and kissed the tears away.

Chapter 22

-YOU KNOW WHAT IT IS-

Tank and Rock pulled into the alley on Kenyon Street after circling the block looking for Malik's car.

"Rock, this nigga ain't even home," Tank said, checking the scenery while patting his gun against his lap.

"Yeah, his car ain't nowhere around, but that don't mean he ain't there."

"So what are you saying? You wanna go knock on the door or what?" Tank asked.

"Nah, let's just lay low for a minute and see if he comes through." Rock decided.

"We gonna give it about thirty minutes, and if he don't come through, we going up in there."

Rock and Tank's timing was right. It was noon and most niggas would just be getting up. As they sat parked in the alley waiting for Malik to come home, Malik was parked on Wisconsin Avenue impatiently waiting for Lee's call.

"Damn. Where the fuck is this nigga at this early?" Tank asked impatiently.

"I dunno, but I tell you what. If he comes home within the next half hour, before the rest of these niggas start coming out, then we got him. All we gotta do is walk his ass in, and bingo! We rich!"

Tank lit a Newport and blew out a perfectly round ring of smoke. "I hope his bitch ass hurry the fuck up, 'cause I'm tryna cop me a Lexus coupe before the day is over."

They both smiled an evil grin and clutched their guns.

After about ten minutes, a pearl white SL500 pulled up in front of Malik's building. Tank and Rock were slumped down in their seats looking at the Mercedes.

"Rock, who is that?"

"I dunno, but that joint is tight as hell."

"Yeah, it is, but I hope he ain't just gonna be sitting there. If so, it'll fuck up our whole caper."

The door to the Benz opened and a short, stocky, older guy got out. Rock immediately jumped up.

"Look Tank. Oh shit! That's the nigga, Lee. Malik's connect."

Tank looked up at the man he'd heard had millions of dollars for the taking. "If that's Lee, then where the fuck is Malik?" Tank asked.

"Man, fuck Malik right now. He's small change compared to this nigga," Rock said.

"Well, what the fuck are we sittin' here for? Let's get him now."

"Hold up. Let's see what he's about to do first."

Lee got out of his car and walked toward Malik's building with his keys out as if he lived there.

"He's going in Malik's building! He probably got a spare key or Malik's up in that joint."

"Good, then we can kill two birds with one stone," Tank replied, his adrenaline pumping.

PRINCE OF THE CITY

"Come on then."

Tank and Rock got out the car, walked out of the alley, and yelled out to Lee as he opened the front door with his key.

"Hey, main man. Can you hold the door for me please? I lost my security key."

Although Lee didn't recognize the two, he didn't think of anyone doing harm. After all, the owner did rent apartments to some Howard University students during the school semesters.

Lee held the door open, letting Tank and Rock inside. As soon as the door closed, Tank turned and placed his .357 Desert Eagle in Lee's face, while Rock grabbed his collar and placed his .45 automatic in Lee's back.

Smack!

Tank smacked Lee across the jaw with his Desert Eagle.

"Nigga, shut the fuck up. You know what it is. I do all the talking. You listen."

Lee nodded, letting them know that he was willing to cooperate. After all, they must have come for money and not his life, because if so, they would have killed him already.

"Now, I know you got a spare key to Malik's apartment, but what I don't know is if he's in there or not," Tank said.

"Nah, slim, he ain't there. I dunno where he's at. I just stopped by to holler back at him 'cause my cell phone battery went dead."

"A'ight then, nigga, we gonna go in there, and if you're lying, I'm killing both y'all. You go first."

They led Lee up to Malik's apartment and made him open the door, pushing him in first.

"Get on the floor!" Rock ordered while Tank checked the apartment.

"Nah slim, he ain't here," Tank said.

"Well, Lee, that's one point for you. As long as you keep cooperating like this, I promise you'll live."

The first thing Lee noticed was that his robbers knew his name, and if they knew him, then they did their homework. They knew he was holding onto millions. So there was no way he could give them what they wanted and still come out alive. Lee knew he was going to die.

"A'ight, it's like this. First, where's the money at in this apartment? And I mean all of it," Tank said.

"Man, Malik keeps his money in the air vents and the lining of his refrigerator. He also keeps his coke right there in front of your face."

Tank kicked Lee in the head. "Nigga, don't get smart with me. Now, where's the coke at?"

"Look under the couch," Lee told him.

Tank flipped the couch over and saw three perfectly wrapped, duct-taped bricks and a Taurus 9-millimeter handgun. He then got the money out of the air vents and the refrigerator and placed everything in two pillowcases and set them by the door. Then Tank went into Malik's room and found his Rolex and bracelet while turning the room upside down looking for more money.

"A'ight then, Lee, that's another point for you. Right now, you're on a roll. Now listen, this is the most important info we need right now, and we expect you to be honest with us. Where is your money located?"

When Lee didn't answer, Rock kicked him and said, "Nigga, where your bank at? Don't make me kill you 'bout some money. Where's it at?"

Lee flinched and rubbed his head. "Come on, slim, you ain't gotta kill me. I'd be glad to give you some money, but the sad thing is I can't get to it. Even if I told you where it is, you couldn't get to it."

"See Tank, I told you this nigga ain't giving up shit."

At that, Lee knew for certain that he was going to die. His attacker revealed his partner's name, and there was no way they would let him live with that information.

As Lee tried to get up off the floor to make a run for it, Rock emptied two bullets in the back of Lee's head. Lee lay dead in the middle of Malik's living room, sprawled out in a pool of his own blood.

"Come on, Tank. Let's go!"

As Rock reached for the pillowcases, Tank placed his .357 to the back of Rock's head. "Nah Rock, you staying here with him."

Then Tank pulled the trigger one time and Rock's brains splattered all over Malik's walls. Tank walked out the door with two hundred thirty thousand dollars plus three kilos of pure Columbian cocaine.

For Lee, it was a matter of being in the wrong place at the wrong time. For Tank, it was the ultimate come up, but for Rock, it was a lesson well learned. Trust no one!

Chapter 23

-TEARS OF A HUSTLER-

L ee never called back, and after about fifteen minutes, Malik's mind was racing about what to do next. He knew he had to do something fast, but Malik wanted to let Lee know before he started putting his murder game down.

Malik knew Rock, but he didn't know Tank. His first mission was to find out who Tank was. He wanted to kill Rock and then kill Tank, or catch them both together.

As Malik headed back home, his pager was blowing up with 911. The only person who would put a code in without a number was Linda. So Malik pulled over and called Linda on her cell phone.

"Hello?"

"Yeah, what's up?"

"Thank God, boy. You're safe."

"What you talkin' 'bout?" Malik asked.

"Peaches told me what happened."

"Damn, Peaches got a big mouth."

"Peaches got love for you, and I do too. Where are you?"

"I'm in Georgetown right now, but I'm headed back home."

"I'm already at the Madness Shop, and I advise you not to come here."

"Why? What's up?" Malik asked, growing more concerned.

"We need to talk."

"What's up? What's going on?"

"Malik, it's bad."

"Aunt Linda, what's bad and why can't you tell me now?"

"'Cause, baby, I don't want you to flip out. Just meet me at my house while I take care of this mess."

"What mess? What the fuck are you talking 'bout? Did the Feds raid my joint?"

"No."

"Well then, what the fuck is going on? Tell me now. You know I ain't with no guessing game shit."

"Just meet me at my place. Okay, Malik?"

"No, Aunt Linda! I wanna know now. What the fuck is going on?"

"Okay then, I'm a give it to you raw. After all, I know personally you've become immune to this shit."

"Spit it out then."

"Well, I was coming to your place, and when I got here, the building was evacuated and police and ambulances were everywhere. At first, I thought something happened to you. But Peaches called about ten minutes ago and told me what was up and that she left you on Wisconsin Avenue. So I knew you couldn't be here that fast."

"So what happened?"

"When I got here, they were bringing two bodies outta your apartment."

"What!"

171

"Yeah, and Lee was one of them."

"Who? Lee? Awwwww, hell naw! Not my man . . . I know these niggas ain't kill my man. Who was the other one?"

"I can't identify him. I've never seen him in my life."

"Did you go in there?"

"Yeah, I had to, 'cause my name is on the lease."

"Did the police fuck with you?"

"Nah, but I do have to go down to homicide to get interviewed. Don't worry though, baby. I've been through this before. I can handle it. Did you have any ID in there?"

"No, I got my license on me. But I did have money and shit."

"Well baby, you already know that's gone. You can always get that back. But when your life's gone, ain't no coming back. I thank God you weren't in there."

"Damn, Aunt Linda, these bitch-ass niggas done killed my man."

"I know, baby, but the only thing we can do right now is lay back and find a way to resolve this shit. Now, Lee and I were good friends, but my main concern is you. Whatever decisions you make from this point on must be done wisely and executed to the fullest degree."

"Yeah, I understand."

Malik knew Linda was right. He couldn't just go out and look for Rock and Tank. He had to do his homework and develop a plan. The main thing was to retaliate and get away with it.

"Now that you understand, go to my place and stay there. I will try to find out who this other person is. Don't worry 'bout nothing, baby. I got it under control. Just wait for me till I come home, and then we'll discuss this in a strategic way."

"Okay," he replied sadly. So many emotions were going through his mind at that moment that all he could do was listen." Malik found himself, sad, depressed, angry, worried and helpless all at once.

"Hey, Malik?"

"Yeah, what's up?"

"I love you, baby. You're all I got."

"I love you too, Aunt Linda. I love you too," he said before hanging up.

Malik knew that regardless of how much of a man he had become, it was Linda who had given him the game, and whatever decision she made was the wisest of all. Linda was a true gangsteress, and if she had been a man with those qualities, she would be the boss of all bosses.

On the drive to Linda's place, Malik lit his blunt as Scarface's "Never Seen a Man Cry" blared from his speakers. As the lyrics sank into his ears, Malik sat back and collected his thoughts. He knew he was prone to death, and so were those around him. He had lost the people that he loved the most to the game.

Linda was the only person on earth that he had left, and Malik refused to lose her. With this thought, Malik tried to decide whether he should get out of the game. He also wanted to know the true story about his parents.

Malik knew there was more to life than the life he was now leading, and if he continued on this path, he'd end up in the same place as his parents, Sonny James, Smitty, and Lee. Death was no enemy to Malik. It was a good friend who came at any given moment. Malik decided he didn't want death to visit him yet. His only problem was how Linda would take it. Malik knew he couldn't live without her.

* * * * * * *

After hanging up with Malik, Linda walked back to the crime scene to see if anything else was left in the apartment. On her way in, she was stopped by detectives. "Excuse me, miss? Are you Linda Wells?" a homicide detective asked.

Linda paused for a moment, looked around the crowded hallway filled with detectives and forensics. She gave it a thought to ignore him and just walk past the scene and knock on another apartment door, but she knew she couldn't. She had already talked to one officer earlier, so it was obvious they knew who she was.

"Yes, I am."

"Well, we need to talk to you. Can you step over here, please, and place your hands on the wall?"

"Place my hands on the wall? For what? I wasn't there. That was my boyfriend."

"Yes, we know that, ma'am. But your name is on the lease and officers found cocaine in your kitchen cabinet under the sink."

"So what! That ain't mine! You can't charge me with that!"

"Ma'am, please. Don't make a scene. Just place your hands on the wall."

"Fuck no! I ain't doing shit. You muthafuckas are tryna plant shit on me."

When the officer grabbed Linda, she tried to tussle away.

"Ma'am, you're under arrest for possession of narcotics, and if you keep trying to fight me, you'll be charged with resisting arrest."

"Fuck you, you white bitch! Get the fuck off me!" Linda fought helplessly, while the two plain-clothes detectives placed her in handcuffs.

"Get the fuck off me, bitch!" Linda spat at them as they threw her in the backseat of their unmarked vehicle. "Let me go, you white bitch! You can't put that shit on me! Let me go!"

Everybody looked on as they drove Linda away. Some speculated she had something to do with Lee's murder, while others knew she didn't and it was just a coincidence that there was still coke left in the apartment. Linda was just in the wrong place at the wrong time, and there was nothing she could do about it.

* * * * * * *

As Malik pulled into Linda's back parking lot, he passed a crowd of young hustlers indulging in a game of craps. The back parking lot had become a profitable strip after the Feds closed down the Bowling Alley. Most of the guys who worked for Malik moved it over on Seventh Street.

Fat Keith had become the head nigga on Seventh Street. He moved from Ninth Street over to the parking lot and renamed it The Pit. The Pit was a good strip, but it had also come under investigation since Fat Keith had come over. Bodies would pop up at least twice a month.

Malik found out that Fat Keith brought a bloody beef with some of the Ninth Street niggas who would come through and blast every chance they got. Malik grabbed his keys and placed his gun on his side as he headed around the front of Linda's apartment.

"Hey, Malik. What's up?" Fat Keith yelled out as Malik passed the dice game.

"Hey, wassup, Keith? How you doing, slim?"

"I'm chillin'. Just bustin' these young niggas' asses," he replied, shaking a set of dice.

Malik started to walk away.

"Let me holla at you for a minute."

Malik turned back. Even though he wasn't in the mood for conversation, he still gave Fat Keith a few minutes.

"Yeah, what's up?"

"Slim, you know I got this spot jumpin', right?"

"Yeah, I know. What about it?"

"Look, Malik. I ain't gonna beat around the bush, but a nigga needs a connect. Now all these niggas out here movin' shit, but nobody won't sell me no powder. And I've known you for a while. Shit, we used to box together, and from what I see and hear, you got that shit. I'm just tryna get down. I don't give a fuck how high the number is. I just want some powder. I'm tired of these niggas serving me this already cooked up shit. All I need is a little help, and I'm asking you like a man. Throw a dog a bone."

"Keith, I'd love to help you out, slim, but right now, I'm kinda fucked up. I don't even know when the next time I'm a get down myself. When I do, you'll be the first nigga I come see. A'ight?"

"That's good enough for me. Thanks, slim. You won't regret it."

Malik and Keith shook hands, and at the moment they turned from each other, four unmarked police cars pulled up, blocking off the vicinity.

"Everybody get on the ground!"

Malik tried to walk away as if he wasn't part of the crowd.

"Hey! Take another step and I promise your whole family will be walking behind you real slow. Now get your ass on the ground before I bust a cap in your ass. I'm just itching for one of y'all to try me today."

As soon as Detective Cowboy threatened Malik's life, without hesitation Malik complied with his orders. He knew Cowboy meant every word.

The officers searched the crowd of hustlers one-by-one. Some they let go and some they locked up. Malik was one of the ones that got locked up. He had in his possession a sixteen-shot Smith and Wesson .45 automatic.

Malik was arrested, charged as a juvenile, and sent to the receiving home for boys on Mount Oliver Road in Northeast until his eighteenth birthday. Just like Linda, Malik was caught in the wrong place at the wrong time, and there was nothing he could do about it.

* * * * * * *

At the same time that Malik was sent away, Linda was found guilty of possession with intent to distribute and sentenced to five years in federal prison. She was placed in the Danbury Federal Correctional Institution for women in Connecticut.

After Linda and Malik were arrested, Peaches was their only family left who lived by loyalty. Peaches took all of Linda's things and placed them in storage. She also had Malik's car towed to an auto garage in Clinton, Maryland. She often visited Linda on holidays and her days off.

Peaches took all the money she'd saved up, and with an advance loan of twenty thousand dollars from Linda, she opened her first nail shop on Martin Luther King Jr. Avenue in Southeast. Peaches gave up her old life and buried her past as if it never was. She gave herself another shot at life and what it could offer. Although Peaches had changed, there was still something from her past that she wanted. Something that would always be planted deep in her heart. That something was Malik Jabril Perry.

Peaches wrote and sent pictures to Malik at least three times a week. She hoped that after giving up her life in the streets, Malik would look at her differently and accept her for who she truly was. She hoped he would understand her pure love for him. She showed Malik her loyalty and trust in every way. Peaches opened up to Malik in letters, exposing her whole life to him, uncut and leaving no stone unturned. She often wrote him poems, hoping it would brighten his day. She badly wanted to visit Malik, but because he was a juvenile, the only people able to visit were his parents or legal guardian.

Malik had nine months left before his eighteenth birthday, and Peaches did everything she could to make sure Malik would be comfortable when he came home. She saved up all the profits from her business and slowed down on her spending just to have enough money so that when Malik came home, he wouldn't have to struggle as hard to get back on his feet.

Peaches always knew Malik was a great hustler. She just didn't want to see him start from rock bottom again.

* * * * * * *

Black Sam and Chevece pulled off the sweetest three-million-dollar caper ever. Chevece's divorce became final within months, and she and Sam married in a private ceremony in Atlantic City, New Jersey, not far from one of his favorite casinos, the Taj Mahal. After Sam gambled away at least five hundred thousand of their newfound wealth, they bought a house in Fort Washington, Maryland, twenty minutes outside of D.C. Then he put the remaining money with his drug profits and continued to drop off bricks of Mexico's finest to the Southeast Jungle. Sam was king of the Jungle, crowned in 1988, which was the longest run ever heard of in the game.

Chapter 24

-BROTHERS FROM ANOTHER-

Months later . . .

Malik lay back on his bunk reminiscing about his parents and the hand of life dealt to him. He had no beefs about how his cards were dealt, but he often wondered if there was a God, then why?

Rico came bursting into the cell, interrupting Malik's thoughts. "Get up, nigga. Heard 'em call your name for mail," Rico said.

Malik went out into the hallway where the counselor, Ms. Wilson, was calling out mail. "Perry! Perry!" she called loudly.

"Damn, Malik, you always get mail," Soup, a youngster whom Malik grew to love as a lil brother said.

"Yeah, I know, young Soup. I guess they still love a nigga out there," Malik said.

"Yeah, from all them stories you told me, I imagine they would still love your ass," Soup responded.

Malik rubbed him on the head. "They gonna love you like that one day too, Soup. Just watch and see."

"I know, 'cause I'm gonna be the richest nigga in D.C. by the time I'm twenty-one."

"Yeah, Soup. You got seven more years before you turn twenty-one, so until then, move your lil ass over and let me holla at my man," Rico said, interrupting Soup and Malik's conversation.

"Man, Rico. You swear you got all the sense, always tryna bust me and Malik's convo like you got something important to say! Nigga, you ain't talking about nothing, you fake ass wannabe Al Capone!"

"Don't worry about what I'm talking about! You just take your lil ass over in the rec room and go play some ping-pong or something."

"Man, fuck you, Rico. You fat punk!"

"Soup, I'm a fuck your lil ass up; keep playing, a'ight!" Rico said, getting angry.

Malik laughed at the courageous, but funny youngster. Soup always had a way of making Rico mad and Malik loved it, often putting a stop to it before it got out of hand. "A'ight, Soup, that's enough. I'm a talk to you later, okay?"

"Just make sure you're by yourself. I don't want no suckers around," he replied, indirectly insulting Rico.

"Keep it up!" Rico threatened Soup.

Malik laughed again.

"Fuck is so funny?" Rico asked, clearly pissed off.

"You, Rico," Malik responded.

"Me? How am I funny?"

"'Cause, man, you be letting that lil boy get under your skin."

"Man, fuck that lil nigga. His ass too fucking smart out the mouth!"

"Go 'head with that shit Rico. He a'ight. He just a young soldier. You gotta respect that."

PRINCE OF THE CITY

"Yeah, in some ways I do respect it, but in most I don't, because he don't know who to say that shit to."

"I know. I know," Malik said. "But what is it you wanted to talk about?"

Rico and Malik were the best of friends. They met at court while awaiting the outcome of their arrests and were both admitted on the same day. Rico was also arrested on a gun possession, and just like Malik, Rico had no parents. Rico never knew his mother or father, and was raised and adopted by a family friend in Spanish Harlem, New York. Rico came to D.C. in 1991 when he was thirteen, with a Puerto Rican for whom he was working. They took over the major clientele for bricks while D.C. was in its worst condition.

In 1991, the city's coke supply was dry due to the fact that D.C.'s number one drug kingpin was convicted of conspiracy and serving a life sentence. The city needed a connect, and that connect was the Puerto Rican who brought Rico to D.C. This same connect later became D.C.'s biggest snitch, but he was a great teacher for Rico, showing him that regardless of how solid and loyal a friendship might be, never trust anyone. Rico saw how his connect sold his soul and ratted on those who killed for him, those who put their families before him, those who remained loyal to him, and those whom he once called friends. What he did broke down all levels of respect Rico ever had for him. At one point in his life, he eagerly wanted to be like the connect, but after witnessing him pull a Houdini on his comrades, he eagerly wanted to kill him. Often he wished that he had. Rico was angry with himself for not being able to spot the weak and lame earlier.

After the connect got locked up, Rico stayed in D.C. He started messing with this girl named Tasha who lived on

Robinson Place in Southeast, and eventually moved in with her and began hustling at the bottom of the hill. He fell in love with D.C. and made it his permanent residence.

Rico and Malik shared everything. They often talked about how they would get together when they got out, and how much money they were gonna make, and the places they would go, and how many bitches they were gonna fuck. They were preparing to take over the world together, and were so compatible that everything they did or wanted to do, they did together. Rico and Malik became like brothers, something that neither one of them ever had, but always needed.

* * * * * * *

As the weeks went by, Peaches wrote more and more. Her letters became more intense, and Malik started to give in to her. After all, he didn't have any place to go when he got out, and he needed someplace to chill while he and Rico got their plans together.

Peaches had moved into a townhouse in Oxon Hill, Maryland, right across the D.C. line, and just five minutes away from the Southeast Jungle. Malik began to write Peaches back, telling her all the things she wanted to hear. He told her that he'd give it a chance, but not to go too fast. And he reminded her that no matter the outcome, he'd still have love for her for the things she did for him while he was away. Malik liked Peaches, but the only thing that drew him away was her past profession. He didn't like the idea of Peaches having been involved with the same type of niggas he dealt with in the streets, so he stayed focused on his and Rico's plans to take over the whole Southeast side.

Rico was a couple of months older than Malik, so when he turned eighteen, he'd get out first. Their plan was for Rico to chill out and just open Robinson Place back up to keep the money flowing until Malik came home and found the connect. Rico was holding around twenty thousand dollars to his name while Malik was broke. However, Malik still had his Benz, an asset worth about a hundred thousand. That Benz was going to bring Malik back to life.

"Now, Malik, you know I go home next month."

"Yeah, Rico, I know. How can I forget?"

"I'm not saying you forgot. I'm just going over our plans, that's all."

"What's there to go over? It's plain and simple. You go home, cop half a brick, and keep flipping that shit for the next three months. Then, bam, I come home and sell the Benz. We put our money together, find a connect, and get rich like we supposed to, nigga."

"Malik, all that sounds good, but you forgot one thing."

"What's that, Rico?"

"We gotta find that bitch-ass nigga Tank and give 'im what he deserves."

"I ain't forget that part. I just try not to say it, 'cause I want it so bad."

"I feel you, nigga. I feel you."

They both pressed each other's palms hard and embraced one another as if they were brothers bound by blood. After Malik and Rico finished going over their plans, the counselor called count.

"All right, you young niggas know what time it is, and if you don't know, then you know now. It's count time!Baby boy, get in your room," the counselor told Malik.

Malik went into his room, sat on his bed, and opened up the mail he'd received. It was a letter from Linda, and whenever

JASON POOLE

Linda wrote, Malik took his time reading it, because her letters always contained lessons well learned.

Dear Nephew,

By the time you receive this, you'll be on your way out the door back into the world of reality where only the strong survive. However, I cannot be with you on this journey due to my lengthy sentence. Malik, I raised you from a boy to a man. I no longer can be there to guide you through pitfalls. This is the reason I raised you the way I did. I always knew that one day you were gonna have to make it on your own. So I prepared you at a very young age. Malik, you are very skilled physically and mentally. Use what you have wisely and judge others by their character, but never give in to their sweetness. Remember, sweetness is a man's weakness. Peep game and recognize it before it's been played. That way, I guarantee you won't fail.

You know, Malik, it's kinda funny that I'm writing to you this way. I always thought I'd be telling you this at home before purchasing your own house or something. Don't worry about me. I'm OK. I can weather this storm and my bankroll is still fat. I took this charge mostly because I wanted to see you on your own, and for real, I need a rest from them streets as well. But I'll be back in three and a half years, looking and feeling better than ever. Hopefully, you'll be in a position to buy me that house you always talked about. ☺

Malik, do right by Peaches. You know she's a soldier and they don't make 'em like her no more. If you have any problems with tryna get down when you first touch down, just go to the Howard Inn on Georgia Avenue and holla at Butter. He'll do something for you on the strength of me.

So now, my darling nephew, I'm going to end this letter. I pray that you hold deep in your heart every lesson I gave you.

PRINCE OF THE CITY

Use it to your advantage. Stay wise and strong, and remember this always, maintain your composure, master your condition, and forever keep the haters within the bounds of moderation. TRUST NO ONE, not even me. I bear witness that if you live according to these principles, there will be no room for error.
Love Always and Forever Loyal,
Aunt Linda

After count was clear, lil Soup came into Malik's room. "What's up, Malik? I thought you was gonna come down my room and holla at me?"

"Well, Soup, ain't no need for me to come down to your room since you already here."

"Yeah, you're right," he responded with his head low.

"So what's up? Why you so anxious to talk?" Malik asked.

Soup sat up on Malik's bed and looked him in the eyes. "I know you are leaving in a couple more months, and I know Rico leaves in a couple weeks."

"Yeah, so what about it?"

Soup paused for a few seconds and looked away, trying his hardest to hide his emotions before he spoke. "I ain't got nobody. My pops is dead and moms is strung out on that shit! You and I know that ain't nobody gonna come and rescue me from this joint. I'm stuck here till I turn eighteen, which is three more years, 'cause I'll be fifteen next month anyway."

"So what are you trying to say?"

"Maaan, take me wit' you, please?" he begged.

Malik looked at young Soup. He could see how strong this youngster was. No matter how much Soup wanted to let his tears fall, his face remained dry.

185

"Please, Malik, take me wit' you, man. I promise I won't be a burden. I ain't got nobody but you and Rico. Y'all my only family, man. Please don't leave me in this joint."

"How am I supposed to take you with me? I just can't say 'all right, I'm leaving, and Soup's coming with me.'"

"All you gotta do is pick me up from around the corner in Ivy City apartment complex."

"How are you gonna get there?"

"Easy. You know right before count time, Ms. Wilson goes out front to take her smoke break, and you know the gate be locked, but there's enough room on the side that I can slide my body through the gap."

"And what if she sees you?" Malik asked, cutting him off.

"Man, you know Ms. Wilson's fat ass can't catch me. All you gotta do is be at Ivy City waiting on me. I guarantee I'll be there."

Malik took a long look at Soup. As much as he loved this youngster, he couldn't say no. He knew that Soup would end up in a more fucked up spot if he stayed. Also, he could use Soup in his plans to take over Southeast. Soup was from a neighborhood called Third World, and Malik wanted it. "Okay, I'll do it, but one thing."

"What's that?"

"When you get out, you living with me," he said with a smile.

Soup was so happy that he jumped on Malik as if he was his big brother. "Thanks, Malik, man. I love you!"

"Yeah, I know."

At that moment, Rico burst into the room. "Yeah, nigga, I got your lil ass now. Come here, chump!" Rico grabbed Soup and began pounding his legs.

"All right, Rico. You got it, man. C'mon, stop, Rico. You got it!" Soup pleaded, trying to guard his legs.

"Nah, little nigga, say you sorry." Rico slamed his fist in Soups leg harder.

"Okay, I'm sorry."

Rico hit him again.

"Ouch! Man, I said I'm sorry," Soup whined.

"Nah, say you sorry, Uncle Rico."

"Okay. I'm sorry, Uncle Rico. I'm sorry."

Malik saw that Rico was hitting Soup in his legs kinda hard, and Soup was on the verge of crying, but his pride wouldn't let him. "Okay Rico, that's enough. I think he learned his lesson," Malik interrupted.

"A'ight, lil nigga. I'm a let you go, but the next time you get smart wit' me, I'm a put it on you worse than that."

"I'm sorry, man. Just let me up!" Soup pleaded.

Rico let Soup get up. "Now get outta here!" Rico demanded.

As Soup got up and walked close to the door, he turned and cursed Rico out once again. "Fuck you, you fat, curly headed bitch! You hit like a girl!" Then Soup ran down the hall while Rico and Malik sat back and laughed.

Chapter 25

-A QUEEN ON A RISE-

Summer 1996 . . .

Rico was home two months before they let Malik out the gate. While he was home, he executed every part of the plan, plus more. Rico was now copping at least two bricks a week from one of Kojack's main lieutenants named Pee-Wee. Rico was serving dime and twenty rocks hand to hand for the first month, and then moved up to serving half ounces until he developed a healthy clientele serving six deuces and eighths of kilos. Rico and Tasha rented a townhouse in Clinton, Maryland, and Rico also rented a condo in Wingate Condominiums for the stash house, which served as his and Malik's new headquarters. Before Rico left, Malik asked him to get a condo at the Wingate and to make sure it was on the tenth floor facing the back parking lot. Rico didn't understand why Malik was so particular about the apartment, but he still managed to get it. Malik had made up his mind that if he was going to take over Southeast, then he was gonna do it the right way, the way his father did, the way it was taught to him, overlooking the Jungle.

* * * * * * *

PRINCE OF THE CITY

The day Malik came home, Peaches picked him up from the receiving home in his Mercedes Benz. Although his car was now a year old, it still looked like showroom furniture. Peaches had it detailed at the Auto Garage before picking him up. Malik stepped out of the front door dressed in his gray Hugo Boss sweat suit and tennis shoes. His hair was pulled back into a ponytail at the request of Peaches, because she wanted to be the first to do his hair.

Outside, as he walked toward his car, Peaches leaned up against the driver's side with the door open, blasting Tupac's song "How Do You Want It." She was dressed in a thin, tight, Chanel mini dress that fit her body like another layer of skin, and she wore matching lace-up Chanel sandals, exposing her perfectly manicured toes. Peaches looked good. She was a natural dime piece with a head on her shoulders and a troubled past. Malik pulled her into his arms and began kissing her passionately as if she were his queen.

"Hey baby, I missed you," she said, looking into his eyes.

"I missed you too, Peaches," he responded, kissing her again.

Peaches felt all over Malik's body. "Damn boy! You have gotten bigger. What you doin'? Lifting weights or something?"

"Nah, boo, just pushups and calisthenics."

"Well. It looks good on you. Damn, I can't wait to see it all!"

"You look like you been working out too. Is your ass getting phatter or is it the way you're wearing that dress?" Malik asked, patting her on her ass.

"I don't know. Why don't you take me home and find out for yourself," she replied seductively.

JASON POOLE

On the drive to Peaches's townhouse, Malik sat in silence, staring at her the whole time, wondering where this would take him and why he felt the way he did. He also wanted to know why Peaches felt the way she did, and why she changed for him.

"Why are you staring at me like that?" she asked, turning briefly to look at him.

"Like what?"

"You know, like you got something on your mind."

"Well, I do."

"What is it then? Can we talk about it?" she asked, sounding concerned.

"Let me ask you a question."

"Go ahead."

"Why did you change your life around?" he asked seriously.

Peaches pulled the car over and parked on a side street before answering. "I'ma be straight up with you. Like I told you two years ago, I love you, and I mean it. I know you would never let me be your woman if I was still doing what I used to do. I also know that if I changed for the better, it wouldn't be just for you, it would be for me also. Malik, I've had these plans way before I met you. I just fell in love and ask that you be a part of them."

"So tell me this. Why sell pussy to achieve your goals?"

"Oh, I see what this is about now. You're worried about how niggas gonna look at you if you accept me as your girl. Put it this way, if I was just some pretty ass hood rat bitch fucking niggas for free or for pocket books and shit like that, would it make a difference? No! It's just that I refuse to fuck for a dinner at the Cheesecake Factory or some cheap jeans. Malik, I didn't like what I did at all. I never got any satisfaction from it. I just needed the money so I could finish

190

school and start my own business. I was all alone until I met Linda. My past is as dark as yours, and I want to leave it there. That way it can never harm me. If only you can accept me for who I am and not what I used to be." Peaches became overwhelmed with telling her story and began to shed tears. "Malik, I love you, and I've done everything in my power to have you accept me. I don't know what else to do."

Malik wiped Peaches's tears and kissed her forehead. "Baby, you did enough. I accept you. Now stop that crying. I don't need no crybaby. I need a soldier," he replied with humor.

"Shut up, Malik," Peaches said, hitting him on his arm.

"If we gonna be together, you gotta be able to handle certain situations. You gotta go the whole nine yards plus more. You gotta be a gangsta's wife, and a whole lot comes with that, you understand?"

"You ain't telling me nothing I don't already know!"

"The reason I'm telling you this is because my own mother took two bullets in the chest for being a gangsta's wife. Now are you willing to take that risk?" he asked, looking into her eyes.

"I already did when I told you about Tank and Rock. Can you imagine what they would have done if they caught me eavesdropping on them?"

"Yeah boo, I feel you. Now let's go home. We got some making up to do."

Peaches smiled and drove out to their new home in Oxon Hill. As Malik and Peaches entered the house, Malik was greeted with balloons and a welcome home sign.

Malik looked at Peaches. "All this for me?" he asked.

Peaches grabbed Malik's hand and led him upstairs to their room. "No, Malik, all of this is yours. This whole house and everything in it." Peaches unsnapped her dress, letting it fall to the floor, exposing her tight, milky smooth body. Her breasts were firm and round while her nipples were erect as a baby's pacifier, waiting to be sucked. The curves in her stomach rippled as if she did sit-ups on a regular basis while her hips and thighs were sculpted like a prized horse.

Peaches turned and posed for Malik. Her ass jiggled as if it were Jell-o. "All this is yours, and you can do whatever you want to it."

Malik's dick swelled in his pants. He grabbed Peaches and began kissing her passionately, tonguing her mouth. He caressed her breasts and nipples while he kissed her. He then laid her down on the king-sized bed and massaged her whole body. Malik kissed her thighs and ran his hands under her legs until he reached her round ass cheeks. He cupped them, pulled her legs back, and began fingering her pussy while licking her clit like an ice cream cone. He sent chills through her land of pleasure, which she'd been long waiting for. The more he licked and sucked her clit, the deeper his fingers went. He positioned his fingers upward and motioned his index finger as if telling her to come to him. As Peaches's screams began to get louder, Malik knew that he had found her G spot.

"Oh Malik! Oh my God! Malik, what are you doing to me? Malik, I can't take it no more. I'm about to cum, baby! Oh, yes boo. I never felt sooooo good. Damn! Baby, baby, I'm cumming. I'm cumming! Malik, oh yy-eee-sss. Malik Ma . . . lik, ooooooh, baby!" Peaches ran her hands through Malik's hair as her body quivered and shook for about five minutes, letting out the most extensive orgasm she had ever experienced. This was the first time Malik had performed oral sex on Peaches, and it was way more than what she imagined.

After a few minutes of letting Peaches get herself together, Malik put one of her legs on his shoulder and spread her pussy, sticking his hard, throbbing dick sideways into her warm, wet center. His first few strokes were slow and long, penetrating every inch of her walls. As her pussy became wet and moist, his rhythm became hard and fast. Malik pounded Peaches until she was drowning in her own moans. Finally, Peaches became speechless as she came all over Malik's dick while tears raced down her cheeks like waterfalls.

"Malik, I love you. Please don't stop."

Malik pounded her until he couldn't take it anymore. Peaches's pussy was so good that even after he exploded, his dick was still hard. "Damn, your pussy wet as shit!"

"I know, Malik. I can't stop cumming. Even when you pull out, I cum." She blushed.

"Turn around."

Peaches got into doggie position, arched her perfectly round ass upward, and spread her cheeks exposing her pussy and asshole to Malik. He slid his dick into her wet pussy and instantly began pounding her pussy while smacking her ass.

"Yes Malik. This your pussy, boo. I'm your bitch for life. That's right. Fuck me till I'm sore. Fuck me, boo."

Malik took flight at the sound of her voice. The more he pushed his dick into her, the more she pushed her pussy toward him. Both created a rhythm of friction, ecstasy, and eroticism. Her pussy was so wet that her juices were dripping off Malik's nut sack.

"Does it feel good, boo?" Malik asked.

"Yes, baby! Can you please fuck me like this all night?"

"I'm a fuck you like this every night."

193

Malik was the king of Peaches's castle while she eagerly became his queen.

After they both exploded together, Malik lay back on the bed while Peaches snuggled under his arm, caressing his chest as they discussed their future.

"So, I guess it's good to say that we're finally a couple?" Malik said, surprising Peaches.

"You made it official the moment I picked you up. And I promise from this day until the day I die, I'll love you and do whatever I gotta do to keep you happy," Peaches said.

"I feel the same way. It just took me a long time to realize it," Malik said.

"Why? Was it because you were ashamed of what I did?"

"Nah, I was just scared of what the outcome would be. Like I told you, my mother lost her life being married to the king of Southeast."

"Well, I'm willing to give my life for the prince of Southeast."

"And who's the prince?" Malik grinned.

"Come on. If your daddy was the king; then that makes you the prince."

"Yeah, you're right, but what if he had another child by someone else?"

"There can only be one prince born by the king and queen, and that prince is you."

"Yeah boo, I'm the prince. Just like my pops used to say," he proudly announced while looking up at the ceiling.

"Okay then, Mr. Prince. Just tell me when you'll be king, so we can get married and I can claim my spot as queen."

"Soon boo, real soon."

Malik smiled as he caressed Peaches. He thought back on the lessons Linda gave him. The one that stood out was: "Trust no one."

PRINCE OF THE CITY

While falling asleep with Peaches, Malik thought of her devotion to him, which also brought Rico to mind because he was just as loyal. Malik fell victim to her sweetness and the bond he formed with Rico. When it came to them both, he felt deep in his heart that their loyalty should never be questioned. He wondered if he was unconsciously breaking one of the major rules Linda gave him as a child. If so, only one entity would know his mistake—God.

Chapter 26

-SOUTHSIDE'S MOST WANTED-

The next morning Rico pulled up to Peaches's house ten minutes later in his black, fully equipped Yukon Denali. He called Malik, who came outside and embraced his comrade. Malik got into Rico's truck, amazed by the interior. The truck had black leather seats, wood grain, two TVs, a PlayStation, and a surround sound system that held twenty CDs. Malik sat back as Rico fired up a neatly rolled blunt.

"Damn, Rico, this is tight. How much you pay for this joint?" he asked, admiring the vehicle.

"About thirty-five. And guess what?"

"What?"

"This joint is fully loaded. Plus, it got this." Rico opened the glove compartment and pushed a button on the stereo. The whole dashboard rose, exposing a very large hydraulic stash box.

"Got damn, Rico! What the fuck is this? Some James Bond shit?"

"Nah, nigga. We call this our ten thousand dollar ticket away from jail."

"That's how much it cost to put that in?"

"Yeah, slim. And for real, that's cheap. I got a man in New York named Mike Gadget, who's a beast with this shit." He always look out for a nigga.

"Yeah, I can tell. How much does this shit hold?"

"About ten bricks and a few guns. Speaking of guns, which one do you prefer?"

Rico reached in the stash spot box and pulled out two handguns—an eighteen-shot SIG Sauer 9-millimeter, and a sixteen-shot Smith and Wesson .45 automatic. The Smith and Wesson was loaded with hollow-tip bullets and was the exact gun Malik had been arrested for carrying.

"Damn, Rico, you found Prince? Let me get that."

"Here, nigga. I knew you was gonna pick this one anyway. That's why I bought it."

"Thanks. Now a nigga feels warm in these cold-ass streets."

"Yeah, a nigga needs to stay strapped twenty-four-seven 'cause these niggas in Southeast be lunchin'. Only the strong survive."

"In that case, I guess we gotta be the strongest muthafuckas out here then."

"We are, Malik. They just don't know it yet."

"You got that right. Now take me uptown so I can holla at this nigga Butter, and we can get down to business."

"Where we headed uptown?"

"To the Howard Inn on Georgia Avenue."

As Rico and Malik pulled up to the Howard Inn, Butter was getting out of his 850i BMW. Malik rolled down the window and waved.

"Hey Butter."

Butter looked at the young boy who had grown into a well-groomed young man. "Hey! What's up, Malik? How you doin', boy? I ain't seen your ass in a while. Now get your ass out that truck and let me see what you look like."

Malik jumped out of the truck.

"Damn boy, your ass got big, huh?" Butter said, getting a good look at Malik.

"Yeah, a nigga been eatin' good. You know." Malik nodded.

"I see. So what brings you over here? It gotta be something, 'cause your lil ass ain't been around here since the pool hall closed."

"Yeah, I know. And to tell you the truth, I do need something, and I hope you can help me out."

"Go ahead. Spit it out."

"Man, I'm fucked up, and I need some help."

"What kinda help?"

"Well, first of all I'm broke, but I'm not broke."

"Now how the hell can you be broke, but not broke?"

"It's like this. I just got out of the receiving home and I know you heard what happened to Lee in my apartment."

"Yeah, and?"

"Well, them niggas took everything I had but my car. My car is worth at least a hundred thousand, and it's only a year old."

"Sounds to me like you ain't broke. Now, are you asking me to buy your car from you?"

"You can do it either way. You can either buy it straight up, or you can front me the bricks and keep my car for collateral."

As Butter observed Rico waiting for Malik, he figured Malik and Rico had to be business partners and Malik seriously needed the help. Butter also knew this would be a good opportunity to make some extra money, mostly because he had a friend who owned a dealership in Virginia. Butter figured that if he offered Malik four bricks worth seventeen-five apiece and sold the car, he would come out on top since he planned to sell bricks to Malik at twenty-two anyway.

"What you want for it?"

"Give me five bricks."

Butter stepped back and looked at Malik like he was crazy.

"Now, you said your car is a year old, meaning the value went down. I don't plan on keeping the car. I'm just doing you a favor. But I can't give you five. The best I can offer is four."

Malik knew Butter was running game, but Butter had the bricks and Malik needed them badly. Malik needed to open up shop fast, and Butter was the only person he knew who had bricks like that. Fuck it.

"How much you chargin' for them bricks?"

"Well, if I purchase your car that means you'll have to keep coppin' from me. After all, you do need the connect, and since Linda is locked up, ain't too many muthafuckas uptown gonna wanna deal with you. You know niggas still think you had somethin' to do with Louie getting locked up."

"Man, these bitch-ass niggas got me fucked up. What the fuck I look like snitchin' on my man? Matter of fact, who the fuck is spreadin' rumors?" Malik's anger began to boil and Butter noticed.

"Hold on, Malik. You know I've known you all your life. You ain't never gotta defend no shit like that to me. I know where you stand, and I know Linda ain't raise no rat. Let alone your father. But what I think you should do is go visit Louie at Lorton and explain what really went down. He's the one spreadin' the rumors."

"Man, fuck Louie! That nigga assassinated my character."

199

"I ain't tryna get all into what you and Louie are going through. I can see you getting upset. Why don't you just clam down and finish conducting business with me?"

After a few seconds, Malik calmed down. He took a deep breath.

"A'ight Butter, what you movin' them for?"

"Twenty-two a pop."

Instantly, Malik felt Butter was getting over on him. "Got damn, Butter! I used to get them joints for seventeen-five last year."

"I used to pay fourteen back in '89. But it's a new era. It's going into '97 and shit high right now. In Florida they going for eighteen right where they dropping that shit off. In New York they going for twenty-one, and here in D.C., they going for twenty-five. But I'm cuttin' you three thousand. Just work with me, Malik. It's gonna get greater later."

"Okay, if you say so. Now how you wanna do this?"

"Just bring me your car tomorrow when you come get them joints."

"A'ight, thanks."

"Yeah, no problem. Just stay focused, youngin', and keep your eyes open, 'cause everybody ain't what they seem to be."

"I'll remember that."

"You do that." Butter watched Malik get in the SUV with Rico and then they peeled out.

Chapter 27

-RUTHLESS-

H ow much you say you working with?" Malik asked Rico on the drive back to Southeast.

"I got like sixty thousand, plus a half key left."

"Okay, now Butter gonna give me four bricks in the morning. We can put the whip game down and make at least an extra half off each joint. We sell nothing but six deuces and eighths and come out wit' no less than two hundred thousand, and we keep copping shit from Butter until we find a better connect."

"Well, right now Robinson Place is locked down. Homicide been swarming that joint ever since the nigga Froggy got killed. But I got Tenth Place and Congress Park blowing my pager the fuck up."

"Good, then I'll get Third World and work my way to Fourth and Sixth in no time."

"How the fuck you gonna get Third World?"

"Finesse, Rico, finesse. You just watch and see how I do it. I'm a work my way through this whole fuckin' Southeast wit' finesse, but the first thing we gotta do is pick up Soup tomorrow."

JASON POOLE

"Soup! How we gonna pick up Soup?" Rico asked, looking confused.

"He's gonna escape tomorrow at count time. I promised we'd pick him up at Ivy City Complex."

"Where is his lil bad ass gonna stay?" Rico asked.

"He staying wit' me, and that's how we gonna get on Third World. That's Soup's hood."

"Yeah, but you also know that the dude Rock was from Third World. How you gonna mingle your way in that spot?"

"Rico, them niggas know I ain't kill Rock. All they know is that Tank and Rock went on a caper and Rock never came back. So if anything, they beefing wit' Tank for killing they homie. It don't take a rocket scientist to figure that out."

"Speaking of Tank, I got some info on him," Rico said.

"Oh yeah. Why you wait so long to let me know?"

"I was waiting for the proper time to tell you."

"Rico, this nigga killed my man and took my money. My aunt doing time because of his bitch ass! I'm out here broke, tryna sell my car just to get back on. Any time is the proper time! I hate that nigga. I want him bad, slim. Just like I want my parents' killer."

"Well, all I know is that the nigga I be getting my coke from be hitting Tank off too. I think Tank getting like seven joints, 'cause he got a lot of clientele out here."

"So you know where he be at?" Malik asked.

"I only saw him twice outside the barbershop, but I be seeing his Lincoln Navigator truck parked on the side of this building on Chesapeake Street, too."

"You think he lives there or what?"

"Nah, that nigga's getting too much money to be living in the hood. I think that's his stash joint where he be cooking up his shit. Or it's some hood rat's spot where he just be laying up."

202

"Come on. Let's ride past the barbershop and see if we can spot his bitch ass."

When they arrived, Rico and Malik parked in an alley across from the barbershop. "Let's just sit here for a while and see if he pops up. You got a hat or something?"

"Yeah, grab that Bulls hat right there," Rico replied, pointing to the backseat. He then handed Malik a black bandana, keeping one for himself. They tied the bandanas around their necks. They waited for about an hour until it was almost noon.

"For real, I don't think this nigga be getting up this early."

"Man, I ain't movin' till I get this nigga. Fuck that. Let's just wait."

"I ain't got no problems with killing this nigga, but I think we need to check his other trap first before we start laying on him."

Malik knew Rico was right. There was no sense in waiting for Tank if he could be somewhere else.

"Let's go past that joint to see if he over there."

As soon as Rico pulled onto Chesapeake Street, Tank's shiny burgundy Navigator was the first thing they saw.

"I told you his ass was gonna be here. You know he's in there, 'cause he owns that Lexus coupe, too," Rico said, pointing in the direction of the luxury vehicle.

"Well, let's just hope you right, 'cause we gonna sit here until his ass comes out. I'm a put sixteen in his face. Watch me."

"Damn, Malik. You tryna overkill this nigga, huh?"

"Nah, I just wanna make sure he's dead twice—once for me and once for Lee."

"I wanna kill this nigga just as bad just for trying his hand with a real nigga. Let's just run up in there and kill everybody. Just go in blasting shit."

Malik laughed. "Nah, we can't go in like that. We don't even know which apartment he's staying in."

As Rico and Malik talked, a short, brown-skinned girl came outside and headed toward Tank's truck. She got in and pulled off.

"Damn! I told you we should've stayed at the barbershop. This nigga probably ain't even in there," Malik said with disappointment.

"Nah, I bet his ass is in there. Whenever that bitch comes back, we're walking her ass inside."

"Yeah, but what if we do and he ain't there?"

"Then we kill the bitch and get whatever's in the apartment."

"Man, I ain't killing no bitch, especially if she ain't got shit to do with it."

"Man, ain't no fuckin' morals in an immoral game. Shit just happens. That's how it goes out here in the Jungle. A nigga gotta be ruthless in order to survive this shit. Man, we gangstas. That's just how it is in the life we chose."

"Yeah, you're right. But I ain't tryna kill nobody who ain't got nothing to do with it."

"Man, you think that bitch don't know Tank's a cold killer? That's probably the only reason she fuckin' with the nigga."

As Rico's reality hit Malik, he wondered if his mother's killer thought the same way.

"Hold up, Malik. Looks like she coming back. She must've forgot something. Come on, let's go."

Malik and Rico walked into the building as if they lived there and waited for the girl to come in behind them. Malik held the door open for her while Rico stood inside. The girl approached the doorway and thanked Malik as she walked past. Rico slipped behind her and reached his left hand over her mouth while putting his 9-millimeter to her temple.

"Don't make a fucking sound. We ain't gonna hurt you. Now, I'm gonna ask some questions and you're gonna nod your head yes or no."

The girl nodded in compliance.

"Is Tank in your apartment?"

She nodded yes again.

"Is anyone else there?"

She nodded her affirmation.

At that moment, Malik was unsatisfied with the move they had just made, but he knew there was no turning back. He motioned Rico to have her lead them to the apartment.

"Okay, now we're gonna walk right behind you. And I swear to God, if you make one sound, I'm a smack your head clean off. Understand?" Rico asked. She nodded.

The girl opened the apartment door with her key. As Rico and Malik entered with their guns drawn, Malik put his finger up to his mouth signaling Rico to be silent. Malik then motioned Rico to stay in the living room with the girl while he walked back to the half closed bedroom door.

Almost simultaneously, Malik lifted his foot to kick open the door, and the girl let out a halting scream, alarming Tank, but not in enough time.

Malik kicked open the door with his Smith and Wesson .45 pointed directly at Tank, who did the most cowardly thing any so-called gangster could do. Within a second, Malik pulled the trigger while Tank picked up his two-year-old daughter and used her as a human shield. There was no way Malik could avoid it. The bullet had already made its exit from the barrel, ripping straight through the little girl's heart.

Malik blacked out. As he ran toward Tank, he kept pulling the trigger.

Boom!Boom!Boom!

The first three bullets hit Tank in the chest, causing him to fall back on the bed. Malik then stood over his body and began emptying his clip into Tank's head, shooting him five more times at close range.

Boom, Boom, Boom! . . . Boom!Boom!

While Malik was in the bedroom with Tank, Rico was in the living room scuffling with the girl. Rico didn't want to kill her just yet. He wanted to hold off until she showed them Tank's stash. But after hearing the gunshots, the girl began screaming and hollering for her baby.

Rico couldn't take it. "Shut up, bitch!" he screamed before pulling the trigger.

Boom! He splattered the girl's brains all over the living room walls, and then ran back to the bedroom where Malik was.

Rico saw Malik standing over the little girl's body, crying.

"Oh shit! Come on, man. Let's get the fuck outta here," Rico said, looking disturbed.

"Look, Rico! Look what the fuck this bitch-ass nigga made me do."

"I see, Malik. I see. Now let's go before the police come."

"Nah, Rico. Look what he made me do," Malik repeated while tears fell down his face.

Rico knew Malik was tripping. As he heard sirens, he grabbed Malik.

"Come on. Snap outta that shit. Let's go before the police get here."

Malik instantly snapped out of his trance. Once they left, Malik and Rico rode in silence. Rico took glances at Malik, trying to figure out what was going on in his friend's head. Rico felt that what happened was supposed to happen. It wasn't their fault Tank had used his daughter as a human shield. As Rico saw the silent tears run down Malik's face, he had to say something. Rico was a cold-hearted gangster and had to let it be known.

"Ah, Malik, fuck that shit! Shit like this happens. This is the life given to us. It ain't like you did the shit deliberately. It was a fuckin' accident on your part that sent a message."

Malik still remained silent.

"Look, Malik! That broad put herself and her daughter in that situation by even fuckin' with a nigga like Tank. You think that bitch ain't know what type of nigga Tank was? Shit, we in Southeast—the fuckin' Jungle. Ain't no morals in an immoral game. They were supposed to get blasted. That's just the way it goes."

Malik looked up at Rico. He knew Rico was telling the truth, although he felt bad about the child. Malik thought about his mother. This was the same type of situation that had gotten her killed. Malik made up his mind that if he ever had a child, he wouldn't bring it or the mother into his vicious lifestyle.

"Yeah, Rico, I hear you. But that bitch-ass nigga just fucked up my head with what he did."

"Yeah, I know, man. That's what you call a real live bitch nigga. Well, a real dead bitch nigga now."

They smiled lightly. "What do we do now, Malik?"

"Let's just go somewhere and chill. I need to get my thoughts together."

"I know the perfect spot for you, my nigga."

When Rico pulled into the Wingate Condominiums parking lot, Malik's heart began to race. They walked through the lobby, entered the elevator, and Rico pushed the button. Instantly, Malik's legs trembled as the elevator moved its way up to the tenth floor.

When they exited the elevator, Rico led Malik straight to his old apartment where his parents were killed. Malik had told Rico that his parents were killed, but didn't tell him where.

Once they walked inside, Malik's heart raced faster. The way Rico had the place laid out reminded him of his parents and instantly made him feel like a child again. The black carpet, cream furniture, and the bedroom was laid out like a Taj Mahal suite. Malik walked around looking at the apartment, and then came into the living room.

"Man, I hope you like it. I went through hell getting this spot," Rico said.

"Rico, I love it. It's beyond perfect."

"Good, then you can stay here and chill. Break this joint while I go pick up Tasha and get the baby from the babysitter. I should be back in an hour or so."

"Go 'head. I'm cool. Just give me some of that smoke."

Rico threw the bag of weed on the table and proceeded to leave.

"Look, nigga, what happened today let them niggas know that we're two niggas willing to kill whoever or whatever's standing in our way."

Malik looked at Rico. "Yeah slim, we 'bout to lock it down for real."

They embraced.

"Malik, I love you, nigga. You're just like the brother I never had."

"Same here. Till death do us part, nigga. We're gonna ball till we fall."

After Rico left, Malik rolled a blunt, poured some Remy, and went out on the balcony. He looked out over Southeast and began to have a conversation with his father. Yeah Pop, it's my turn now. Now I understand the meaning of a prince. I understand the shit you went through to get here. I also see what must be done to stay here. I'm a rule this muthafucka with style and finesse. I bear witness while I'm still living, I'm gonna make it my business to avenge you and Mommy's deaths. I promise to learn from mistakes and capitalize on them in the process of claiming the throne.

* * * * * * *

The next morning, Rico came to pick up Malik. As Malik opened the door to Rico's truck, the front section of the Washington Post lay on the passenger's seat. He picked up the newspaper and started reading while Rico passed the blunt.

"Yeah nigga, read that. We made the paper."

Malik read the article out loud. "Twenty-one-year-old Timothy Smith, twenty-one-year-old Tearra Blackwall, and their two-year-old daughter were killed mafia style yesterday around 12:15 pm. This is the first time in years a child has been a victim of a crime like this. Police believe the killings are drug related. They found weapons, narcotics, and money. Mr. Smith was also suspected in several homicides in the Southeast area. Police have found no witnesses or motive for the slayings."

Rico smiled, and Malik shook his head in satisfaction. Rico was happy that the Jungle would recognize their work, while

209

Malik was happy that there were no motivesor witnesses mentioned.

"A'ight, we gotta take the Benz to Butter, get the bricks, go to thestash joint to cook shit up, and then move that shit like hotcakes," Malik said. "Nigga, we 'bout to be rich. Just follow my lead. I'm like the MichaelJordan of this shit."

"Guess I'm Scottie Pippen then, huh?" Rico asked.

"I imagine so. Now gimme that blunt and let's go get my nigga Soup, so we can hurry up and take over this city."

An hour later, Rico was growing impatient as he and Malik pulled in the back of Ivy City and waited for young Soup to call Malik's cell.

"Man, what time is it?" Malik asked Rico.

"Why the fuck Soup ain't called yet?" Rico looked at his watch. "It's twelve o'clock count time."

"I dunno, slim. I just hope his lil ass ain't get caught tryna use the telephone," Malik answered.

"Man, it's count time. Soup probably in his cell right now. Knowing him, he probably fucked up his own move."

"Nah, not shorty. He ain't tryna be in that joint. If anything, he waiting for the right time to call." As Rico and Malik were talking, young Soup crept up to Rico's window and surprised them.

"Boo!" he yelled. They both jumped and reached for their straps while Soup's face pressed against Rico's window with the biggest smile ever. "Ah-ha, y'all niggas some bitches. I scared both of y'all."

"Nah, nigga, your lil ass was about to get your head blown off playing," Rico said, opening the door for Soup. "Get your lil ass in!"

"Fuck you too, Rico. It's nice seeing you."

"Man, why you ain't call?" Malik asked Soup.

"'Cause, man, Ms. Wilson's fat ass took her smoke break early, so I had to make my move then."

"Did she see you?"

"I don't think so, but if she did, who gives a fuck. Nigga, I'm free! Now let's get the fuck outta here before we all get locked up."

They laughed and hugged young Soup before pulling off.

Chapter 28

-THE PLOT-

As Malik desperately climbed the ladder to his throne, the real king, Black Sam, was making and losing millions.

While Sam and Chevece vacationed in Aruba, Sam got a call from home and knew it had to be important. Kojack never called Sam while he was out of town unless there was an urgent problem.

"Hey Sam," Kojack said when Sam picked up the call.

"What's up? Why you calling me? Is something wrong?"

"Well, yeah and no."

"What the fuck you mean, yeah and no?"

"It's like this. You know Pee-Wee got locked up and Tank got killed. Because of that, business been a lil slow for the past month."

"What!"

"Yeah, slim, and they fucked him up too. Killed his kid and baby's momma."

"Damn, that's vicious. Who the fuck did that?"

"Word on the street is that a young nigga from uptown did it. Tank supposed to have killed his peoples and robbed him. Plus, I hear he moving shit on Third Street and Robinson

Place. They say the young nigga gettin' money. Supposed to be a real smooth nigga."

"Oh yeah? Well, find out who the fuck he supposed to be and let me know. I don't give a fuck what Tank did. That was our number one youngin', and somebody gotta answer for that. Now what's up with Pee-Wee? Did you get him a lawyer?"

"Nah, he don't want one. For real, I don't know what to say about Pee-Wee, slim. He got caught with twenty bricks, and they got him on tape serving an undercover two keys of crack."

"What? Crack?"

"Yeah, and you know anything over five hundred grams carries life."

"Damn! You think that nigga Pee-Wee gonna hold water?"

"I dunno, Sam, but we got enough information to make him reconsider his actions."

"Yeah, if he love his mama, huh? A'ight. Don't forget to find out who that youngin' is. Maybe since Pee-Wee gone, we can put him on the team and then decide what to do with him later."

"Yeah Sam. Bake a big ol' cake for his ass."

"And blow out the candles at the right time."

Chapter 29

-GOOD DIE YOUNG-

A year went by, and Malik and Rico were copping at least ten bricks a week from Butter. They were moving so much coke that Butter sometimes had to take their money and cop from somebody else, but Butter never gave Malik a connect. He wanted to make sure Malik continued to need him.

Malik finessed his way around the whole Southeast. Within months, he had Haley Terrace, Barry Farms, Park Chester, Wayne Place, Twenty-Second Street, Parkland, Congress Park, Robinson Place, Brandywine, Sixth Street, Fourth Street, and his most profitable strip was Third Street.

Niggas around Third looked up to Malik. In their eyes, he was a silent, smooth, and vicious killer, who was getting money. The hood regarded him as a good nigga. He played fair with his prices, and if a hustler needed some help, Malik was in a position to provide.

The girls also loved him. Malik bought uptown style and mixed it with his Southeast roots. He became the slickest gangster in the city. He wore a three-carat diamond in his ear, owned several watches, and his dress code was strictly Versace, Hugo Boss, Armani, Prada, and Gucci. With his caramel skin, always fresh cornrows, light goatee, boxer's body with wide shoulders and a six-pack, every girl wanted him.

Rico's looks were opposite Malik's. Although he was a little on the chubby side, he was strikingly handsome too, with high yellow skin and short curly hair. Rico loved money, but he didn't like to spend as much as Malik did on clothes and jewelry. His problem was women. He was known to buy a female anything she wanted. His favorite present was giving a car to the girl who gave him the best head for the week.

Young Soup still looked up to Malik, and soaked up every bit of knowledge Malik passed his way. Malik also taught Soup how to shoot dice. He'd passed on every lesson in gambling that old school Shorty Jeff at the pool hall gave him when he was twelve. Soup was now a bonafide gambler who knew how to cheat to perfection. If anyone wanted to find Soup, all they had to do was go to the nearest dice game in Southeast.

Now that Soup was part of Malik and Rico's enterprise, he was making his own money and was finally going to get his own ride when they all headed to Virginia next week to cop new whips for the summer.

While Soup was cheating Rico out of his money at a game of dice in the Wingate condo, Malik stood on the balcony thinking about all the knowledge his father had dropped on him as a child. His mind began to drift as he thought back on his childhood, until his thoughts were disturbed by Soup and Rico's yelling.

"Man, what you doing, Rico? I gated that shit!" Soup yelled.

"No you didn't, nigga. You gotta knock 'em down."

"Man, fuck that, nigga. I been callin' all this time."

Rico was losing all his money to Soup, so he decided the only way to end this dice game was to cheat.

"Soup, the rule is you gotta knock 'em down when you gate."

"Nah, your ass tryna cheat 'cause I'm breaking your fat ass. That point don't count."

"Yes it do!" Rico yelled.

"No it don't!"

Rico reached for his last two hundred dollars in the pot, but Soup jumped up and grabbed the money before Rico could take it.

"Nah, that ain't your money. You ain't hit that point. I gated that shit."

Malik entered the living room where Rico and Soup were on the verge of a fight. "Man, what the fuck you two fighting over now?" he asked.

"Rico tryna cheat me outta my money," Soup said, trying to get Malik to side with him.

"How much you cheat him for?" Malik asked Soup.

"Nigga! I knew your lil ass was cheating," Rico said. "Give me my money back."

"I ain't giving you shit, you fat, lying, cheating muthafucka!"

"See Malik. That's what I'm talking about. He gonna make me fuck him up."

"Go 'head with that shit, Soup. What I tell you about that?" Malik asked.

"A'ight, Malik, but—"

"But shit. Soup, don't make no excuses."

"A'ight. Man, look. Let me get the truck then. I gotta make a few runs."

"I ain't letting your lil ass drive my shit," Rico said.

PRINCE OF THE CITY

"Go 'head, Rico. Give 'im the keys. We gotta do something anyway."

Rico reluctantly gave Soup the keys to his brand new black Range Rover. "Here, nigga. But don't fuck my shit up and don't be having none of them dirty ass bitches in my ride either."

"A'ight. I can respect that. I'll see y'all later." As Soup headed out the door, he looked back. "Oh yeah. Rico?"

"Yeah, what's up?"

"I still love you, nigga, even though your fat ass cheated me outta my money."

Rico and Malik laughed. Soup would never change.

"Man, get your lil ass outta here," Rico said.

"A'ight, I'll see y'all later," he said.

Once Soup was gone, Malik told Rico to get the bags from the back while he set up the money machine.

Rico left and came back into the living room moments later with two duffel bags filled with money. They began to place the bills together, face up, and feed them through the money machine. After about two hours had passed, Malik and Rico counted seven hundred eighty-two thousand dollars.

"Damn! Malik, pop a bottle of Moet."

"You know I don't fuck wit' champagne like that, but I'll tell you what. I'll take a shot of that Remy."

Rico poured his friend a drink while he popped a bottle of Moet. Then they both went out on the balcony. "Damn. Malik, look at this view. A nigga can see the whole Southeast from up this muthafucka!"

"What you think I be out here all the time for?"

"I dunno. To tell you the truth, you be out here on some different shit. Like you be seeing something else other than Southeast."

"I do. When I look out here I see our future. I see a jungle that's outta order, a jungle that needs a new king."

"Man, you tripping. The only king you gonna see around this muthafucka is Black Sam."

"Who you say? Did you just say Black Sam?"

"Yeah, Black Sam. He is the real King of Southeast. They say this nigga got Bentleys and shit, and all he do is point the finger and niggas move."

"Oh yeah? I thought you told me Kojack was the biggest nigga out here."

"Kojack is Black Sam's lieutenant, so just imagine what this nigga Black Sam's holding. Shit. This punk ass seven hundred stacks we got is probably Black Sam's lunch money."

Malik kept his thoughts to himself. He badly wanted to tell Rico that Sam was his uncle, but instead he kept quiet. He knew that if he was able to talk to Sam, then he and Rico would be set for life. Malik had to figure out a way to speak to Sam.

"If the nigga Kojack working for him, then that nigga Sam is beyond rich," Rico said. "The thing is, how we gonna get plugged in wit' 'im? Man, you know Pee-Wee got locked up, and ever since then Kojack chilled out. That's why we been getting all this money so fast. Now, if we could find a way to holla at Kojack, maybe we could take Pee-Wee's spot, then move from there. Shit, right now we the only niggas out here getting most of the brick, and I know Kojack need that business."

"A'ight then. Tomorrow, we going around Wahler Place where Kojack be posted."

PRINCE OF THE CITY

"I hear even though he getting all that money, he still like to come around the hood and flash," Rico added.

"Well, I hope he be out there tomorrow," Malik said.

At that moment, Malik's phone rang. "Hello?" he answered. In the background was some commotion. Malik wondered who it was. "Hello!" he said again.

"Oh hey. Malik, what's up? This Soup."

"Boy, where the fuck you at?"

"I'm down at Fresh Gear in the back, gambling casino style. Malik, I'm punishing these niggas!"

"Well, I hope you finished, because Rico wants his truck back."

"Damn, man, when we getting my shit? I'm tired of pushing y'all cars."

"Next week, Soup."

"A'ight, slim, I'm on my way. I'm 'bout ready to leave anyway. These niggas mad as fuck at me. I busted they asses for eighteen thousand in like twenty minutes."

"Damn! What'd you do, pull out your gun?" Malik joked.

"Shit, you might as well put it that way, 'cause I came off like the mob. Tell you what. We all going out tonight and everything's on me."

"'Bout time your lil ass spent some money on us for a change."

"Yeah, I think I can do that. Thanks to Bonehead and DonDon, 'cause I punished they asses, Malik!"

"Good. Tell me about it when you get here."

"A'ight, I'll do that," he said, hanging up the phone.

* * * * * *

219

Soup left Fresh Gear with eighteen thousand dollars stuffed in a tennis shoe box. As he headed to the Range Rover parked on Sixteenth and Goodhope Road, out of nowhere, two men armed with 9-millimeter pistols approached him.

"Hey, Soup. Hold up for a sec. I think you owe us something," one of the men said.

Soup turned to face the men and quickly realized they were strapped. He looked around and figured that since Goodhope Road was a busy street, no one would be foolish enough to shoot somebody there, so Soup resisted, not backing down, even at the sight of two guns and the two men that held them—Bonehead and DonDon.

"Fuck you mean I owe you something?" Soup asked through clenched teeth.

"We both know you had trick dice in that game," DonDon said.

"Man, y'all niggas trippin'. What the fuck I need to cheat you niggas for?"

"Look, I ain't tryna hear all that back talk. Just give us the box," Bonehead said.

"I ain't giving you shit, nigga!" Soup then tried to put his key in the door while DonDon reached for the box. "Man, what the fuck you doing, slim? Y'all niggas know who I am. Y'all know you can't take nothing from me and get away wit' it."

"Nigga, shut the fuck up," DonDon said, snatching the box outta Soup's hand. "Nigga, you lucky we don't slump your lil bitch ass."

"Nigga, fuck both of y'all!" Soup then snatched back the shoebox of money and began to run up toward Sixteenth Street. The first two shots flew past Soup's head as he ducked and kept running for his life. After a few more steps, Soup was losing his wind, and his gait became sluggish as he looked back at Bonehead and DonDon. Soup didn't notice the crack in the sidewalk that caught the front of his Nike Air Force 1s, causing him to fall to the concrete.

As Soup tried desperately to get up, DonDon was the first to stand over him and deliver two shots to Soup's body, causing him to fall back down. Bonehead then came over, placed his 9-millimeter in the back of Soup's head, and pulled the trigger, ending Soup's life instantly.

Chapter 30

–DOWN FOR WHATEVER-

Ring, Ring . . .

Malik, answer your phone!" Rico yelled as he fixed himself something to eat.

Malik got off the sofa and reached for his phone. "Hello?"

"Hi, baby," the caller responded.

"Hey, Peaches. What's up, boo?"

"You and me sitting in a tree F-U-C-K-I-N-G," Peaches said, mimicking the old school children's rhyme.

Malik laughed at his girlfriend's sense of humor. "Yeah, boo.Well, tonight we gonna be doing a whole lot of that after we come back from the show."

"Oooh, that sounds good," Peaches cooed.

"Did you get my clothes from the cleaners?" he asked.

"Yes I did, my king. Is there anything else you want?"

"Nah, boo. Just keep that good pussy wet for me."

"Always and forever will this pussy be wet for you. But Malik, I was calling to tell you something."

"Well, what is it?"

"Never mind. I'm not going to tell you now since we going out tonight."

"Is it something important?" he asked in a concerned tone.

"That's for you to decide, but I'll just wait till tonight. Okay, boo?"

"All right."

"What time you coming home?"

"In a lil while. Most likely I'll get there before you."

"Okay boo. I'll meet you there later."

"A'ight."

"Hey."

"What's up?"

"I love you, baby."

"Yeah, I love you too," Malik replied, and then hung up the phone.

"Damn, nigga, you in love like shit," Rico said, teasing Malik.

"Man, that's just my bitch."

"Yeah, right. More like your bitch for life—wifey."

"Nah slim. I ain't getting married to nobody!"

"That's what you say for now."

"Rico, a nigga's too deep in the game to get married."

"Fuck you talking about? Gangstas always get married. That's a part of being a gangsta—having a wife and kids. The best of both worlds. At least that's the way I see it. All them mafia muthafuckas got a wife and kids. That's what this shit's about, Malik. Getting money so that you and the family can live like royalty."

"Well, if I ever decide to get married and have kids, then I'm getting outta the game for good, relocating, and living my life comfortable. Never could I bring this shit into my house where my wife and kids lay. That was my father's mistake, and he paid the ultimate price for that."

"Yeah, I feel you. But for real, nigga. We gangstas and shit just happens in this lifestyle. Ain't but one way in and no way out. A nigga just can't pack his bags and leave after you and your niggas risk your lives to build it. Hell no, man. That's treason."

"I guess me and you see different on this issue then. I don't know about you, but I lost my parents to this shit."

"Man, at least you knew your parents. The only thing linking me to my parents is a funky ass birth certificate. And most likely, my mom was a dope fiend or something."

"Like you say, shit happens."

"That's what I'm trying to get your ass to understand, nigga."

They both laughed at the sad but true humor of both of their lives.

"Man, where the fuck is Soup with my truck?" Rico asked. "His lil ass taking too long. Call his cell."

"Hold on," Malik said, and then dialed Soup's number. After letting it ring about eight times, Malik hung up. "Man, I bet his lil ass done jumped right back in that crap game with Bonehead and DonDon being greedy."

"Who you say? Bonehead and DonDon?"

"Yeah. Why you say they names like that?"

"Them niggas from the Farms, ain't they?" Rico asked.

"Yeah, but why you got that worried look on your face?"

"Because they some sneaky ass niggas. I heard all they do is stand outside the store and try to rob whoever hit the dice game for a nice piece of money," Rico explained.

"Yeah, I heard that too. Soup said he busted both of 'em for eighteen thousand. Sometimes I wish I never taught him how to shoot. This lil nigga got a disease with that shit and can't stop."

"Fuck it. Let's just ride down there and pull his lil ass out."

"A'ight."

Malik and Rico drove down to Fresh Gear on Goodhope Road in Malik's new work vehicle. As the van rolled up on Goodhope Road, a crowd of people gathered on the corner of Sixteenth and Goodhope Road, looking at the dead body being outlined by detectives. Yellow tape divided the crowd from the crime scene as detectives desperately tried to question possible witnesses. The closer Malik's van got to the crowd, the more he felt that something was wrong.

"Damn, somebody got they head hit," Rico said.

"Yeah, I see." Malik parked. Then he and Rico got out and walked toward Fresh Gear. Something told Malik that this didn't feel good. Soup never answered his phone, and Rico's truck was at least fifteen feet away from the crime scene. "Hey, Rico, hold on for a minute. Let me go see what's going on."

"Man, stop being nosey. Let's just go in, get Soup, and leave this muthafucka. It's too many police out here."

Malik ignored Rico and found his way into the crowd to look at the young boy who was sprawled out on the concrete, drowned in his own blood. As Malik got closer, his knees began to get weak. He saw the brand new Air Force 1 tennis shoes he'd just bought Soup the day before. As he looked at his young protégé lying in a pool of blood, he expressed no emotion. Malik calmly turned and walked toward Rico's truck. The moment he got in the truck, a single tear dropped from his eye. Rico followed Malik and got into the driver's seat. He looked at Malik and knew something was wrong.

225

"What's up, Malik?" Rico asked.

"Man, that's Soup lying in the middle of the street in a puddle of blood. Look what they did to our boy!"

"Nah, I know these bitch niggas ain't kill my youngin' over some punk ass eighteen thousand. Man, fuck that. I'm going down the Farms and killing everything out that muthafucka. Lil kids and all!"

"Hold up, Rico. We can't just lunch out like that."

Rico couldn't hold back his anger. "Man, fuck that shit, Malik! Them niggas gotta answer to that. They slumped my youngin'!" He placed his hands over his face and buried his head on the steering wheel.

"Yeah, I know, but we gotta make our move wisely. We just can't go on a mission not thinking. We'll fuck around and get locked up going out like that. Now calm down, slim. It's all gonna work out in our favor. Whatever we do, we do it wisely. Remember, our mission is to get our man and get away with it."

"Man, fuck that! I want blood right now!" Rico shouted angrily.

"I love Soup just as much as you do, and I want blood just the same, but we gotta think before we react. We gotta do our homework."

"What homework? We already know that Bonehead and DonDon did it."

"Then we think of a plan and kill both of they asses first thing in the morning. Now let's just go home for right now and think this shit out," Malik demanded.

Rico looked at his friend in disbelief. Malik was getting soft, especially after the incident with the infant. "Yeah a'ight. But whatever you come up with, let's do it fast before these niggas get to braggin' like they done something slick," Rico said.

"Just go home for now, Rico. I'm a put everything together. Just keep your eyes open and watch your back, 'cause these niggas know that Soup was our man, so they might try to hit us before we hit them," Malik instructed.

"Okay, slim, I'll see you first thing in the morning."

* * * * * * *

When Malik stepped into his house, Peaches stood in the living room fully dressed in her D&G outfit with her arms folded as she glared at Malik.

"Where the fuck you been? We was supposed to be at the show an hour ago!" Peaches ranted.

"Something came up," he answered, hanging his jacket on the rack.

"What the fuck you mean 'something came up'? Malik, we planned this evening two weeks ago."

"Not right now, Peaches."

"Oh, I see. I guess you too tired to go out. What! You was out fucking one of your hood rat ass bitches?"

"Don't start wit' me. I don't feel too good."

"I'm not tryna start no fight. All I'm saying is that we never go out anymore. We used to go out all the time. You're never home anymore. Seems like the more money you make, the more you stay away from home. Shit, Malik, I gotta play with my pussy just to be able to sleep at night 'cause you ain't here. What is it! You got another bitch or something?"

"Bitch, stop naggin' me!" Malik turned and looked at his loving girlfriend with tears in his eyes.

The moment Peaches saw those tears, she knew something was very wrong.

JASON POOLE

"Oh my God. Malik, what's wrong? Baby, what happened?" Peaches asked as she grabbed both sides of his face, trying to look him in his eyes. "What happened?"

"These bitch ass niggas done killed Soup." Malik's anger was mixed with sadness. He blamed himself for Soup's death. He wished that he never showed Soup how to gamble. Soup was like a little brother to him.

"Damn baby, I'm sorry. Why would somebody kill Soup? He was an angel."

"I dunno. Niggas just be out here trippin' sometimes."

"Baby, you gotta be careful out here! I can't lose you to these streets. We need you."

"What you mean 'we need you'?" Malik asked, looking confused.

"We need you, Malik—us," she explained while rubbing her stomach. "Me and this two-month-old fetus in my stomach."

"What! Why you ain't tell me you was pregnant?" Malik asked, apparently shocked.

"I just found out this morning when I went to the doctor to get a checkup."

"Well, why you ain't tell me this morning then?"

"Well, baby, I was, but when I called I was so excited that you and I were going out that I wanted to surprise you after making love tonight."

"Damn, what a surprise."

"If you don't want me to have it—"

Malik instantly cut her off. "Of course I want you to have it, but it's just a fucked up time to talk about it right now."

"Okay, boo. We'll talk whenever you want. Do you need anything?"

"Nah, just leave me here in privacy. I wanna be alone for a minute."

PRINCE OF THE CITY

Peaches looked at her man in his most troublesome moment and placed a gentle, wet kiss on his lips. "Boo, it's gonna be all right. You a king. You know how to handle shit. You were born to address drama. I love you, Malik. Just be careful." Peaches knew her position. She knew that she couldn't pull Malik away from the Jungle. It was something that had to be done by him alone, so she left him alone while praying for his safety, hoping he realized there was more to life now that she was pregnant.

Malik sat in the living room listening to Jay-Z's "Hard Knock Life," which was Soup's favorite song. As he smoked a blunt, he tried to figure out a plan for tomorrow. While sinking into the song's lyrics, his house phone rang.

"Hello?"

"You have a collect call from a federal prison. This call is from Linda. If you wish to accept the charges, dial five now." Malik pressed five immediately.

"Hello?" Linda asked, upon hearing the call go through.

"Hey, Aunt Linda, what's up?"

"Nothin', baby. Just thought I'd call and check up on you."

"Did you get my name on your visiting list yet?"

"Nah, that shit is kinda hard, but I'm still working on it. How are you doing? Is everything all right?"

Malik badly wanted to tell Linda that he was in a fucked up position, that he didn't have the proper connect, and that somebody killed his friend over eighteen thousand dollars. And to top it off, Peaches was pregnant. His life was in a crisis, and he was on the verge of giving up. But he couldn't put his problems on his aunt, at least not while she was in prison.

"Yeah, everything's cool. Are you okay? Do you need anything?"

"No baby, not right now. I was just calling to let you know that they gonna release me a little earlier than my mandatory."

"How early?" Malik asked, excited.

"About six months."

"So then you'll be home before the year is out? That''s good, auntie. Right on time so I can take you to Cancun!"

"No, baby. Been there and done that. I wanna go to Brazil, lie on the beach, drink wine coolers, and smoke my Js."

"Hahaha! Yeah, I feel you," Malik said, smiling. "I'll be glad when you get here, because I miss you. I miss our talks."

"I miss you too, Malik. Just make sure your ass stay alive and keep your eyes open at all times. Them niggas in Southeast some cruddy muthafuckas."

"I knew this at the age of eight, something I learned from my father."

"I'm just making sure your ass don't forget."

"I won't."

"How's Peaches doing?"

"She's doing okay. The shop is starting to pick up a little more."

"Have you been keeping her happy?" Linda asked, knowing how hard it was to get Malik to realize that Peaches was a good girl.

"Oh yeah, she's happy. She gets on my nerves sometimes, but it's all good. She just shows a nigga she loves 'im."

"That's good. But are you happy?"

"As far as me and Peaches, yeah, that's my boo. A nigga's lucky to have her by his side. She's a good soldier. For real, Aunt Linda, one day I might fuck around and marry her."

Linda laughed. "Well, I hope I'm alive to see it, 'cause boy, your ass know you be running them streets."

"Yeah I do. But believe me, I know where home is."

"That's right, Malik. Just stay focused," Linda stated seriously.

"Trust me, I will. You wanna talk to Peaches? She's upstairs."

"Yeah, put her happy-go-lucky ass on the phone."

"After Malik handed Peaches the phone, he went back into the living room, sat down in silence, and contemplated his next move.

Chapter 31

-HIT 'EM HARD-

The next morning Rico and Malik met at the stash spot in Wingate Condominiums. While Rico loaded his Mac-11 with the extended clip, he eagerly waited to hear Malik's plan.

"So what's up? How we gonna do this?" Rico asked Malik.

"You know I sat up all night thinking about how we gonna kill these niggas."

"Shit, that ain't hard. They from Barry Farms, so you know they gonna be around back on Stevenson Road or on the court."

"Well, I guess that's the first place we look."

"Shit. Nigga, we could've done that yesterday."

"I know. I just wanted you to cool down so we could do it right."

"Well, I'm cooled down now. So what do you want—the Desert Eagle or the Mac-11?"

"Give me the Desert. I'm tryna flip me a nigga."

"Good, 'cause I'm tryna make swiss cheese outta a nigga." Malik and Rico both dressed in dark clothing. Before they left for their mission, they embraced.

"Nigga, this for young Soup," Malik said.

PRINCE OF THE CITY

"That's right, slim, and when we hit, we hit 'em hard. We 'bout to send the Southside another message," Rico said.

"Yeah, let's just make sure no mistakes this time."

"Fuck these niggas. I'm killing whoever out there."

Malik shook his head and ignored his hyper friend, knowing Rico meant every word.

As Malik and Rico smoked their last blunt before entering Barry Farms, they made a right turn off Martin Luther King Avenue onto Summer Road. Rico sat slumped down in his seat while Malik drove at a very slow speed, looking around to make sure the area was safe from any possible witnesses or police.

"Oh shit! Hold up! Slow down, Malik. I think I see DonDon's car over by the basketball court," Rico said, pointing.

Malik slowed the car down while Rico double-checked to make sure the black BMW was DonDon's car.

"Yep, that's it. The black BMW with tinted windows," Rico said.

"You sure, Rico?"

"Nigga, I'm positive. I know this nigga's car when I see it. Plus, he the only one in Barry Farms wit' a car like that. Pull up a lil closer. I think I see him."

DonDon stood in the middle of two other guys engaged in a serious game of craps.

"Bingo! What I tell you? There they go right there. That's DonDon bending down shooting the dice."

Malik looked over at the men. "Yeah, that's him, but where the fuck is Bonehead?" As soon as Malik asked, Bonehead appeared out of nowhere and began shooting dice.

"There he go right there! We can peel they wigs right now. Let's just ride through the alley and punish they asses," Rico said, anxious to get at them.

"Nah, that might draw too much attention. Let's just get out and walk through. That way we can get all the way up on 'em before they're able to pull out their straps."

"However you want to do it, let's just do it."

Malik parked the car on Summer Road. He and Rico put on their caps and pulled them down over their eyes while tying bandanas around their faces. Before they got out of the car, they embraced each other with a look in their eyes of both fear and love.

Rico was the first to get out. He walked down the alley six steps ahead of Malik. As they got closer, butterflies grew in both of their stomachs. Even though they'd both killed before, they were still a little fearful of their fates, not knowing if these four men were strapped. The closer Rico got, the more tension he felt. Malik trailed right behind him with his Desert Eagle ready to blow. Rico was at least fifteen feet away from the men before one of them noticed that he and Malik were creeping up.

As DonDon rolled his last shot, one of the young men that was gambling screamed, "Watch out!" alarming Bonehead, who reached for his strap. Immediately, Malik ran toward him while reaching for his gun. He delivered two shots, hitting Bonehead in the neck and chest.

The impact from Malik's gun lifted Bonehead from his feet, making him fall flat back with his eyes wide open. While the other two men fled, Rico was focused on DonDon. DonDon tried to get up and run, but Rico chased closely behind him. DonDon had only taken eight steps before Rico cut him down with the Mac-11.

DonDon fell on the ground face first. He was hit, but he wasn't dead. The shots Rico fired hit him from the waist down. As Rico ran up and stood over DonDon, he pulled the trigger and found out that his gun had jammed.

"Fuck!" he yelled, desperately trying to unjam his gun while DonDon rolled over and reached in his waistband for his own gun. Before DonDon could get out his gun, Malik came up behind Rico and placed his Desert Eagle right between DonDon's eyes. Before he pulled the trigger, Malik pulled down his mask and revealed his identity.

"Look at me, bitch!" Malik demanded. "Look at me! I want you to witness your own murder, nigga."

Boom!Boom! Two shots emptied from Malik's gun as DonDon's head jerked back and his brains oozed out of his head and onto the concrete.

Ten minutes later while driving up Martin Luther King Avenue, Malik sat in silence as Rico continued to try to unjam his gun.

"You gotta take out the clip, then pull back and shake it until the jammed bullet falls out."

Rico followed Malik's instructions and unjammed his gun in seconds. "Thanks."

"You just put too many bullets in the clip. Next time don't overload it. Leave some room so the bullets can breathe."

"I ain't talking about the gun."

"What you mean?" Malik asked, looking confused.

"Back there. Thanks for saving my life. Man, if you didn't come behind me, that nigga DonDon woulda got out his strap."

"Don't thank me for shit like that, nigga. You're my best friend. Real niggas do real thangs. If it was me you woulda done the same thing."

Rico didn't respond. He was just grateful for having a friend like Malik. Malik was the brother that Rico always wanted, and he couldn't live in this game without him.

Chapter 32

-DIVIDE AND CONQUER-

Black Sam called Kojack out to his mansion in Fort Washington, Maryland for a meeting as soon as he and Chevece were back in town. Sam poured himself a drink while Kojack lay back into the soft leather sofa in Black Sam's conference room.

"Did you find out who this young kid is going around killin' niggas and takin' over strips?"

"Yeah, Sam. Come to find out it's not just one, but two of them. They're partners. One's named Rico and the other is Malik. Now, from what I hear, Malik is the one who's supposed to be the boss. He makes all the moves while the other one puts in the work."

"Yeah. Well, that's a plus for us."

"Why you say that?"

"'Cause, we can use the old divide and conquer move. All we gotta do is pump up this guy Rico to make him think his man ain't playin' fair with him."

"Oh, I see. Then we get them to beef with each other while we sit and watch 'em kill each other, and we make money off both of 'em."

"Now you get the picture."

"But how we gonna get 'em down with the team?"

"Easy. They gonna come looking for you. Believe me. I've been in this game long enough to know what the next nigga's move is gonna be. If they wanna keep making money, they gonna want a good connect, and from what I know, we the only niggas who got it the way they want it."

"Tell you what I'm a do, Sam. I'm a throw a small party at Bryan Manor and wait for them to come and try to cut into me."

"After you meet them, start giving them shit. Then drop the number, and after a few months, tell them that I wanna meet them."

"Okay, I can do that."

"Whatever you do, make them feel real comfortable."

"Yeah, I got you. I'm a get 'em some pussy, free drinks, and all the good shit that makes a nigga feel like he's on top."

Sam laughed at his partner and only friend.

"A thought just hit me. You ever hear anything about that broad, Linda?" Kojack asked.

"Last thing I heard was that no-good, scheming bitch was locked up on some murders or something."

"Damn! That bitch be killin' like that?"

"Jack, you'd be surprised at what that bitch is capable of doing. She's a master of deception. Why you ask about her anyway?"

"Nothin'. I just saw a bitch that looked like her in a swimsuit magazine. She was looking good as shit too."

"Well, it might be her conniving ass. She probably fucked the photographer for a shot."

Kojack laughed. "Nah, it wasn't her. She just favored her. But I always did wanna fuck her pretty ass, though."

"No you don't, 'Jack. That bitch is the devil. I'm telling you."

* * * * * * *

Six months later . . .

Malik and Rico counted the profits for the remaining bricks, and then they counted every piece of money they had left in the streets.

"This is one million. Now you can pull out the champagne," Malik told Rico.

"Nigga, you ain't said nothing." Rico pulled out a chilled bottle of Cristal while Malik rolled some blunts. "Nigga, put on some music."

Malik turned on the CD player and Tupac and Scarface's "Smile for Me" came blaring from the speakers, enhancing their mood to celebrate their first million dollars.

"Nigga, this is a toast to our success," Malik said.

"Yes, our success," Rico responded. "We built this shit together like we said we were gonna do."

"Smile for me, Rico."

"Smile for me, Malik."

They toasted and fired up blunts while dancing and bobbing their heads to the lyrics.

"Nigga, we rich," Rico said.

"Not yet, Rico. Not yet. But we're on our way, and when we get there, we'll know it, 'cause we ain't gonna have to do this shit no more."

"Nah, ain't no such thing as quitting. You could never have enough money. It takes money to generate money. Once your money stops generating, it starts deteriorating, and I definitely don't want that."

"Whatever, Rico. Drink your champagne and enjoy the rush of having a million."

After Malik and Rico celebrated, Malik went out onto the balcony and began to think about his future. He knew there was something more that life had to offer, but he didn't yet know what it was. He wondered what his father felt like when he made his first million. He wondered how his life was going to end. If he could just sit back and focus, he knew there was a way out the game other than jail or death.

Malik needed a voice. He needed his mother's opinion. He needed his father's guidance, and most of all, he needed the woman who raised him from a boy to a man. Malik missed Linda. She was his only advisor, the only one whose judgment he held deep in his heart.

As Malik looked out into the Jungle, Rico, who made it a habit, crept up behind his friend and whispered in his ear. "Hey, Mr. Spooky Man, who are you out here talking to?"

"Nobody. You know I just be out here chilling, thinking, and putting shit in order."

"Yeah, whatever. I think you be out here talking to a ghost or something."

Malik laughed. "Man, you stupid."

"Yeah, whatever. But anyway, guess what, homie?"

"What's up?" Malik asked.

"The nigga Kojack is having a party tonight at Bryan Manor. You tryna go or what?"

"Fuck yeah! We might be able to cut into him at that joint."

"Yeah, that's the move, 'cause everybody in Southeast gonna be there. But we're the only ones getting that real money. For real, Malik, the nigga probably wanna talk to us more than we wanna talk to him."

"Yeah, you right. Look, I'm a go home and change, and you can meet me back over here tonight."

"A'ight. I'm a get the Range cleaned up and put on something fly."

"Do that, and call me when you're ready to go."

"A'ight nigga, but in the meantime, don't jump off the balcony."

Chapter 33

-LETS DO IT-

Malik looked in his closet at his huge wardrobe, trying to figure out what to wear to Kojack's party. He pulled out a pair of tan slacks with a Gucci print shirt and matching Gucci print shoes. He laid his outfit on the bed to take a second look without noticing Peaches standing in the doorway of their bedroom with her arms folded.

"I guess you ain't gonna be home tonight, huh?" she asked.

"What's up, Peaches?"

"Don't 'what's up, Peaches' me. I asked you a question."

"To answer your question, Ms. Nosey, I got a business meeting to attend."

"A business meeting at night with a five-thousand-dollar outfit and a hundred-thousand-dollar's worth of jewelry? I guess this must be a hell of a meeting, huh, Malik?"

"Why the fuck you keep naggin' a nigga? What do you want, huh? You got a nice house, nice car, and nice clothes. I put a ring on your finger worth eighty thousand. Bitch, what the fuck do you want from me, huh?"

PRINCE OF THE CITY

Peaches reared her head back in shock, she couldn't believe how harsh Malik could be. "Malik, you've changed. You're not the same. Ever since I told you I was pregnant, you act like you don't wanna be bothered with me. What do I have to do? I love you. Can't you see that?"

"I love your ass too. Probably too much. Boo, you've done what you're supposed to do. You're the perfect woman for me, and I know one day you'll be the perfect wife and mother. Now, you always talking 'bout me going out, and you don't even understand the reason a nigga spending all his time in the streets is because I'm trying to build up a bank, so we can step the fuck off like we planned. You think I put that ring on your finger for fun, huh? When I asked you to marry me, I meant it. Now stop complaining and follow my lead. Okay?"

Peaches fell into Malik's trap. He knew whenever he mentioned marriage and their child, Peaches would calm down and fall in place.

"Okay, baby. But I just be worried about you. I ain't trippin' off them other bitches out there 'cause I know can't none of 'em fuck with me. I'm the one you come home to every night. Well, at least almost every night. But the fact of the matter is that I own a nail salon and I hear shit. Bitches gossip, and whenever I hear one of them bitches come in there talking 'bout this nigga got killed and this bitch is fucking this bitch's husband, all I do is think of you."

"As long as my name doesn't come up in those conversations, you ain't got nothing to worry about."

"Your name has come up before."

"Oh yeah? What did you hear then?" he asked.

"Something you don't wanna know."

"What? Who am I supposed to be fuckin' now?"

"It ain't who you're fucking. It's who you killed," she said with her arms folded while leaning against the wall.

"What! You heard somebody mention my name in a murder or something?"

"Relax. It ain't nothing you haven't heard before, 'cause everybody talking 'bout it. It's all over D.C. Muthafuckas respect you out here, and you know the streets be speculating."

"What did you hear?"

"Well, put it like this. I heard something 'bout a guy, a girl, and a kid, which I know you didn't do, 'cause my boo can't be that ruthless. Hell no, not my boo. You wouldn't do no shit like that. So when I hear it, I make sure I straighten that shit out real quick."

"Good, 'cause muthafuckas out here will say anything just for conversation. Boo, you know I ain't never in my life killed nobody. I mean nobody."

"I believe you, but even if you did, it still wouldn't change nothing with me. I love you the same."

"Well, in that case, I guess we can do a little something before I go out. That way I might come home a little earlier so we can finish up where we leave off."

Peaches smiled and untied her robe, revealing her perfect figure.

After Peaches and Malik made love, Malik took a shower and got dressed. He then called Rico to let him know to meet up.

"What's up, fat boy? You ready?" Malik asked.

"Give me 'bout a half hour."

"Damn, Rico! What were you doing all this time?"

"Nigga, I had to smash Tasha off some dick. She was trippin' 'bout a nigga going out."

Malik laughed. "Yeah, I had to do the same thing."

244

"So meet me at the stash spot in about a half hour."

"A'ight. I gotta get Peaches to do my hair anyway."

"Cool. Nigga, what you wearing?"

"Just put it like this, nigga. I'ma be the flyest thing walking 'round that joint. Niggas gonna think I'm the one giving the party."

"Yeah, whatever nigga."

"What are you wearing?"

"Nigga, I got an Iceberg sweat suit from Atlantic City. Don't nobody got this joint."

"Man, don't put on no sweat suit. Wear something slick. We gotta represent our positions out here."

"A'ight. I got a Ferragamo shirt with the matching shoes."

"Yeah nigga, put on that shit."

"You ain't gotta tell me what to wear. I know how to get fly."

"A'ight whatever. Just hurry your ass up, okay?"

"I'll see you in a few."

* * * * * * *

Rico pulled into the Bryan Manor parking lot alongside BMWs, Benzes, 'Vettes, and Caddies.

"Damn! Malik, look at these bitches," Rico said as a beauty walked inside. "And we ain't even go in yet."

"But we ain't come here for the 'hos. We came to do business."

"Yeah, whatever nigga. If I find some pussy, I'm taking it."

"I know you will."

As Malik and Rico entered the party, niggas whispered when the pair walked past.

"Who dat?" one nigga asked.

"Oh, that's that nigga Malik. He gettin' it. He the new nigga who supposed to be runnin' shit. Plus, he go hard as a muthafucka."

"Oh, so that's the nigga everybody keeps talkin' 'bout. They say he killed Tank."

"Yeah, he peeled his wig back. Him and his whole family. Now that's what you call vicious."

"Yeah, but I hear he supposed to be a good dude too."

Malik smiled as the young hustlers admired his character. As he walked past them, they spoke to him as if they knew him already. Malik nodded at the crowd of hustlers, acknowledging their respect for him.

On the other hand, Rico was mugging them down, instilling fear in their hearts. Rico wanted to be feared more than respected while Malik wanted a little of both.

As Malik was looking through the crowd for Kojack, females constantly walked up to him.

"How are you doing, Malik? I'm Keisha."

"Hello Keisha. How do you know my name?"

"Come on, Malik. Who don't know your fine ass?"

Malik smiled at the nice-looking girl.

"Well, Keisha, I'd love to sit here, talk to you, and have a drink, but I'm looking for somebody right now."

"Who are you looking for?"

"Kojack. You know him?"

"Yeah, he's over there by the bar being flanked by all them bitches," Keisha said as she pointed toward Kojack.

"Look here. Can you do me a favor?"

"Yeah, what is it?"

"Go over there and whisper in Kojack's ear. Tell him that Malik's here, and he'd like to speak with him in private."

"Okay, but where you gonna be at?"

"Right here at this back table." Malik peeled off three hundred-dollar bills. "Get me a bottle of Cristal and keep the rest."

Keisha took the money and went on her mission. About ten minutes later, she returned with the champagne.

"Here you go."

"Thank you. Where's Kojack?"

"I don't know, but I told him though."

"Did you tell him where I was?"

"Yes. I guess he's busy right now. You want me to stay here and keep you company?"

"That won't be necessary. I think me and Malik need to talk in private," Kojack said.

Keisha looked back. "Oh, there you go. Kojack, this is Malik. Malik, this is Kojack."

As Keisha played host, Malik figured out that this was all a plan. Keisha was sent to him by Kojack in the first place. Malik got up and pressed Kojack's hand with a firm and hard press like his father had taught him. From the handshake, Kojack knew the young nigga had been around some true gangstas in his lifetime. The only niggas he knew who greeted each other in this fashion were the legendary Mike Perry and Black Sam.

"So Malik, I've heard a lot of things about you."

"Yeah? Well, I hope they were good things."

"Oh yeah, they're good. I've heard some other things too. But to me, that's still good, 'cause a nigga gotta do what he gotta do to survive in these streets."

"Yeah, I know what you mean." Malik knew Kojack was referring to Tank.

"So where's your partner?" Kojack asked.

"Oh, Rico? He's over there talking to some bitches, probably tryna find a bitch to take to the hotel tonight."

Kojack laughed. "Well, he ain't gotta worry 'bout that. I got plenty of pussy around here beggin' to get fucked."

"Yeah? Well, I don't mean to be rude, but I ain't interested in no pussy. I came to talk business."

Kojack looked the young gangster in the eyes. Something about Malik reminded him of how it was in the old days when Mike Perry ruled the Jungle.

"I like that in you. I see you're about money. Not many young niggas out here are like you. So what part of town you from?"

"I'm from uptown, but my folks are from Southeast. I was raised by my aunt, but I don't think my life history is necessary in order for us to do business. I'm just a young nigga tryna get money."

"How old are you?"

"Twenty."

"I see, and with the mind of a forty-year-old gangster."

"However you see it. I was just brought up in the game by some good people."

"Yeah, I can tell. Anyway, what is it you wanna talk about?"

Malik smiled. "Now we're getting somewhere. Well, first of all I wanna know what them birds flying for?"

"It all depends on how many you tryna get." Kojack smiled and poured himself a glass of Malik's Cristal.

"Well, let's say I want thirty of 'em."

Kojack immediately put down his glass and looked Malik directly in the eyes.

"Now, that's a lot of joints. If you wanna do business on that type of scale, then our relationship must be a marriage. You can't never cop from nobody but us."

PRINCE OF THE CITY

"What you mean by us? I thought I was just dealing with you."

"I have a partner. You may have heard of him before, but he doesn't normally come around. If you gonna be copping shit like that, then it's a must you meet him also."

"Oh, I see. So who's your partner?"

"I'll let you know in time. But for right now, let's get these prices established." Kojack then leaned forward, rubbed both hands together, and looked Malik directly in the eyes. "I can give 'em to you for seventeen-five, and after a while, the more you cop, then the price is gonna drop."

"Damn, that's a good number. In that case, we tryna get thirty-five of them thangs."

Kojack's eyes lit up at the young hustler's request. This was his biggest client ever. The most shit Kojack had sold to one person was fifteen bricks. Kojack was only getting fifty at a time anyway. He badly wanted Malik's business. Even though Kojack lowered the number from nineteen just to satisfy the young nigga, he would still be coming out on top. Black Sam was getting shiploads from Mexico for twelve thousand a key and giving it to Kojack for sixteen. Kojack would normally sell for twenty, but at the request of Black Sam, he lowered the number for Malik to seventeen-five.

"Now, this is how we gonna do this. I deal with you and only you. Give me an address where to drop 'em off, preferably a storage spot or a house with a garage."

"I got the perfect place already. You know the Auto Garage in Clinton, Maryland?"

"Yeah, I know where it's at. That's a good spot. My partner used to keep his Bentley in storage out there."

"Good, then when can I cop?"

249

"First thing tomorrow morning. I'll call you. Now since the business part of this meeting is over, let's make a toast to a good future."

Malik held up his drink as Kojack happily touched his glass. Malik thought of the riches soon to come his way, while Kojack wondered how long Black Sam would do business with the youngin' before he decided to end his life.

Chapter 34

-NO MERCY-

By the winter of 1999, Malik and Rico were copping a whole load of bricks from Kojack on a monthly basis. Their clientele grew larger and spread throughout the city. Those who used to cop two or three bricks at a time eventually moved to ten bricks a week.

Malik and Kojack's relationship was getting even closer. Sometimes they would go out to parties together and introduce each other to different women. As Kojack and Malik started getting along, Rico and Malik started disagreeing more. Rico became jealous of Malik and Kojack's relationship. He started to view Malik as a possible traitor.

While sitting in the stash house, Rico began to indirectly question Malik's loyalty. "Man, did you know Tasha's having her baby shower next month?"

"Yeah, and what about it?"

"Are you coming or what?"

"Niggas don't go to baby showers."

"Man, fuck that. It's gonna be a lot of bitches there."

"Well, guess we gonna be the first niggas ever to go to a baby shower, huh?"

251

Rico laughed at his partner and friend. "Now, don't forget. You know it's important to me and Tasha."

"Man, how can I forget to come to my soon-to-be godchild's baby shower?"

"I don't know. You and that nigga Kojack been hanging real tough lately."

"So what are you saying, Rico? You think I'd put this nigga before my own family? Nigga, you're like my brother out here. I only fuck with this nigga 'cause he got what we want. After we meet the real nigga, Black Sam, I'm cutting his bitch ass off," Malik said, not yet wanting to reveal that Sam was his uncle.

Malik didn't want Rico to start asking more questions that he couldn't answer. He didn't want to come to Sam empty-handed. He wanted to show his uncle that he remembered every lesson Michael Perry taught him as a child. But if Rico knew about Sam and Malik's relationship, he would want Malik to use that relationship to take short cuts.

"This nigga's a ho for real, Rico," Malik said about Kojack. "I can see it in his eyes. I can tell by the way he be tryna hang around me just to let other niggas know that we down with him. Niggas out here don't respect this nigga. The only reason they ain't robbed and killed his ass yet is because they're afraid me and you gonna retaliate."

"Yeah, I know. But for real, I'm thinking 'bout robbing his ass. Fuck him and Black Sam. Their time is up. Those niggas are old heads now. Time for them niggas to go. It's some new, up and coming niggas out here now running Southeast with an iron fist, and their names are Malik and Rico."

Malik smiled. "Yeah, I feel you. But first, let's get to Black Sam, find a real number for these birds, and then establish a connect. That way we'll knock Kojack out the way without moving a finger. Then after a while, Black Sam is gonna have to step down and let a real nigga get that spot. Always remember, Rico. Whatever we do, we do it with finesse."

"Yeah, I know. You've been saying that shit ever since I first met you."

They both laughed. Rico grabbed his keys, got up off the sofa, and headed for the door.

"Malik, come on. We gotta pass Wahler Place. This nigga Lil Dave ain't paid me the rest of my money yet."

"How much he owe?"

"I gave him five joints about two weeks ago. So far he only put down forty, and he's owed a nigga sixty thousand for the last two weeks. Now either he got locked up, which I seriously doubt, or he just feels like tryin' a nigga. Regardless of what he's tryin' to do, he gotta pay a nigga his money."

"Don't be so quick to kill a nigga. Let's just go 'round there and see what's up first. After all, he might have your money."

"Yeah, well, it's only one way to find out. Come on, let's go."

Malik pulled up on Wahler Place in his brand-new Cadillac truck. It was pearl white with light gray leather interior, TVs in the headrests, and a seven-thousand-dollar sound system.

"Hey, CoCo. What's up?" Malik asked the young hustler as he pulled to the curb.

"Oh.What's up, Malik? My muthafuckin' nigga? I ain't seen you in a while," the young hustler responded as he walked up to Malik's window to shake his hand.

"Yeah, I know. I'm looking for Lil Dave. Have you seen him?"

"Yeah, I saw him not too long ago. He just went in crackhead Bobbie's house, probably getting his dick sucked."

"A'ight, thanks. You be careful out here," he advised after noticing CoCo was strapped with a gun that was too big to conceal.

"I will."

As Rico and Malik entered the apartment building, Rico put his finger up to his mouth to keep Malik silent. He then placed his ear to Bobbie's door to see if he could hear Lil Dave in her house.

"Come on, Dave. Give me the pipe back," Bobbie said. "Your ass been up here smoking all fucking week. Give me a hit before I put your ass out and tell everybody your ass is on the pipe now."

"Bitch, you do that, and I'll kill your ass. Anyway, you're the one who freaked out a nigga and got me on this shit."

Hearing enough, Rico knocked on the door with hard force and then placed his ear back on the door.

"Who is it?" Bobbie asked.

"It's Rico, Bobbie. Open up."

"Bobbie, don't open the door," Rico heard Lil Dave say.

"Why not? Rico will kill my ass if I don't."

"Bitch, I'm a kill you if you do."

"Hey Bobbie. I'll give you an eight ball if you open this door right now," Rico said.

"Fuck you, Dave. I'm opening this door." Bobbie got up, rushed to the door, and unlocked it. "A'ight, Rico, where my coke at?" she asked, standing there with her hand open, waiting to be served.

Rico just gazed at her with an expression that said, "Get the fuck away from me."

Malik then walked in behind him and gave Bobbie a fresh Ben Franklin. "Here, Bobbie. Go 'head down the street and cop you one from CoCo."

254

"Thanks, Malik. You always was one who kept his word," Bobbie said, glaring at Rico with hatred in her eyes.

Malik closed the door behind him as Rico stood over Dave with his .45 Smith and Wesson shoved in Dave's face.

"Nigga, your ass is on the pipe now? This the reason you been ducking me? How the fuck you gonna smoke coke and sell weight at the same time. You should've known this shit was gonna catch up with you."

"Rico, please don't kill me, man. I just got a habit. I swear I'll get your money, man," he pleaded, holding on to Rico's feet as if he was praying to him.

"Nigga, how the fuck you gonna get my money when you on it like a brown hornet?"

"Rico, man, I swear I can get off this shit, man. Just work with me. This bitch Bobbie turned me out. All I need is a few months of rehab. I swear, Rico. I'll pay you, man. Just spare my life, please." Lil Dave then looked at Malik. "Malik, please help me out here, man. I've known you for a while now, and you know I'll pay the money back when I get myself together. Please, Malik, can you help me?"

Malik looked at the helpless, frail man, who once was a short, stocky, well-dressed hustler.

"Rico, give the nigga a chance," Malik said.

"Thank you, Malik. I swear you won't regret it. Thanks, man," Lil Dave said, looking relieved that his life had been spared. If it wasn't for Malik, his brains would have been splattered all over the walls by now."

Rico looked at Malik in disbelief.

"Come on, Rico. Let the nigga live, man."

Rico looked at Malik and then at Dave. "I tell you what. I'm a spare your life, nigga. I'm a help you get off this shit for good. Now, do you really wanna kick the habit?" Rico asked.

"Yeah. Thanks, man. I'll pay you your money."

"Okay, Dave, I'm a help you out. We gonna take you up to Greater Southeast Hospital so you can check into their rehab. Get your helpless ass up off that floor and come on."

Malik smiled now that Rico was finally thinking. There was no sense in killing Dave. If Dave was dead, Rico would never get paid. However, if Dave did the rehab and came back strong, then there was no doubt he would pay with interest. To Malik, this was a smart mobster move. To Rico, it was a weak move.

Malik, Lil Dave, and Rico walked outside in the cold winter weather, ducking their heads in an attempt to hide from the frost.

"Damn, it's colder than a muthafucka out here," Lil Dave said.

"What? You sell your coat for that shit?" Rico asked, but Lil Dave didn't have an answer.

After Malik got into the truck and unlocked the door, Rico opened the door for Lil Dave and stepped to the side.

"Get in the back."

Just as Lil Dave was about to put his feet up on the running board of Malik's truck, Rico's .45 automatic pressed against his temple. As Malik turned the ignition to start the truck, Rico pulled the trigger.

Boom!

Splattering Lil Dave's brains on the cold concrete.

Rico hurriedly jumped in the truck. "Come on! Let's go, Malik."

Malik looked at Rico as if he was crazy. "Man, Rico, what the fuck is wrong with you?"

PRINCE OF THE CITY

"The nigga asked me to help him get off the shit, so I did. I just helped him get off it for good."

"Man, you're a stupid-ass nigga, Rico." Malik shook his head. "You don't think for shit!"

"Man, what's done is done. Ain't no sense in crying over spilt milk, or should I say spilled brains," Rico said as he flashed a devilish grin.

"Shut up, Rico. You're stupid."

"Yeah, I love you too, Malik."

"Fuck you, Rico. You a stupid-ass nigga." Malik looked at Rico in disbelief while putting the truck in gear and speeding off.

Chapter 35

-WELCOME HOME-

L inda Wells was released from prison early in the morning on New Year's Eve 1999. As she walked outside the heavily guarded razor-wire fences, she was greeted by a tall, long-haired, handsome man. He was wearing a light brown, hip length fur coat imported from Africa. By his side stood a short, big-bellied, pretty woman, who was at least seven months into her pregnancy. The woman wore a full-length fur coat to match the one the man wore. They stood beside a green Cadillac Escalade with a bow and ribbon tied to the front grill.

As Linda hugged Malik and Peaches, the tears on her face turned to icicles from the cold weather.

"I missed you two," she said.

"We missed you too, Linda," Peaches responded.

"And look at you. He got you out here in this cold all pregnant."

"Nothing in the world could stop me from coming to get you."

After the two friends laughed and hugged each other, Linda turned toward Malik.

"Boy, you look just like your daddy. Come here and give me a hug."

PRINCE OF THE CITY

Tears fell down Malik's cheek as he embraced his mentor, teacher, aunt, advisor, and only family. His embrace was so tight and affectionate that Linda was the one who had to break it.

"We'll talk later," Linda told Malik. He nodded okay.

"But in the meantime, who's the owner of this pretty-ass truck?" Linda asked.

Peaches held up the keys. "This here is your Christmas present."

Linda hugged and thanked them both. "This is nice, y'all. But I was looking for something like a new house."

Malik and Peaches smiled.

"Now, Aunt Linda, you're gonna have to pick that out yourself. Shit, I almost had to fight Peaches over the color of this truck."

"Girl, I keep telling Malik that your favorite color is green."

"Malik, you forgot?"

"Nah, I ain't forget. But they had a burgundy one that looked better to me."

"Well, for your info, I love whatever you two get me."

"Come on. Let's go home now," Peaches said.

Malik looked at Peaches and saw how happy his fiancée was. He, too, was happy.

On the drive back to the house, Malik's cell phone rang. As Peaches and Linda sat up front talking about everything Linda had missed, Malik was laid out in the back asleep after a long night out with Rico.

"Will you wake him up, please, and tell him to answer his phone?" Peaches asked.

Linda shook her nephew. "Malik, get up. Here, boy. Your phone is ringing."

"Hello?"

"What's up, young nigga?"

"Who dis?"

"Kojack, nigga. What? You high or something?"

"Nah man. I just woke up. What's up?"

"Look, my partner has decided to finally meet you and Rico. He's inviting you two out to his house tonight for New Years. So whatever you already got planned should be set aside. This is a one-in-a-million chance and you don't want to blow it."

"What is it? A party or something?"

"Yeah, a small party, or more like a celebration of a new partnership. He's quite impressed by you and Rico and wants to proposition you."

"Well, tell him we'll be there. What time does he want us there?"

"About eleven o'clock. He first wants to discuss a few things, and then bring in the New Year with a new resolution."

"A'ight, I'll talk to you later."

As Malik was talking, Linda acted like she was listening to Peaches, but she was really ear hustling on Malik's conversation.

After hanging up with Kojack, Malik dialed Rico's number.

"Yeah, big daddy speaking," Rico answered.

"Nigga, you stupid."

"What's up, baby boy?"

"Where you at?"

"I'm in Tiffany's picking out some earrings for Tasha's fat ass. You know she's due next month."

"How can I forget? You tell me almost every day."

PRINCE OF THE CITY

"Fuck you, Malik. What you call me for anyway? I thought you were supposed to be picking up your aunt?"

"I did, and we're on our way back home now."

"So what's up, nigga?"

"Guess what?"

"What?"

"We've just been invited to the muthafuckin' man's house tonight."

"Black Sam?"

"Yeah nigga. This is it."

"So I guess you feel like Tony Montana when he first visited Sosa, huh?" Rico asked, laughing.

"Fuck you. Your ass just be ready to roll tonight."

"What time are we going?"

"About eleven o'clock. He wants to bring in the New Year with us."

"A'ight. I guess I should spend as much time with Tasha as I can, 'cause you know she gonna be a pissed bitch. It's New Year's Eve, Malik."

"Yeah, I know. You act like I ain't gotta go through the same thing. They just gonna have to be mad, 'cause this here is our chance of a lifetime."

"Yeah nigga, we about to blow up like the World Trade Center," Rico said in his Biggie Smalls voice.

"You better say it."

"See you later then."

"Come by the house around ten because I want you to meet my aunt before we go."

"A'ight then. I'll see your long-haired ass at ten."

"A'ight."

Chapter 36

-TRUTH BE TOLD-

After Peaches cooked dinner, they all ate while reminiscing about old times. Soon Peaches started to get sleepy.

"Excuse me, but I've been up all day and I'm a little tired," Peaches said. "I need to take my butt to bed. Somebody better come wake me up for New Year's."

"Okay, baby. Go 'head and get you some rest. You've been carrying that big ol' luggage around all day."

"Shut up, Malik. I'll sure be glad when I drop this load, 'cause it's killing me."

"I'll be glad too, boo. Maybe then a nigga can get some you know what."

"Now, don't be nasty, Malik," Linda said.

"A'ight, Aunt Linda. Peaches, I'll be up to rub your stomach in a lil while. I gotta talk to my aunt for a minute first."

"I already know you two got some catching up to do. See you later on tonight, and welcome home, Linda."

Linda kissed her former protégée on the cheek before she went upstairs. "Now, Malik, what's up?" Linda asked.

Malik sat back in his chair and smiled. He couldn't wait to tell Linda everything that had happened while she was away.

First, he told her about Rico and how close they were. He also told her how Butter treated him, and how he didn't want to turn him on to his connect. Malik even told her about the murders he'd committed and how he'd always thought they were justified.

Linda smoked her Newport while listening carefully to Malik tell his story, detail by detail. "I wanna ask you a question," she said.

"Go 'head, Aunt Linda. What's up?"

"Over all these years of being in the streets, what's the most valuable lesson I taught you?"

"Never trust no one."

"And what else goes with that phrase?"

"Trust no one. Not even you, Aunt Linda."

"That's right."

"Man, it's kinda hard not trusting you. You're the only one I can trust. You're my only family. You're more than my aunt. You're my mother, father, sister, and brother wrapped in one."

"I know, Malik, I know."

"There's something else you don't know that I wanna tell you."

"What's up?" Linda asked.

Malik began to tell the story of how Sonny James tried to trick him out of his life. Linda smiled as she listened to the young man's life of crime. She was pleased that Malik turned out to be one of D.C.'s most ruthless but smart gangsters.

After he finished telling his story, Linda blew out a cloud of smoke.

"You wanna know something, Malik?"

"What's up?"

"I always knew it was you who killed Sonny James and Smitty. I just never said anything because I wanted to see how long you could hold water."

Malik looked at Linda with surprise. He wondered how she knew. There wasn't a witness in sight except Booga, and he didn't think Booga saw anything. Plus Booga ended up dead two weeks later.

"How did you know?"

Linda flashed a devilish grin. "Let's just say I went around the Bowling Alley one night looking for you, and I ran into Booga."

"So Booga did see me, huh?"

Linda smiled. "He won't be able to tell nobody though."

At that moment Malik knew that Linda was Booga's killer. Linda was too smart to straight up tell Malik that she had killed Booga. She stuck to her principle of trusting no one.

"So tell me. Who's your connect?"

"Oh, you won't believe this shit. I get my shit from this dude named Kojack, and guess who he works for?"

"Who?"

"Black Sam. Uncle Sam doesn't even know it's me that's dealing with Kojack. I'm supposed to meet him tonight at his house. When I get there, I'm a see if he remembers me. It's been thirteen years now," Malik said with excitement.

Linda's expression suddenly changed from happy to sad, and tears began to drop from her eyes.

"What's wrong? Why are you crying?" Malik asked Linda.

"There's something I want to tell you. Something that you've been longing to know since you were ten-years-old. Because of where you're going tonight, you need to know this. Malik, I'm a give it to you raw and uncut."

"Give it to me then." Malik prepared himself to hear whatever Linda had to say.

264

"Black Sam ain't your uncle. He's your enemy."

"Why you say that?"

"'Cause he's the one who killed your parents. He killed your father because he wanted to keep hustling and your father wanted to quit."

Malik's eyes began to fill with tears. "Then why'd he kill my mother?"

"She was in the apartment and was the only witness."

"How do you know all of this, Aunt Linda?"

Linda looked down at the floor where her tears became a small puddle. "I was on the phone with your mother when it happened, and you were sitting right beside me playing cards with Butter."

Malik's anger boiled as tears came rushing down his face. "Is there anything else I need to know before I kill this nigga tonight?"

"Well, I wanna tell you something your father didn't know. Before he met your mother, he had a girlfriend, Chevece Jones. She was his high school sweetheart. She got pregnant but never told your father. After your father met your mother, he dumped her. Chevece was so ashamed and hurt that she wanted a way to get back at your father, so she left town and had the baby. I don't know if it was a boy or girl, but I heard she put it up for adoption, ran away to Las Vegas, and married some rich white man."

"So you're telling me that I got a brother or sister out here?"

"I don't know, Malik."

"Damn. Is there anything else?" he asked, looking confused.

265

"No, that's it. Just remember the golden rule. This is why I constantly tell you not to trust anyone. You never know what someone else is thinking. Your friend Rico is probably a really cool dude, but look at your father. He and Sam grew up together. They'd known each other since preschool, and Sam turned around and killed your parents over some money. The love of money is truly the root of all evil, Malik. Remember that."

Malik sat back and looked at Linda while savoring everything she had held back from him over the years.

"Is Sam having a lot of people over tonight?" Linda asked.

"No. It's only me, Kojack, Rico, and Sam to my knowledge," Malik replied.

"Do you think your friend Rico is down with what you're about to do?"

"Of course. The nigga loves this type of shit."

"Good then. Most likely Sam has his money close by. If he's been moving shit all these years, I know for sure he gotta be a multimillionaire by now."

"You think he's gonna give up that money?" Malik asked.

"Yes, but he won't give it up if you let him know that you know he killed your parents."

"Why do you say that?"

"'Cause he's gonna figure out that you came to kill him anyway."

"So you're saying to play it off like a robbery until he gives up the money?"

"Yes. And whatever you do, don't give him a chance to talk."

"Why?"

"'Cause he'll try to talk his way out of you killing him."

"Yeah, I understand."

PRINCE OF THE CITY

Malik looked at Linda as she instructed him on how to pull the biggest caper ever. Linda was extremely careful of how it should be laid down properly, as if she'd done it before. Malik was impressed by her wisdom in the game. He always thought if Linda was a man, she would be the most ruthless gangster of all time.

After talking to Linda, Malik went upstairs to check on Peaches. "Get up, boo. I need to talk to you," he said, waking her.

"What's up, Malik?"

"Remember when you said you would risk your life for me?"

"Yes, baby."

"Did you really mean it?"

"Of course I mean it. What's wrong?"

"Nothing, just listen. I need you to do something for me."

Malik explained to Peaches what he wanted her to do. Peaches was the mother of his child, and so far the only person he could trust. Malik gave her all the details and instructed her to make reservations for a flight out of town.

"Where to? Where do you wanna go, baby?"

"Anywhere you wanna start a new life. You name it."

"Okay, baby. Please be careful."

"I will. You just do your part and wait for my call."

"Okay, I will. Malik, I love you."

Malik cupped Peaches's face in both his hands. "And I love you too, Peaches. I promise I'm a make you the happiest wife on earth after all this is over."

Malik then went into his closet and pulled out his P-13, sixteen-shot .45, and armor-piercing bullets. He put on a pair of black Versace jeans, a black Versace sweater, and some black Versace suede boots. He wore his mink coat, Frank Muller watch, and three-carat diamond earring.

Ring.

"Hello?" Malik said after he answered his phone.

"What's up, nigga? It's ten o'clock and I'm out front. You want me to come in or what?" Rico asked.

"Nah, you can meet Aunt Linda later."

"A'ight. You got directions to the joint?"

"Yeah. Kojack gave them to me about ten minutes ago."

"Well hurry up and bring your monkey ass out here."

"Fuck you, Rico."

As Malik descended the stairs, Linda was at the bottom waiting for him. "You know what to do, right?"

"Yeah. Just make sure you come pick up the money at Wingate Condominiums when I call you."

"Okay, I'll be here waiting for your call. Be careful, Malik. Sam is a vicious and sneaky man. Watch him carefully. Okay?"

"I know what to do." Malik and Linda embraced.

Ten minutes later, Malike slid into the passenger seat of Rico's Range Rover and slammed the door.

"There's been a change of plans," Malik said once he was inside.

"What's up?" Rico asked.

"Nigga, we 'bout to pull off the biggest caper of our lives."

Rico's eyes lit up. "What are you getting at?"

"We gonna rob Black Sam blind."

"Yes!" Rico said with enthusiasm shining brightly in his eyes. "Nigga, that's what I'm talking 'bout. We're taking over this muthafucka for real." Rico pulled his gun and waved it around like a maniac.

"Calm down, Rico. Calm down."

"Okay, I'm calm. It's just that I was wondering when you was gonna come around to your senses."

"Now is the time to claim our spot on the throne. You ready?"

"Nigga, I was born ready. Let's get the ball rolling and hurry up and get this shit over with. I can just smell the money." Rico inhaled and briefly closed his eyes.

"Good then. Now pull over and let me drive."

Chapter 37

-CROWN ME KING-

Rico passed Malik the blunt as he turned into the Tantallon neighborhood in Fort Washington, Maryland.

"Damn, it's some big-ass houses out here," Rico said, admiring every house they drove past.

"Yeah, this is where all the rich, white folks stay. They only let a select few blacks in."

"I hear Riddick Bowe lives out here."

"Yeah, he does. And the broad who played Laura on Family Matters lives out here too." Malik turned onto a dark street, which revealed a house that took up half the block. He smiled at Rico.

"From the directions, this one right here is Black Sam's joint," Malik said as he pulled through the open gate, which was guarded by two life-sized statues of lions with their mouths wide open. As he drove through, lights automatically turned on, giving him directions to his parking spot.

"Malik, this here is some real fly shit. I swear, in all my years of hustling, I've never seen no shit like this before. This joint reminds me of Tony Montana's house in Scarface."

"Yeah Rico, this is a serious joint."

As Malik parked, he looked to his right at the fleet of cars lined up.

"Oh, shit! Rico, look at this. I know this nigga don't got no Bentley."

"Damn, that's a grown man's car."

Kojack came out to greet the two young men as they sat marveling at the dark blue Bentley Azure with cream interior.

"Hey fellas. Glad to see you made it. Did you have trouble finding the joint?"

"Nah. We were just sightseeing on the way through," Malik said.

"Yeah, it's some real fly houses out here. Ain't it, Malik?"

"Yeah, Jack."

"Don't worry about it. After tonight, the two of you will be able to live out here."

"I know we will," Rico replied in a sarcastic tone.

"Come on, fellas. We've been waiting for you." Kojack led them to the front door where Chevece stood dressed in an all-black Chanel gown. Around her neck was Connie's diamond necklace, which Black Sam took after killing Connie in the apartment thirteen years prior.

As she greeted the two young men, Malik almost broke down in tears at the sight of the necklace his father had bought his mother for their anniversary. Now he knew for sure that Sam was his parents' killer.

"Hello fellas. I'm Mrs. Bennett. Let me take your coats. Please make yourselves at home. My husband will be down in a minute. Is there anything I can get you?"

"No thank you," Malik said, eyeing the necklace.

"Yes, ma'am. A glass of champagne will be fine," Rico responded.

Chevece looked at Rico. "Well, young fella. What kind do you prefer?"

"Anything," Rico said as he lusted over her body.

Chevece smiled at the young, curly-haired boy, who she thought was handsome.

"Come on in the guestroom, you two," Kojack said. He led Malik and Rico into Black Sam's conference room."

"What time is it?" Rico asked.

Malik looked at his watch. "It's eleven o'clock."

"Rico, you got somewhere to be?" Kojack asked.

"Nah, 'Jack. I just wanted to know how long we got before the ball drops. I'm tryna bring in the New Year with a bang," Rico responded with a smile.

"Yeah, I know what you mean, man," Kojack said.

Chevece came into the conference room with five glasses on a tray and a bottle of Dom Perignon champagne. Malik knew from the glasses that there were only five people in the house, which was perfect, because soon they would all be in one room together.

"Here you go, young fella. That's Dom P, the best champagne around," Chevece said as she smiled at Rico.

"Thank you, ah . . ."

"Call me Mrs. Bennett."

"Oh, I'm sorry. Thank you, Mrs. Bennett."

"Sure."

As Rico reached for the glass of champagne, a strong, tall man resembling Michael Jordan came into the room. He was dressed in an all-black Armani tuxedo with a six-carat yellow diamond in his ear and a handcrafted Audemars Piguet watch iced in yellow diamonds on his wrist.

"Hello, fellas. I see you've made yourselves at home." The first person he reached out to was Rico. His presence was bold as he walked straight up to Rico, looked him in the eyes, and pressed his palm firmly but not tightly.

"Hello, I'm Sam, but my friends call me Black Sam. And you are?"

"R-Rico . . . I'm Rico," he stuttered, intimidated by Black Sam's presence.

"Well, pleased to meet you, Rico. Why don't you have a seat?"

Rico sat down on the plush leather sofa, admiring the strength of the older gangster while envying his position. Rico wanted desperately to be like Black Sam.

As Sam walked up to Malik, he looked him hard in the face. He stood for a fews seconds and looked even harder. From the way Sam was acting, everyone sensed something was wrong. Malik stood firm and looked Sam in the eyes, the same way Michael did before Sam pulled the trigger. Sam was in shock. This young man resembled his best friend and one-time partner so much that he uttered his name without realizing it. "Mike!"

At the sound of his father's name, Malik acted on instinct, pushing Sam back with his left hand and drawing his .45 to Sam's face with his right.

"Nah, nigga, it's Malik. Mike's son."

Rico got up off the sofa, drew his Desert Eagle .357, and pointed it at Kojack and the lovely Mrs. Bennett. "Don't nobody move or say nothing. If you do, I'm a put a hole in your ass so big they gonna have to bury you in a closed casket. Now, everybody on your knees," Rico instructed as he checked Kojack and Sam for weapons.

Malik held his gun firmly on Black Sam. "Now look, Sam. We came for the money, not your lives. So please don't make me kill you and your wife."

At the statement, Chevece started crying. "Oh my God, please don't kill me! Please. Please don't kill us! Oh my God, help me!"

"Shut up, bitch, before I put a bullet in your head," Rico said.

"Yes, okay. I'll do anything you want. Just don't kill me."

"Hey, Malik. Do you know what you're doing? Man, you can't rob us and get away with it," Kojack said.

"Nigga, shut the fuck up. I run this shit. You talk when I say so. And since you're the first to jump out there, I'ma ask you where the money's at, and if you don't tell me, you die. Kojack, where's the bank?"

"All I know is that I got like three million upstairs, but I don't know where Sam put it though."

"Well, since you don't know, then you die." Malik walked over to Kojack and put his .45 against Kojack's forehead.

"Fuck you, Malik!" Kojack said, showing no fear.

"Fuck you too."

Boom!

The .45 exploded, blowing out Kojack's brains.

Chevece let out a loud scream. "Oh my God! Sam, do something! Tell them where the money is! Please don't kill me!"

Sam remained silent and calm while Chevece was panicked and disturbed by the murder she'd just witnessed.

"Bitch, shut up before I blow your fucking head off," Rico said as he placed his gun to her head.

"Okay, okay, just please don't kill me," she cried out, holding her hands in the air as if to say stop.

"Now, Sam, listen closely. I'ma ask you one more time where the money is, and if you give me the wrong answer, I'm sending your lovely wife straight to la-la land," Malik said.

Chevece instantly got hysterical. "Oh no! Please don't kill me! Please, Sam. Do something! Tell them where the money's at!" she screamed.

Sam still remained calm, never saying a word. From the way Sam was acting, Chevece knew Sam didn't care if she lived or died.

As Rico cocked back his gun and placed it in Chevece's face, one second away from pulling the trigger, she yelled out, "Nooo! The money is upstairs in the master bedroom. There's a secret wall behind the closet."

"What's the combination?" Malik asked.

After Chevece quickly revealed the combination, Rico ran upstairs to retrieve the money. Malik still held his gun on Sam and Chevece as he began to talk.

"Now, Sam, I can understand you killin' my father, but I have one question. What did my mother have to do with it? Why did you kill my mother?"

"Oh my God, Sam. You killed his mother!" Chevece yelled.

"Shut the fuck up, Chevece!" Sam yelled.

After hearing Chevece's name, Malik now knew who Mrs. Bennett really was. "Did he just call you Chevece? Is your name Chevece Jones?" Malik asked.

"Yes. How did you know my maiden name? Who are you?"

"You knew my father."

"Who's your father?"

275

Malik looked at Chevece. He could see her pain. She was innocent, yet caught in a web of destruction just like his mother had been.

"My father was Michael Perry."

"Oh my God! Sam, you son of a bitch! You killed your best friend?"

"Yeah, he killed him. He also killed my mother, and the necklace you're wearing belonged to her."

She glared at Sam with a look that could maim. "You heartless muthafucka! You said you bought this necklace from Europe."

"Look, Malik. You got it all twisted. I didn't kill your parents. Where did you get that shit from?" Sam asked.

"Linda told me, and it was Linda who raised me to take revenge."

"What! Linda? Man, you don't even know Linda's the one who orchestrated the hit."

"Man, fuck you! You'll put it on anybody. Nigga, you took the crown from my father, and now it's time for you to give it back to its rightful owner. Nigga, you stole it, and I inherited the shit. Nigga, I'm the king." As Malik placed his gun between Sam's eyes, Rico came down the stairs with two suitcases.

"Fuck you, Sam!" With that, Malik pulled the trigger twice. *Boom!Boom!*

Chevece hollered again at the top of her lungs. "Oh my God! No, no, no, no! Please, don't kill me! Oh my God! Sam!"

Frustrated with the scared woman's screams, Rico placed his Desert Eagle .357 to her temple. Before Malik could stop him, Rico pulled the trigger. "Bitch, shut the fuck up!"

Boom!

PRINCE OF THE CITY

As Chevece's brains blew all over the conference room floor, Malik yelled, "No, Rico! What the fuck is wrong with you, you crazy muthafucka?"

"Man, fuck that bitch. She was getting on my nerves with all that fucking crying and screaming."

Malik looked at Chevece and then back at Rico. "You don't even know what you've just done."

"Fuck that bitch. Now get your ass upstairs and help me with these suitcases. Nigga, we're rich!"

Malik and Rico packed the suitcases in the back of Rico's Range Rover, and then headed back to the stash house to count and divide the money. On the drive back, both Malik and Rico were silent. Both wondered what was going on in the other's mind.

Chapter 38

-THE THRONE-

11:40 PM . . .

Malik and Rico opened the first suitcase. At the sight of so many Ben Franklins stacked and bound with rubber bands, they hugged each other and then spoke their first words since leaving the scene. "Nigga, look at this. We're rich," Rico said.

"Yeah, now we can say we're rich." Malik looked deep in his eyes. "Nigga, I couldn't have done any of this shit without you."

"Me neither, Malik. Nigga, I love you. We're bound for life."

"Hold up, Rico. Look at this." There was a tag on the side of each suitcase that read THREE MILLION DOLLARS. Malik looked at Rico. "Nigga, its three million in each suitcase."

Malik and Rico hugged again before they opened the next case.

"Nigga, this is twelve million dollars, plus the two million we already got," Rico said. "We're rich for real. Nigga, pop a bottle. We're bringing in the New Year right. Fire up them blunts, Malik."

"A'ight, but first let me call Linda real quick."

Malik dialed the house number and Peaches picked up.

"Hello?"

"Peaches, it's me, baby."

"Malik, are you okay?"

"Yeah, boo. Everything went as planned. Now do you remember what to do?"

"Yeah, I did everything. We got a flight booked for California first thing in the morning."

"Good. Now let me speak to my aunt."

"Hold on. Hey Linda, telephone."

"Hello? Malik, are you okay?" Linda asked after taking the phone from Peaches.

"Yeah, I'm cool."

"Did you get the money?" Linda asked, sounding excited.

"Most definitely. Now why don't you hurry up over here so you can take it back to the house? I'll meet you back there later."

"Okay, I'm on my way. I'll be there in ten minutes," Linda said, and then headed out the door after hanging up.

After Malik rolled a couple more blunts, the house phone rang.

"I'll get it, Rico. Hello?"

"It's me, Aunt Linda. You want me to come up or what?"

"Nah, I'll be right down," Malik replied, and then hung up. "Rico, I'll be right back. I gotta go give my aunt something."

"A'ight, but hurry up, nigga. We got ten minutes before the ball drops."

Linda double-parked her brand-new Escalade in front of the building. Malik came out and placed two suitcases in the back, and then went up to the driver's side window and kissed his aunt.

"I love you, Aunt Linda."

"I love you too, Malik."

"Call me when you get back to the house and let me know the six million is safe."

"There's six million in those suitcases?" Her eyes lit up like a Christmas tree.

"Yeah, and I'm a get you that house you want too."

"Boy, I love you, Malik." Linda kissed her nephew on the forehead before leaving.

Malik went back upstairs. "Hey Rico. We need to talk."

"What's up, homie?"

"Man, we got fourteen million dollars. If we keep hustling, you know we gonna end up getting locked up or some vicious niggas coming up in the game are gonna end up killing us just like we did Black Sam."

"So what are you saying?"

"Rico, I'm saying I'm quitting this shit. I'm out. I'm rich, my fiancée is pregnant, and I've put in enough work. A nigga's getting tired of this shit, all this killing and shit. Man, fuck that. I can't raise no child like this. I told you before that I would never bring my family into this shit."

"So what are you saying? We ain't family enough to stay together? Nigga, you can't quit. We built this shit together. Man, fuck that, Malik. We're gangstas. Gangstas don't retire. They die still a gangsta. How the fuck you just gonna roll out and leave me like that? Whatever happened to 'ballin' till we fall' and 'we're in this for life,' huh? You remember that? Those were your words, Malik."

"Yeah, Rico, but that was years ago. A nigga's a full-grown man now. A nigga's got a family now and wise decisions gotta be made."

PRINCE OF THE CITY

"Fuck that! I got a family too. My girl is pregnant too. But do you hear me crying 'bout getting out the game? See, Malik, you're getting soft, man."

"Rico, ain't nobody soft. I'm just smart. I don't wanna die early. I know what it feels like to take a life. I've been killing since I was sixteen. That shit's over for me now. I wanna live my life. I wanna know what it feels like to bring a life into this world."

"Yeah, whatever. I see I can't change your mind. So do what you wanna do. But me, nigga, I'm a real-live gangsta. I'm a die in this shit. Regardless, you're still my nigga, although I don't respect your decision."

"That's good enough for me," Malik said. He then poured himself a glass of Remy XO and went onto the balcony to look over Southeast one last time. As he took in a deep breath of the cool winter night, he looked out into the Jungle and thought of his parents. He said goodbye to his kingdom. Although it was his first day on the throne as king, it was also his last. Malik no longer wanted any part of the life.

As he took a sip of his Remy, he suddenly felt the cold steel of a gun pressed against the back of his neck. "Rico, before you pull that trigger, there's something you need to know," Malik said quietly to his best friend.

Malik then began to tell Rico his life story.

Chapter 39

-LIKE FATHER LIKE SON-

W hen Malik finished telling Rico his life story, the hard, cold steel of the gun remained pressed on the crease of Malik's neck, waiting to be fired.

"Now, I've stood here and told you everything about me. I gave it to you raw and uncut, and if you were listening, you'd know this. You once told me that the only thing you have linking you to your parents was an old birth certificate. I've read the birth certificate. Remember how you kept it tucked away under your pillow at the receiving home? Well, one day Soup was going through your things, and he found it and brought it to me. Your mother's name was Chevece Jones. That woman you killed today . . . her name was Chevece Jones. And if that was your mother, she only bore one child by a man named Michael Perry. The woman you killed today was your very own mother, and the man you're about to kill is your only brother."

As Rico listened to Malik tell him about his past, Malik took a sip of his liquor while smoothly pulling out his .45 automatic. Malik held the gun close to his front, not revealing to Rico that he had just slipped it out.

The more Malik talked, the less pressure Rico exerted with the gun. Malik knew that Rico's mind had to be racing. He just discovered that he'd killed his own mother. And now Rico was about to kill his brother. As tears fell down both their faces, only about ten seconds remained in 1999. "Rico, if you're gonna kill me, then do so. But just remember, I'm still your brother, your blood."

After a few seconds, Rico lowered his gun from the back of Malik's neck and stood there looking at his only brother, the brother he'd always dreamed of having. This was the only life Rico had ever spared, and the only life he ever would.

"Malik, you're my brother and I love you," he said.

"Rico, you're my brother and I love you too."

With that, Malik turned face-to-face with his only brother. Before Rico noticed, Malik's gun was pointed at him. Rico took two shots to his abdomen at exactly midnight.

The gunshots didn't disturb the rest of the building. At midnight on New Year's Day, all of Southeast sounded like Beirut. Rico clutched his stomach and looked at Malik with shock. "Rico, there was something I learned from a whore, and that was never trust no one. So I came to this meeting prepared, which is something our father didn't do when he met with Black Sam."

With that, Malik placed his gun on Rico's forehead and pulled the trigger. Malik then called Peaches.

"Malik, you okay?" she asked him.

"Yeah baby. Did Linda ever come back?"

"No, she didn't. She's been gone for a good while. She should've been back by now."

"I kinda figured that. You ready?"

"Yeah. You want me to come now?"

"Yeah, and drive my truck. Call me when you get downstairs."

"Okay, baby. I'm on my way."

"Hey, Peaches?"

"What?"

"I love you."

"I love you too, Malik."

After instructing Peaches to pick him up, Malik grabbed a towel and wiped down the whole apartment. He then wiped off his gun and placed it on Rico's chest.

Malik placed all four suitcases by the door. While he waited for Peaches to call, he went outside on the balcony one last time. He sat upon his throne, a king, and silently began to talk to his father.

Dad, now I'm the king. I now understand what it took to get here, and I understand what it will take to stay. Therefore, I'm doing what no other king has done. I'm leaving the throne without dying, which is something you always wanted to do.

I know I just killed my own brother, but there was no other way. I pray that you forgive me for killing the son you never knew, but even in the real jungle of beast and animals, this is part of the law of nature.

I don't ever wanna live like this again. So I'm taking off my crown and bowing out gracefully. I love you, Dad, and I promise I'll live out the same dream you had for me and Mommy through Peaches and my unborn child.

He then blew a kiss to the sky.

Chapter 40

-TRICKED-

After picking up the suitcases of money from Malik, instead of going to Peaches's house, Linda got on the I-495 and headed toward Florida. She'd planned to escape to Florida thirteen years earlier, but couldn't because Black Sam never gave her the money from the move she'd helped him pull on his best friend.

Linda and Sam had been secret lovers since high school. They were both jealous of their best friends' relationship. Connie was prettier and smarter than Linda. Everything Connie had, Linda wanted. She envied her best friend while Sam envied his.

Sam would kill Mike, take the money, and the two would get married and live in Florida. But Black Sam didn't live up to his end of the bargain. He'd killed Connie which Linda begged him not to do and took the money and ran off with Chevece.

Linda knew she couldn't find anyone to kill Sam for revenge, so she raised Malik to do it. She knew that the only way to get Sam back was through Malik, a well-trained gangster. Linda's plan took thirteen years, but to Linda, those thirteen years had paid off well. She was now six million dollars richer.

She smiled as she looked at herself in the rearview mirror of her truck, happy and satisfied. Even though she'd turned an innocent child into a gangster, she still felt relieved that Malik came out the way he did. In the beginning, she didn't think Malik would stand a chance, but to her surprise, he sucked up every game she gave him.

As Linda pulled into a rest stop off the highway, she lit up a fresh Newport, sat in her truck, and thought about what she was going to do with her six million. She decided to take a look at her money before she got back on the road. She wanted to see what six million really looked like.

As Linda walked to the back of her truck and popped the hatch, she looked around for any nosey spectators before opening the suitcases. Her eyes lit up as she opened the first case. The suitcase was stuffed with towels and washcloths.

As Linda's anger built, she rushed to open the second suitcase. Once she opened it, Linda instantly felt dizzy and confused. The second suitcase was stuffed with rolls of toilet paper. There was a note attached to the inside of the suitcase. Linda picked it up and read:

Dear Linda,

I always knew it was you. You gave yourself up with the most precious jewel you could ever give: Trust no one, not even you! Now take this toilet paper and wipe yourself, 'cause you some shit!

The Prince of Southeast, soon to be King

Linda immediately fell to her knees crying. She'd been tricked twice by those whom she'd tried desperately to trick—Black Sam and Malik.

Chapter 41

-ME AND MY GIRLFRIEND-

Peaches pulled up to the front lobby of the Wingate and called Malik, who picked up on the first ring.

"Hello?"

"Malik, I'm downstairs. Are you ready?"

"Yeah, I'm coming right now. Give me a sec."

Malik got off the elevator and walked through the building's lobby lugging two suitcases. He couldn't help but notice Peaches's beautiful smile as she sat behind the wheel of the pearl-white Escalade listening to Tupac's "Me and My Girlfriend."

"You need some help, boo?" she asked.

"Nah, this shit is heavy. Just pop the hatch."

After Peaches popped the hatch, Malik threw in the first two suitcases.

"I'll be right back. I got two more suitcases to get."

"Okay, baby, but hurry up. You know I'm double-parked."

Malik rushed back downstairs lugging the other two suitcases while smiling at his soon-to-be wife. He felt relieved that he was through with the life. His past would be buried, while his new life was just being born.

287

As Malik put the last suitcase in the back of the truck, a tall, thin, gray-haired man approached him.

"Excuse me, Malik," the man said.

Malik jumped in shock. He couldn't believe he was slipping that much to let someone creep up on him like that. He wondered for a second if Peaches had seen the guy, but he knew she couldn't have because she would have warned him. Peaches was stuck in Tupac's lyrics as she waited for Malik to finish loading the truck.

As the man moved closer, Malik looked him up and down, trying to figure out who in the hell this person was.

He then said to the man, "Look, I don't think we know each other."

"Nah, you don't know me. However, I'm an old friend of your father's."

"Look, man, whoever you are, this ain't a good time right now," Malik replied as he slammed the hatch door, hoping the noise would warn Peaches to look in the rearview mirror.

When Peaches looked up at the sound of the hatch closing, she saw Malik talking to someone, but she didn't think anything about it. She figured the man was probably someone Malik knew. Still, she kept her eyes on the man.

"Oh no, Malik. This won't take but a minute. I came for my brother."

"Your brother? Who's your brother—"

"My name is Slim. I just came home from Lorton where I did twenty-three years. My brother was the only family I had."

"So. What the fuck that gotta do with me?"

"I'm Slim James, nigga! Sonny's brother!"

Instantly, Malik reached for his .45, but realized he had left it upstairs lying on Rico's chest. As Slim James reached into his waistband, Malik knew he was dead. After all the years of sucking up the game from his father, Linda, and Lee, he was going to die anyway.

Malik knew he had failed. He knew everything he went through in life was for nothing. The pain and suffering, the love and revenge, it all meant nothing. He tightly closed his eyes as Slim James pointed his gun at Malik's head. Malik was fearless as he stood face-to-face with death, waiting patiently to receive his final blow.

The first bullet fired sounded like a cannon exploding.

Boom!

When it hit, Malik didn't feel anything. He began to wonder what it really felt like to be dead.

The second bullet sounded. This time Malik felt a wet splash on his face like someone was throwing water on him. He opened his eyes, but couldn't believe what he was seeing. Now he knew that the choices he'd made in life were correct and valuable. He knew there was someone that he could always trust. That someone was the mother of his child and his soon-to-be wife, Peaches.

Before Peaches left the house that night, she wasn't sure if everything was completely safe. So she went into Malik's closet and pulled out his 9-millimeter. It was the very same gun he'd taught her how to load and fire. Peaches never thought she would use the gun, but still, she played her position.

When Malik slammed the hatch of the Escalade, Peaches was instantly alarmed. As she looked on, she turned down the music to overhear the conversation with the strange man who'd appeared out of nowhere. She could sense from Malik's body language that something was wrong. Then when she saw Malik reach for his gun and come up strapless, she knew she had to do something, and fast. She literally saw their future flash before her eyes. Quickly, she eased out of the truck, hoping her pregnancy wouldn't get in the way of her moving fast and efficiently.

Just as she reached the back of the truck, she saw the man pull his gun and point it at Malik's head. Peaches moved even faster, hoping she'd be able to creep up from behind just in time. Peaches thought she'd failed as she saw the man on the verge of pulling the trigger. After the first shot, though, she realized he wasn't fast enough. She fired one shot to the back of his head, instantly killing him. She then stood over his body and delivered another bullet to his face, just to make sure.

The blood from the impact of the bullet splattered on Malik's face, making him open his eyes and witness the realest shit he'd ever seen in his life.

As Peaches stood over Slim James's body with the smoking gun still in her hand, Malik smiled inside as he thought back to how he'd taught Peaches well and how she'd listened to every lesson, never ignoring his wisdom. There she was, the true queen of his castle and savior of his life, someone whom he would always hold in the highest esteem and give the greatest honor.

"Malik, are you okay, baby?" Peaches asked as she frantically looked over at the love of her life, hoping and praying that he wasn't hit.

"Yeah, I'm all right. Give me the gun and get in the truck," Malik instructed while easing the gun out of her hand.

As Peaches started the engine and put it in gear, Malik stood over Slim James's body and emptied the rest of the clip in his head before jumping in the truck.

As they fled the scene, Malik looked into Peaches's eyes. "I love you, Peaches. You're my queen and I promise to treat you like royalty forever."

"I already know this, Malik. I love you too. You were always my king, even when you were the prince. Now let's get the fuck outta here, boo, while we can."

"You got that right," Malik responded with a smile.

Dear Readers,

As you can see, once again, I have delivered another classic. And although this novel may give you a harsh sense of reality and expose certain parts of the game, it is my duty to inform you that this is not a true story. These are only recollections of a lifestyle I once lived.

Jason Poole

PRINCE OF THE CITY

 Jason Poole is the author of three urban best-selling classics: Larceny Part I, Convict's Candy, and Victoria's Secret. He is also a screenwriter, who has written several movies as well as the executive producer of a budding reality show slated for production. Now serving as president and CEO of his own publishing house Gangster Chronicles Books, Jason is currently working on his memoir titled, Products of Our Environment, and the release of his first novel under his own imprint.

JASON POOLE

- Seat of Power -

"If its one thing I've learned in this industry, it is to become your own boss," says Best-Selling Author Jason Poole. Hailing from the notorious streets of Washington DC, this former hustler turned Best-Selling Author, Screenwriter and Executive Producer used setbacks as his motivation to succeed. While serving a federal prison sentence Jason went on to become an Essence Best-Selling Author with his first street classic *Larceny*. Then again with the very controversial collaboration of Convict's *Candy*, and later with the international Best-Seller *Victoria's Secret*, a novel that gained notoriety as far away as Jamaica and Amsterdam.

"When I received my first piece of fan mail from another Country that's when I knew my work was classic material." The author states. Now becoming C.E.O. & President of his own imprint Gangster Chronicles Books, a subsidary of his best friends music label, and armed with a distribution deal from *Wahida Clark, (The Queen of Street Literature)*, Jason brings his loyal readers as well as new comers another cult classic, *Prince of The City* and tells us why his novel is gaining such notoriety and is considered one of the most anticipated novels in Hip-Hop fiction. So much, that major label rap artist and actors have tweeted their stamps of approval. Some even name-dropped his novel in recent songs.

"Everyone that's involved with this project is gonna prosper." The author confidently stated. My whole objective is to create opportunities. This is why this project is evolving from novel to soundtrack and ultimately a major motion picture and I wanted to do something exclusively for my City. I wanted to give them that project that would fully represent our moniker *Drama City*. I'm bringing gangster back in a major way," he proudly boasts. He says this because nowadays the majority of Urban Novels are now packed with unrealistic story lines and illogical action.

"Had to bring'em back to that *True to The Game & B-More Careful* era. Novels that had substance and story lines we all could relate to. Poole also says that he wants *Prince of The City* to serve as an inspiration to others, showing that regardless of where you are in life whether its in prison or society you can still become your own boss and create a project that can reach millions. All you have to do is believe . . . just believe the author advises.

And this isn't all for the self-made entrepreneur and Executive Producer. Jason also has a reality show in Hollywood in the works as well and a T.V. drama series *Torch* that's slated for pre-production.

"Torch is a three part series that plunges deep inside the criminal lifestyle of our nation's capital during the late 80s, 90s, and ultimately the new millennium. I'm working with director A.J. Johnson for the Torch project. Everybody's really excited about it. I wanted to bring some source of authenticity to the legendary street tales that you often hear about D.C."

The author plans to adapt screenplays to all novels published under his Gangster Chronicles imprint and promises that when signed under his label you're not just signing a book deal, you are signing onto a legacy.

After digesting all of this, it becomes crystal clear why this man has been hailed as the savior of Street Lit Fiction and the person who's regarded as *The man who brought Gangster back*. Without doubt or contradiction this business man, C.E.O and President of Gangster Chronicles Books definitely deserves his right to sit in the ***SEAT OF POWER*** ...

To order *Prince of The City* go to amazon.com or www.wclarkpublishing.com or anywhere books are sold. Also you can contact Jason Poole at:

Gangster Chronicles Books
C/O Jason Poole C.E.O & President
P.O Box 31086
Washington, DC 20030

Made in the USA
Middletown, DE
04 October 2022

11895696R00187